Ne(

Cherry
Tarts
at the Cosy Kettle

BOOKS BY LIZ EELES

New Starts and Cherry Tarts at the Cosy Kettle

LIZ EELES

Bookouture

Published by Bookouture in 2019

An imprint of StoryFire Ltd.

Carmelite House
50 Victoria Embankment
London EC4Y 0DZ

www.bookouture.com

ISBN: 978-1-78681-634-4
eBook ISBN: 978-1-78681-633-7

This book is a work of fiction. Names, characters, businesses,
organizations, places and events other than those clearly in the
public domain, are either the product of the author's imagination
or are used fictitiously. Any resemblance to actual persons, living or
dead, events or locales is entirely coincidental.

This one's for you, Rachel x

Chapter One

Honeyford is waking up. Curtains are drawn back in golden-yellow cottages, pale spring sunshine is glinting on the old market house, and the washed stone doorstep of the Pheasant and Fox pub is dripping with soapy water.

Beyond the huddled buildings, sheep are tiny white specks on hills that roll gently towards a purple horizon. It's a glorious view, and one that usually fills my heart with peace and joy – but this morning I couldn't give a monkey's.

Rushing along the High Street, I check my watch for the umpteenth time and body-swerve a mum who's pushing a sleeping baby in a pram. Poor woman. She could do with clambering into the pram and getting some kip herself if the lines of exhaustion etched across her face are anything to go by.

Normally, I'd flash her a sympathetic smile, because I can't help feeling sorry for new parents. My best friend, Sarah, insists she'll never be a mother because it sounds so awful – a never-ending round of sore nipples, broken sleep and nappy brain.

But right now, nothing must distract me from getting to work on time. My new boss starts today so rocking up after nine o'clock is not on. And I can hardly say, *Sorry I'm late but Gramp is threatening to do a sponsored parachute jump for endangered butterflies.* Even though he is, and I'm late because I spent twenty minutes trying to talk him out of it.

The frazzled mum sinks onto a bench outside Honeyford Post Office, as I wonder whether caring for a baby is harder than looking after a relative who's gone barmy since hitting the big eight-oh. One minute, he was a normal seventy-nine-year-old bloke who spent his time watching re-runs of *Midsomer Murders*. Then, at midnight on his birthday, he morphed into Bear Grylls.

He's taken up jogging (very slowly) and joined Greenpeace 'to save the world from plastic bags'. Last week, he went wild swimming in a local lake until the police brought him home in sopping wet underpants. So it's hardly surprising that I'm on tenterhooks, wondering what Gramp will get up to next.

Though surely he wouldn't be allowed to skydive at his age. Would he? I hurry past the centuries-old market house, picturing hordes of octogenarians flinging themselves from planes at twelve thousand feet.

Oh, no! Further along the High Street, I spot that my new boss Flora has already pulled up the window blinds at Honeyford Bookshop. The leaded panes are sparkling and two potential customers are checking out the window display. Breaking into an awkward half-walk half-run, I pull out my phone and glance at the jiggling screen, in case my watch is fast.

Nope, it's eight fifty-nine, which means I have exactly sixty seconds to leg it along the road and hurtle through the shop door.

I wasn't planning on rushing into work on Flora's first day. In my head, I'd planned to be there, all calm and collected, before my new boss arrived. She'd walk in to find me re-arranging the stock or welcoming her with a steaming cup of coffee, and she'd thank her lucky stars that Callie Fulbright was her new assistant. But I hadn't allowed for another of Gramp's madcap schemes throwing me off course.

I'm about to shove my phone back into my pocket when I notice that Sarah's sent me a couple of texts.

Good luck, amiga! Hope your new boss isn't a total cow who works you to death, I read, stumbling slightly on the uneven pavement. And despite my new-boss nerves, I have to giggle – I can always rely on Sarah to give it to me straight and make me laugh.

The second text simply says: *Check out Sophie's Facebook!* followed by a line of smiley-faced emojis with their tongues hanging out.

That's intriguing. Checking out anything right now is unwise because I'm still in a mad rush, and the shop door is in sight. But my old schoolfriend Sophie's updates on her fabulous fashion job in Milan are hard to ignore. Her *Woohoo! It's so brilliant in bella Italia* posts give me a vicarious thrill – a taste of how life could have been if I'd taken a different path.

Sophie's probably posted another selfie in a string bikini with some gorgeous Italian man drooling in the background. I've seen plenty of those already. But, as I rush past the sweet shop with its jars of sugary old-fashioned treats in the window, I open Facebook anyway – and do a double-take at the screen. Oh, my! There's not one, but *two* gorgeous Italian men drooling in the background, and they're wearing teeny, tiny swimming trunks that leave absolutely nothing to the imagination. I stop dead on the pavement and squint at the photo. That is absolutely obscene!

As I'm staring at the screen, equally transfixed and horrified, I hear, 'Hey, watch out!' and someone barrels into me from behind. The jolt knocks the phone from my hand and it skids face-down across the pavement, before dropping off the kerb into the gutter.

'I'm so sorry,' I gasp, gazing in horror at my phone, which is now resting in a shallow puddle of grey water.

'I should think you are sorry,' snaps the sturdy fifty-something woman, smoothing down her deep purple gilet. 'What kind of moron causes a pile-up on the pavement?'

My stomach does a flip because upsetting people is one of the things I hate most. It's right up there with dog owners who don't pick up after their pets, and cheese. How anyone can enjoy food that smells of old socks is beyond me.

But right now I'm too busy sending up a silent prayer to the God of Apple to care: *please don't let my phone be broken!* A huge heating bill arrived yesterday – something to do with Gramp trying out Hot Yoga in the front room – and there's no way I can afford to mend a shattered screen this month.

The woman huffs, picks my phone out of the gutter with her thumb and forefinger as though it's contaminated, and hands it back. It's sod's law, of course, that she glances at the screen, and her eyebrows shoot towards her hairline as she clocks the Italian stallions in their indecent swimming trunks. Unfortunately, as the phone hit the pavement it appears to have zoomed in on the crotch area, and Sophie is no longer in sight.

Fantastic! Now she thinks I'm a moron *and* a pervert.

'Thanks so much,' I mumble, clicking off the photo and shoving the phone into my trouser pocket. 'And I *am* sorry for stopping so suddenly.'

'Hhmm. I should think so.' The woman sighs and stares at me over the top of her enormous sunglasses. 'There's no damage done, I suppose. But can I suggest you watch where you're going in future?'

She gives another small sigh and suddenly looks so sad I'm tempted to ask her what's wrong. I don't – partly because she'd only bite my head off, but mostly because the market house clock is striking nine behind me, which means I am now officially late.

Flora's probably waiting with her arms folded and my redundancy letter on standby.

'Sorry, but I've got to go,' I shout over my shoulder, running off at full pelt with a carrier bag over one arm and a Tupperware box of ham sandwiches banging rhythmically against my thigh.

'Oy, Paula Radcliffe!' yells local postman Mark, who's pushing envelopes through the letterbox of the pub. 'What's the hurry? You're not in training for the half-marathon like Stanley, are you?'

What half-marathon? Jeez, Gramp's not signed up for anything else, has he?

But there's no time to ask questions because the final chime is echoing across the town. So I just smile at Mark and wave like a crazy woman while I sprint past.

'Go for it, Callie!' His shout bounces off the Cotswold stone all around me and shatters the early morning calm.

What a morning! And it's only just begun.

Thirty seconds later, I arrive at the bookshop, out of breath and panting. Maybe I should get fit and join Gramp in training for his half-marathon after all.

'There you are,' says Flora, the woman I've met only twice before, but who now controls a major part of my life. She steps out from behind a tidy display of Anne Tylers and runs her hand along the light oak counter that holds the till.

'I'm so sorry I'm late,' I puff, fighting the urge to add: *Please don't sack me, because I have a bonkers granddad to feed.* 'I would have been on time but I bumped into someone.'

'Literally,' says Flora, raising one perfectly plucked eyebrow. 'How's your phone?'

'Ah, you saw that, did you? I think it's fine.'

I pull my phone from my pocket, examine it properly and wince. The screen's not fine at all. There's a feathery silver crack I didn't notice in my haste to click off the photo – before angry gilet woman got a proper eyeful of Italian stallion and marked me down as a sexually frustrated saddo.

'Is it damaged? That's a shame. But never mind, you can always get it mended.' Flora taps her long fingernails on the grained wood. 'And I know you couldn't help it today, but please try not to be late in future.'

She says it pleasantly enough but I haven't got my jacket off yet and I've already been told off. 'Of course,' I mumble, feeling cross with myself for being distracted by Sophie's Facebook post.

Flora gives a tight smile, sits down on the stool behind the counter and crosses her legs. She's wearing a moss-green dress that fits her beautifully and a necklace of large wooden beads that rests just below her collarbone. Not a hair is out of place in her glossy, shoulder-length black bob and I can almost see my face in her polished court shoes. She's practically perfect.

I wipe a hand over my hot cheeks, tug at my shirt which is riding up, and deliberately slow down my breathing. But I still feel out of my depth and slightly intimidated.

My new boss exudes confidence and maturity, though she can't be that much older than me – fifteen years maybe? I'd guess she's in her early forties. But she comes across as a person who has her life sorted. A woman who never wears mismatched socks or sniffs her T-shirt to see if it'll do another day. A woman who doesn't get obsessed with *Love Island* or cause pile-ups in the street.

I bet she lives in a posh house and drinks Chablis with her evening meal, rather than the can of lager I usually share with Gramp.

'Don't mind me.' Flora's wedding ring catches the light as she pulls a publisher's catalogue from underneath the counter and sets it down in front of her. 'Just do whatever you normally would on a Monday morning and we can have a proper talk later.'

She starts flicking through the pages while I take off my jacket and dump my carrier bag in the shabby kitchen. My face still looks flushed in the cracked mirror above the sink and dark blonde tendrils of wavy hair have escaped from my ponytail and are sticking to my neck. I'm a bit of a mess, to be honest, and am seriously regretting opting for Converse trainers and new skinny jeans this morning. A suit would have been over the top – the only one I own is years old anyway – but maybe I should have worn a dress. First impressions, and all that.

Ah well, it's too late now. I pat cool water onto my cheeks and head back into the shop where I start faffing about with the window display – all the while worrying about what Flora's 'proper talk' might entail.

The next few hours pass quickly because there's an influx of locals who come in to 'browse'. Which in effect means gawping at Flora to see what this Honeyford newcomer is like, and nudging me when they think she's not looking. I spend the rest of the time replenishing stock on the shelves, which doesn't take as long as it used to because sales have gradually declined over the last year or so.

Watching sales figures plummet to new lows was what finally pushed Ruben, my old boss, to sell the shop to Flora and move closer to his daughter and grandchildren in Margate.

There were no buyers for the business at first and I thought the shop might close. After all, who in their right mind would want to take on a failing bookshop in a tiny Cotswolds town? But then Flora rode in on her white charger – actually a pristine white Ford Fiesta – and saved the day.

Though I think she might already be regretting her impulse buy. There's been a fair amount of swearing under her breath all morning as she gets to grips with Ruben's idiosyncratic stock system, and watches locals checking her out.

Just before one o'clock, I'm rearranging Kate Atkinsons near the front of the shop when a blonde woman I don't recognise wanders in. She's clasping the hand of a small boy in uniform whose knee-length grey socks are bunched up around his ankles. The heel of his hand is pressed hard against his jaw and he's blinking like he might cry.

Standing in front of the bookshelves, the woman shrugs at the choice and turns to Flora.

'Do you have any Harry Potter? My grandson's just had a filling at the dentist and I promised him a treat.'

'I'm sure Callie can help you.' Flora tilts her head at me and raises one dark eyebrow like it's a test or something. Which it hopefully isn't because I'm about to flunk it, big time.

'I'm afraid we don't have any Harry Potters in stock,' I tell the boy, whose face screws into a tight, *What, no Hogwarts?* pout. Working here for the last three years, it's a look I've become all too familiar with.

'Really? That surprises me.' The woman tightens her grip on her grandson's hand and starts pulling him towards the door. 'Never mind, Henry, I'm in Cheltenham tomorrow and can try a bookshop there. Thank you, anyway.'

'Or you could have a look at our other children's books,' I say, putting on my best smile. 'We've got a great selection at the back of the shop. What sort of stories do you like, Henry?'

'Dunno,' mumbles Henry, a silver trail of saliva dribbling down his chin as the anaesthetic starts wearing off. He wipes it away with the back of his hand.

'Well, we've got all sorts of books about spies, or racing drivers, or secret societies. Does that sound any good?'

When Henry nods, I gesture for him and his gran to follow me across the sloping flagstones to the rear of the shop. It's darker back here and harder to see the coloured spines of the books lining the walls.

'Here you go,' I tell Henry. 'There are lots of fabulous books to choose from so take your time and see which story you like the most.'

The boy's eyes open wide as he runs his finger along the paperbacks, and he nods when I whisper in his ear: 'It's magic back here, isn't it?' He can feel it too.

This is my favourite part of the shop because it's like a portal to exciting, unfamiliar worlds for young readers. Sarah's eyes glaze over when I get all passionate about children's books – but every one offers a glimpse of somewhere new. And that's not to be sniffed at when you're growing up in a small town where nothing much happens.

The fact that *the industrial revolution was the last even vaguely interesting thing to happen around here* – Sarah's words, not mine – means that most of my school friends have moved away. Emily's now teaching English in Japan, Jess is dancing in a West End show, Sophie's fighting off suitors in Portofino, and Sarah's living and working in Cheltenham.

But I'm still here. I know my friends must occasionally wonder if that points to some sort of character flaw on my part – a lack of bravery, perhaps, or curiosity about the big, wide world. So I let them believe that I only stay in Honeyford for Gramp's sake. And I don't mention that the setting sun casting a golden glow over the town's ancient buildings, or ribbons of cloud drifting over distant hills, fills me with joy. I'm not sure they'd get it, and Sarah would definitely take the mick.

'I can't choose between this one and this one,' says Henry, getting my attention by waving two paperbacks in my face. 'Which one's the best?'

The two books are crammed full of thrills and adventure so it's hard to pick between them, and in the end his gran does the right thing and buys both. Henry will love them.

Flora drops the books into a paper bag and waves at Henry as he disappears through the front door with a dribbly smile. Then she turns to me and folds her arms.

'No wonder that lady was surprised. Why are some of the best-selling children's books of all time out of stock? It's not as though we haven't got the space.'

She waves her arm around the shop. In contrast to the exciting, musty bookshops I visited as a child, where novels overflowed from packed shelves and were stacked on the floor in piles, Honeyford Bookshop is ordered and tidy and smells mostly of furniture polish. Its shelves are neatly lined with hundreds of books but there's room for more.

'We've never kept them in stock, Flora.' Oops, maybe I should be calling my new boss 'Mrs Morgan'? She doesn't react so I carry on. 'Ruben didn't approve of books about magic and refused to have them on the shop floor. He was the same about any sort of book that he thought might have a bad effect on his customers.'

'Such as?'

'Books with lots of sex scenes in them, or excessive violence.'

'So he only stocked books that he thought his customers *should* read? That is priceless.' Flora whistles through her teeth. 'Did he ever wonder why sales were slipping?'

I shrug. 'Probably, and I did try to tell him, but he got more particular and entrenched about what the shop should stock as he got older.'

'Hhmm. That could explain a lot, because this shop should be doing better.' Flora sighs, walks to the shop doorway and peers outside. 'Is it always this quiet at lunchtime?' She looks up and down the street as though she might pounce on unsuspecting passers-by and drag them inside.

'Not always, but it's Monday and the tourist season isn't in full swing yet. It'll be busier later on in the week and on Saturday when there are more locals about.'

'Do you think so? Remind me, how long have you worked here?'

'About three years.'

'And you like it?'

'I do, mostly.'

Flora turns and fixes her deep-violet eyes on me. 'Why do you like it?'

Crikey, it's like twenty questions, with the ultimate prize of not peeing off your new boss.

'I love books,' I say, slowly, 'and spreading the joy of literature.' Eew, that makes me sound like a pretentious prat – even though it's true – but Flora just nods. 'And I love talking to people. One of the best things about this job is the conversations I have with the people who come in. Lots of people call in for a chat.'

Flora raises her eyebrows. 'Just for a chat?'

'Loads of them buy books too.'

'Loads' is pushing it because a fair few only nip in to tell me about their medical ailments or to share the latest gossip. But some ask for advice on books they might like to buy, and I'm always happy to give it – just so long as lots of sex, excessive violence and magic aren't their 'thing'.

'You do seem to have a relaxed style with customers,' says Flora, her expression neutral so it's hard to tell if that's a good or bad thing. 'So what do you think of the way this place has been run up to now?'

I shrug. 'It's fine.'

Faint lines fan across Flora's forehead when she frowns. 'No, really. I want you to be honest because I'd like your opinion.'

This is a first. Ruben was a fair boss and didn't mind me having an hour off to drive my gramp to the doctor or his chiropody appointment – just so long as I made up the time later. But he was elderly and old school. He ran the business and I was his employee, who put up and shut up. Any suggestions I had for improvements were dismissed as too expensive, totally unnecessary or completely unworkable. So I ended up keeping my opinions to myself.

'You can say whatever you think. I can take it,' says Flora, fixing me with a hard stare.

'Well…' I hesitate, even though I've always had plenty of ideas about how the shop could be improved. 'I think this place could attract more customers by being more welcoming – with better lighting throughout the store, more chairs so people can browse in comfort, maybe discounts for regular book buyers. That type of thing. And just more books generally – more choice. I'd have books, all kinds of books, everywhere.'

I stop and bite my lip, unsure whether Flora really wants my views. But she nods and says 'interesting' as though she means it.

Then she paces up and down for a few moments, as though wrestling with a decision.

'I need to make this business work,' she suddenly blurts out, her cheeks flushing bright pink as she taps her foot rhythmically against the door frame. 'Malcolm – that's my husband – thinks that taking on a failing bookshop is a foolish investment, especially as I've no real experience of this kind of thing.'

She carries on tapping. Tap, tap, tap.

'I've helped Malcolm run restaurants in the past. He had one in Yorkshire for years until…' she hesitates, 'until we moved to Oxford last summer and he set one up there. So I know about running restaurants, but bookshops, not so much. This is a whole new venture for me, but that doesn't mean it won't work, does it.'

Is that a question or a statement? Flora doesn't seem so confident any more.

'I'm sure it will work,' I say, crossing my fingers behind my back. 'You can make changes for the better, and you've got me here to support you. I kind of know how the shop works so it'll be fine.'

It's only when Flora gives a big smile and her shoulders drop that I realise they've been up around her ears all morning.

'Thank you, Callie. That's what I'm banking on.' She breathes out slowly. 'I'm parched. Do you fancy a coffee?'

This *is* a day of firsts. The only time Ruben ever made me a hot drink was when I slipped in milk on the shop kitchen floor and knackered my knee. And that was purely so I wouldn't sue.

Flora's heels click across the flagstones while it sinks in that maybe my new boss isn't quite so intimidating after all. She seemed nervous when she was talking about her minimal retail experience, and I'm touched that she confided in me about her husband's lack of support.

It turns out she doesn't have a grand plan to turn this place around. She doesn't seem to know much about bookshops at all, which is worrying. But at least I can report to Sarah that she doesn't appear to be a total cow.

Chapter Two

'How was day one with the dragon?' shouts Gramp when I come through the front door of the small house we share. We've lived together since my gran died almost three years ago, which was around the same time that my mum moved to Spain. I shove the door closed with my foot and trudge through the hall with shopping bags in each hand.

'It was OK,' I shout back, dropping my bags onto the kitchen table with a clatter.

Oh dear. He's been washing up the breakfast things again. I chip a chunk of solidified Weetabix from a bowl on the drainer and make a mental note to check over the crockery before putting it away. While I'm sure many women in their twenties dream of romantic mini-breaks with celebs like Ryan Gosling, I'd happily tell Ryan to take a hike if the alternative was a brand spanking new dishwasher.

Abandoning my shopping, I walk to the front room and poke my head around the door.

'What's with the dragon reference? You've never met Flora. And – oh for the love of… what the hell's that on your face?'

Gramp pulls off the huge black rubber goggles he's wearing. They leave deep dents in the wrinkled, papery skin around his eyes.

'What, these? They're swimming goggles.'

'I can see that. But why?'

'Now there's no need to go ballistic, Callie, but I'm thinking of doing more wild swimming so I need the right gear. I've got Clement in the pub to order a wetsuit on the web thing for me, so listen out for the postman knocking. It's second-hand but it'll do, and I've signed up for the sponsored swim in Lower Honeyworth Lake.'

I sink slowly into the chair next to the electric fire, which has two bars blazing even though it's uncomfortably hot in here. 'I'm glad you're planning to take part in a wetsuit rather than your pants, Gramp. But that's quite an energetic swim. Isn't it a few miles long? That's a lot, even for people much younger than you.'

'Excellent! Then it's more of a challenge.' He grins at me and winks. 'After all, you only live once and you should never hold back from being who you are. That's what it said.'

He points at the article he cut out of a magazine just before his birthday – the one encouraging readers to throw caution to the wind and become their 'true selves'. It sets out *rules for being the real you* and ways to *inject authenticity into your life.* I sigh because being my 'true self' would involve strangling the journalist for putting daft ideas into an old man's head.

'I'd just like you to stay alive for as long as possible.' I grasp his hands, which feel hot and clammy in the sauna-like room. 'Taking more exercise is a great idea but don't you think a strenuous swim might be a bit much at eighty?'

'It'll be fine,' he huffs, 'and anyway, I've got to go some time and don't fancy croaking it in a hospital bed. I'd far rather drop off the perch while swimming in a lake or freefalling through space.'

Ah, great. I was hoping he'd forgotten his parachuting plans. I shake my head to dislodge the image of his poor, ancient body lying crumpled in the dirt.

'And talking of going some time,' he continues, 'your mother rang at lunchtime to see if I was dead yet.'

'I'm sure she rang to make sure you're all right. She's very fond of you, you know.'

'Hhmm. She's never quite forgiven me for outliving your dad.'

Gramp's rheumy, grey eyes suddenly look bright and he blinks rapidly while I pat his skinny arm. Behind his head, on the mantelpiece, a silver-framed photo of my dad – his son – keeps watch over both of us.

'How was Mum?'

'All right, I think,' he sniffs. 'Still living it large in Alicante, by the sound of things. I don't think she's *found herself* yet.' He puts 'found herself' in air quotes, and snorts. 'Though I'm not quite sure what she's hoping to find, anyway.'

Poor Gramp. He doesn't approve of Mum moving on, physically and emotionally, after Dad's death. Even though it's been around eight years now since my lovely, funny, argumentative dad died suddenly of a heart attack. I still miss him horribly and wish I'd had a chance to say a proper goodbye.

Gramp was knocked for six by the whole thing and totally floored when my gran, Moira, died three years ago. Loss and loneliness dragged him down, so I moved in to keep him company.

I was only going to stay a while, until he got back on his feet. But it's comfortable here, Gramp and I muddle along nicely, and he needs more looking after than ever these days. Especially since he acquired a death wish as an eightieth birthday present.

Plus, it's the least I can do for my lovely gran, whose presence still inhabits this house – from the half-empty bottle of perfume Gramp keeps on his bedside table, to her beloved copper kettles in the fireplace. She started collecting them when I was a child. And, when I got bored with listening to Mum and Dad bicker for the millionth time, I'd sit on her kitchen table, drumming my heels against the legs, as she polished the kettles with newspaper until they shone.

Make the most of your potential, Callie, she'd tell me as she got stuck in with the elbow grease. *And always follow your dreams* — I guess that's what Mum's doing now in Spain.

'Did Mum say anything about Manuel?'

I pick up the squidgy black goggles and look at them closely. They're still warm from resting against Gramp's skin.

'She didn't mention her boyfriend, no.' He sniffs, takes the goggles from me and drops them onto the coffee table. 'And I didn't ask, thank you very much. Do you think she'll come to her senses soon and come home?'

'I'm not sure when she'll be back but it's good that she's happy again, isn't it?' I say gently, placing my hand on top of his and giving it a squeeze.

'Hhmm.' He lets my hand rest there for a moment before pulling it away. 'Well, at least it's a lot quieter round here now your mother's a thousand miles away.'

Which, much as I miss having Mum around, is a good point.

You always know when my mum's nearby. She's loud, bold and argumentative – a lot like my dad, in fact, which is why the two of them were always bickering. They loved each other but rarely agreed on anything.

Surprisingly – or perhaps not, seeing as I could rarely get a word in edgeways – I'm much quieter than my parents. The thought of being the centre of attention brings me out in hives, and I really, *really* hate arguing. I'll do anything to avoid confrontation, which, according to Sarah, makes me a total push-over. She's probably right, but what can you do?

'Oh, by the way,' says Gramp, brushing stray biscuit crumbs from the white bristles on his chin. 'I heard something interesting today from Ivy in the butcher's. Someone's started work on the old manor house. The one near where your boyfriend Noah Shawley used to live.'

He never misses a chance to refer to Noah as my boyfriend, even though we only went out for a few ill-fated weeks just before university. Back then, I thought wonderfully nerdy Noah was the love of my life – until I overheard him telling his brother he wasn't serious about me because I was too 'rough'. His casual unkindness and snobbery broke my heart and fuelled my insecurity about growing up in the rougher end of town. I ended the relationship immediately, and never told anyone the real reason why we broke up, not even Noah.

'I'm talking about the house directly opposite what was Noah's front gate,' says Gramp, slowly, deliberately bringing up Noah again. He's always been curious about why we split up. 'The one that he and his fam—'

'I know where the manor house is and can't imagine who would take it on,' I butt in, refusing to rise to the bait.

The manor house is the poshest place in town but it's been empty since its owner, Mr Jacob, had a stroke and moved to an Oxford care home two years ago.

'I don't know who's bought it. Some out-of-towner who's well minted.'

'Well minted?'

When I giggle, Gramp gives a shrug. 'Just moving with the times, Callie, and keeping up with what youngsters are saying these days.'

Yeah, youngsters back in the 1970s.

He shuffles in his chair and rubs his hands over his shiny bald head. 'The new owner must be loaded because the place is falling down. He'll probably do it up as a weekend holiday home, skedaddle back to the city and we'll never see him again.'

He tuts, disapproving of Londoners buying up local houses and leaving them empty during the week. He complains local youngsters can't get on the property ladder because there's not enough housing available. But even when places are for sale, people like me who grew up here can't afford them anyway. Especially the handsome Cotswold-stone cottages with thatched roofs that outsiders lap up.

They love the idea of country living and I've seen tourists practically salivating over the old manor house that sits just behind the church. It's a huge, honey-hued building with pillars flanking an imposing front door. The house is set back from the street behind tall, black metal railings, with a gravel drive that winds past box hedges and mature trees.

I used to shove my nose through the railings as a child and wonder why one man needed all that magnificent space while my parents and I were squeezed into a small, unremarkable house on the outskirts of Honeyford.

'Anyway.' Gramp picks up the TV remote and starts jabbing buttons. 'You haven't told me yet how your first day with the old dragon went?'

'My day was fine, and why *are* you being horrible about Flora? You've never even met her.'

'No, but Dick saw her in the post office and says she seems someone not to be messed with.'

'Just because she's a polished, confident businesswoman? I think that says more about Dick's misogynist views than Flora.'

Gramp wrinkles his nose and starts channel-hopping to see if he can find a Western.

'It's good to hear you standing up for your new boss and questioning Dick's motives.' He turns from the TV and gives me a crinkly-eyed smile. 'Maybe you're finding your true self at last, Callie, and not before time. You spend far too long looking out for other people and listening to them burbling on. Aha!'

He drops the remote into his lap as John Wayne's face looms out of the TV screen. 'Anyway, love, chop chop. What are you cooking me for my tea?'

I raise my eyebrows but the irony of his words is lost on my grandfather, who's already engrossed in his shoot-em-up movie.

Chapter Three

The next morning, I get up extra early, ignore talk of Gramp's latest ambitious plans (what is an Ironman challenge, anyway?) and head for work with time to spare.

This is the time of day I love most in Honeyford. The sun is rising in a milky-blue sky scattered with scudding clouds, and spring flowers – purple orchids, cowslips and Cotswold pennycress – litter the grass verges.

The town is coming to life, as it's done for centuries, and it's the permanence of the place that makes me feel safe – because even when the people you love die, disappoint you, or bugger off to Spain, the sun will still rise and cast shadows across weather-worn stone. The circle of life goes on, with me just a tiny, insignificant cog in a ginormous wheel.

Being all philosophical about cogs and wheels means I don't clock that I'm walking the long way to work until I'm halfway along Church Lane. Usually my route takes me straight down the hill, along Weavers Lane, and into the High Street. Twenty minutes tops from door to door.

But, lost in thought, I've taken the turning towards the medieval church and can see the river ahead of me. Further on, just past the tall trees edging the river bank, stand the black gates of the manor house. Damn my subconscious! It's no skin off my nose who's bought the place but I suppose I am a little curious, and the shop will be alive with gossip about it later.

Upping my pace, I cross over the arched stone bridge and avoid looking at the large, picture-perfect cottage opposite that backs onto the water. That's where Noah and his family lived for two years, where we made plans together for university, and where I overheard what he really thought of me. Not that I allow myself to think about that these days.

I march on with my eyes on the road, reach the manor house gates and press my nose up against them.

It's only twenty to nine but there's already a commotion going on. Several vehicles are parked on the gravel drive, including a builders' van and a sleek purple Porsche with personalised registration plates – FS 1. Yep, whoever bought this place is well and truly minted.

'Do you know how long all this is going to take?'

A stocky, dark-haired man in jeans has stepped out of the open front door and is talking to a man in navy-blue overalls. I don't hear the reply but the man in jeans scowls as he runs his fingers through his fringe and looks my way.

Whoah! It can't be! I scoot away from the gates and duck behind the drystone wall that edges the property. When I peep again, the man is taking a drag on the cigarette he's just lit, with his face to the sun. It is! It's Finn Shawley, Noah's older brother. He moved away from Honeyford eight years ago, much to the distress of the local female population. What's he doing here? And, more to the point, who's here with him?

I keep staring but Finn is moving back inside the house and I only catch a quick glimpse of the perfect backside that my sixth-form friends used to lust over. They virtually swooned over his shiny hair, his white teeth and his biceps, and flirted shamelessly whenever he was around.

There's no denying that Finn Shawley is a very handsome man, but he didn't do it for me. His charisma was undeniable, and I was awed by the way he picked up and dropped girlfriends without compunction. But his brash confidence almost frightened me. My quiet personality was overwhelmed by his – and he'd never have given a mouse like me a second glance anyway.

Is he definitely here on his own? Or is Noah here too? Our paths haven't crossed since we broke up and, even though it's been years, the thought of seeing Noah again is making my heart hammer. I do another quick scan of the driveway but there's no one else I recognise. Taking long, deep breaths, I try to calm the fluttering in my stomach.

'Is everything all right, Callie?' Mrs Johnson, the town's biggest gossip, who often calls into the shop to pass on some titbit of information, suddenly looms into view beside me and grasps hold of the gate. 'You look like you're in prison, gazing through the bars.'

'Oh, you made me jump! I'm fine, thank you. Just curious about what's happening at Mr Jacob's old place.'

My cheeks are burning and I feel caught out, like a peeping Tom.

'Apparently someone from London has paid big money for it,' says Mrs Johnson, who I've known since I was a child. Her first name is Lorraine, though I've never used it. My mum was big on children being respectful and thought using first names with adults was out of order. She marched off to the school and complained when one of our teachers told us to call her Debbie.

'Well, it's good that something's happening with the place,' I splutter. 'It would be a shame if it sat empty for too long.'

'Criminal,' agrees Mrs Johnson. 'And empty houses are magnets for those squatting folk.' She peers through the gate and gasps. 'Gosh, whoever's bought the house is getting on with things straightaway. Very efficient and upfront.'

She stands up straight and pushes permed hair out of her eyes. 'Talking of upfront, how's your mother doing these days? Still in Spain, I suppose' – she purses her thin lips – 'with that young lad?'

'She's still with Manuel, who's just had his thirty-ninth birthday,' I say, firmly.

'He's quite the toy boy,' mutters Mrs Johnson, and she looks so sneery I decide not to tell her that the person who's apparently bought the manor is Finn Shawley. The news will set sleepy old Honeyford on fire, and I'm not going to give her the satisfaction of lighting the touch-paper. She already spends far too much time bragging, to anyone who'll listen, about her son who works for some big company in Manchester.

Nope, this is one piece of news I'll keep to myself, in the hope that Finn will realise he's made a terrible mistake and will sell up immedi-ately – hopefully before Noah pays him a visit and starts wandering the streets of Honeyford. Jeez, my stomach starts turning somersaults at the very idea. Just because I'm over the man who callously broke my heart doesn't mean that I ever want to see him again.

Leaving Mrs Johnson with *her* nose pressed up to the manor house gate, I scurry off towards the bookshop.

My early arrival at work results in an approving nod from Flora, who's sitting with her head bent over Ruben's old-fashioned accounts ledger.

'Good morning, Callie. How are you today?'

A beam of sunlight is shining on her smooth ebony hair and casting a halo around her. She looks like an angel – a sophisticated angel in full make-up who's come to deliver Honeyford Bookshop from penury.

'Fine, thanks,' I mumble, brushing my hands over the skinny jeans I threw on this morning and blowing my blonde fringe out of my eyes. My thick, shoulder-length hair is caught up in a ponytail but never looks tidy.

Flora runs a finger along the collar of the exquisite midnight-blue blouse she's wearing. Is it made of silk? The fabric ripples like deep flowing water as it catches the light.

I sigh quietly and tuck in my stripy Primark T-shirt. I'll have to up my game if my boss is going to come into work each day looking like she's stepped straight from the pages of *Vogue*. Maybe I should ditch my trainers and start wearing more make-up than my usual one coat of brown mascara and slick of pink lip gloss.

'I've had an idea,' says Flora. 'What you said about the way Ruben chose his stock got me thinking and I reckon it's about time our customers got a look-in. So we're going to do a survey and ask everyone who comes in to fill in a short questionnaire about their favourite authors and genres, and what they're looking for in a bookshop. What do you think?'

'I think it's long overdue. Will there be an incentive for people to take part? Maybe a book token for whoever's questionnaire is picked out of a hat?'

'What a good idea!'

When Flora writes *token* on the notepad next to her, I feel ridiculously pleased. Like I used to at school when the teacher praised me.

Flora starts working out the survey questions while I deal with customers coming into the shop who want to buy or order books. Being busy keeps my mind off the manor house's new owner and I almost forget the Shawleys for a while.

But my zen is severely tested when Sorrell and Julia come into the shop around lunchtime. We were in the same year at school so they know who I am. But I wasn't part of their gang, not being one of the 'cool' girls. I also lived on the town's small council estate, which was far too common for them to even contemplate, so they always pretend not to recognise me when our paths cross.

They rarely come into Honeyford Bookshop, and, as expected, they don't acknowledge me when they saunter in and make a beeline for the biographies.

I'm behind a stand of Jane Austen paperbacks, wondering if I remembered to put pickle in my corned beef sandwiches, when the name 'Finn' drifts across the bookshelves. Ooh, what do they know about the new arrival?

Sorrell is leafing through a horror thriller as I start creeping closer. And I follow her and Julia when they move on to the cookery section.

It's quite hard being a spy. On telly, espionage looks dead simple – tail your quarry in the street, sit close to them in a restaurant, or drive two cars behind theirs so they don't realise you're on their trail. But it's not so easy when you're trying to follow two women, who know exactly who you are, around an enclosed space. There's only so much tidying of books I can do in their vicinity without coming across as a weirdo.

'I just can't believe Finn Shawley's back in town after all this time,' says Julia, pushing platinum-blonde hair over her shoulder. 'What a treat.'

I pick up the book I've just put down and turn it over in my hands, earwigging shamelessly.

'He must be loaded to buy that place and my uncle says the work he's got planned will cost, like, a proper fortune.'

'Apparently he's some super-rich businessman in London now, so that'll be peanuts as far as he's concerned.' Sorrell's voice is breathless with envy. 'I so should have kept going out with him.'

'Tricky, 'cos I thought he ditched you,' says Julia, sweetly.

'Well, you know Finn.' Sorrell gives a forced laugh and shoots her friend a hostile glare. 'It was a different girl every week with him.'

'Which is why I gave him a wide berth.'

'Really? I thought you were mad about him but he never gave you the time of day?'

'It was more the other way round,' asserts Julia, knuckles turning white as she grips a low-carb, low-fat diet book. 'I didn't want to be just another notch on his bedpost.'

'Are you implying I was easy?' Sorrell slams her hand against the bookshelf, nostrils flaring.

Good grief! Finn Shawley's back in town for five minutes and is already causing tension. Though it's inevitable, I suppose. The gene pool round here is severely limited, so the arrival of a sexy bloke who's mega-minted is bound to cause shock waves.

Julia ignores her friend's mini tantrum as though she's seen it all before, and starts flicking through the diet book. 'His brother's here, too. What's his name?'

The paperback I'm holding clatters to the floor and Sorrell and Julia glare at me.

'Sorry,' I mumble, picking up the book and pretending to read the blurb on the back.

'I can't remember his name – was it Neville or Norris or something? He was always quite sweet but a bit nerdy.'

'Well, you are in for a surprise 'cos he's changed and, oh boy,' Julia fans herself with her hand, 'he's filled out in all the right places. My uncle says he lives in New York now but he's here helping Finn make all the changes.'

'What changes?' I blurt out, all pretence gone. My former classmates stare at me, horrified that I've brazenly broken the unwritten rule that we should never, ever speak.

'Finn Shawley is turning the manor house into a boutique hotel. My uncle's doing some of the building work so he knows what's going on,' says Julia, small grey eyes narrowing.

Which means that Noah will be helping out for a while, and will be in Honeyford for days. Possibly even weeks. Or *months*, if building work doesn't go to plan. And everyone knows building work never goes to plan.

My heart sinks as Sorrell and Julia raise their over-plucked eyebrows. How can I keep my resolution to never speak to Noah Shawley again if I'm likely to bump into him in the post office queue? I can hardly just ignore him.

'Hang on a minute. Didn't you used to hang out with Finn's brother? Back when you were both nerds?' Sorrell smirks at Julia. 'Well, at least one of them has changed for the better since the sixth form.'

What a cow!

You two haven't changed. You're both still bitches. That's what Sarah would say. That's what I should say. But I don't do confrontation. Not ever. So I fold my arms defensively and swallow the words.

Sorrell's plump lips settle into a mean line when she realises I'm not going to retaliate. 'Come on, Jules. Let's go. I can never find what I want in this stupid little shop. It must be so boring to work in such a dead-end place and go home to the Berry Estate.'

'What was that all about?' asks Flora as the girls sweep out of the door, noses in the air. She's hugging a mug of coffee to her chest and steam is wafting in tiny curls under her chin.

'What do you mean?'

I try to sound normal but my hands are a right giveaway. They're clenched into such tight fists, my nails are digging into my palms. How dare Sorrell and Julia dismiss the shop and where I live, and make comments about me and Noah?

'The girls who just flounced out – I couldn't help but notice that you were listening in. Do you know them?'

'Kind of.' I take a deep breath and unclench my fingers because, as my gramp keeps telling me, holding on to anger is bad for the body. 'I don't usually spy on customers, but they were talking about the man who's bought the manor house by the church. I knew him and his brother a long time ago.'

My cheeks are burning and Flora gives me a hard stare, but says nothing. The silence stretches between us, taut and uncomfortable, until I feel obliged to give a fuller explanation. But salvation arrives in the form of a seventy-eight-year-old man in a natty Panama hat.

'Hey, Callie,' shouts Dick from the shop doorway. He adjusts the waistband of his old-man shorts that skim the tops of his knobbly knees. 'You need to speak to Stanley because he's definitely going doolally and won't have any friends left before long. I've tried telling him but he takes no notice of me.'

Flora takes another sip of her coffee and regards Dick over the rim of her pretty china mug. 'I presume he's one of the locals. Who the hell is Stanley?'

'Stanley's my grandfather.'

I scurry over to Dick, who's standing with one sandal-clad foot inside the shop and the other outside. He prides himself on not having read a book since school and won't come into the shop in case so many books in one place worm their way into his head and contaminate him.

'What's wrong with Stanley?' I hiss, guiding him out onto the pavement.

Dick shoves his round sunglasses further up his nose, tilts his hat back, and pulls himself up to his full height of six feet and two inches. His long white beard is streaked with dark grey.

'He's behaving very oddly. You know what a meek and mild fellow he normally is. Wouldn't say boo to a goose. Well, when I asked him this morning what he thought of my new car' – he nods at a rusty green sports car parked badly near the pub – 'he said it was a mid-life crisis car for a man with more money than sense, and I'll look like the Jolly Green Giant in it.'

Dick's eyes open wide in indignation while I bite my lip. It's quite funny really. And accurate. But Dick's right – it's not the sort of thing that Gramp would usually say.

I'm already worried that Gramp's erratic behaviour points to dementia and maybe another sign is telling the unvarnished truth, rather than wrapping it up in half-truths and kindnesses, like most of us do.

'We've been friends for a long time,' continues Dick, still in high dudgeon. 'We've been through baldness and bereavement together. But I'm not going to put up with snide comments about my purchases, so you need to have a word. Pronto.'

With that, he marches back to his car, slides into the driving seat and screeches away with a whiff of burning rubber. Gramp's right. He does look like a giant behind the steering wheel, with his hat squashed flat against the roof.

During my lunch break, I wander along to the town square, sit on the steps of the war memorial, and FaceTime Sarah on my mobile. She answers on the third ring and adjusts her distance from the screen so it's not filled with a close-up of her silver nose ring.

'Hiya, Callie. I was going to call you this evening 'cos we haven't spoken for days. Is everything all right?'

There's a hum of hairdryers and conversation in the background, and the low drone of Cheltenham traffic passing by the hair salon where she works.

'Yeah, fine. Just fancied a chat, really.'

'Well, it's good timing 'cos I'm bored out of my mind,' says Sarah, running a hand through her glossy chestnut curls. 'All I've done all morning is make four appointments, cancel two, and drink coffee. That, and show Sophie's Italian stallion Facebook post to all the girls here. It was much appreciated, let me tell you.' She cackles down the line. 'So tell me what's happening in Honeyford – flood, famine, nuclear apocalypse?'

'Nothing much,' I say, tilting my face towards the sun that's trying to break through thick wodges of white cloud. 'Flora's sorting out a customer survey; Janey Ellison's pregnant again; Finn Shawley's moved into the manor house, and Honeyford's Thursday Market has switched to Fridays.'

'Typical Honeyford!' snorts Sarah. 'How can a Thursday Market be held on a Friday? That's mad. I always thought… hang on a minute.' Her face looms so close to the screen, I can count the freckles on her nose. 'Did you say Finn Shawley's back in town?'

'I did.'

'Wow, that's huge news!' I lower the volume on my phone because Sarah always shouts when she's excited. 'So why is he here?' she bellows. 'I mean, what's the actual fricking deal?'

'The actual fricking deal is that Finn, who's now a very successful businessman, has bought the manor house and is turning it into a boutique hotel.'

'That's amazing. Is he still catnip to the *lay-dees*?'

'He certainly is, if the reaction from Sorrell and Julia is anything to go by. They came into the shop earlier.'

'Urgh, they're a right couple of cows.'

Yes! Thank you, Sarah. When I laugh, a driver with German number plates, who's pottering round the square looking for a parking space, gives me a sideways glance. He thinks I'm a local yokel.

'Is fancy-himself Finn back in Honeyford on his own, then?'

I hesitate. 'Nope, Noah's come over from his home in New York to help out.'

'Noah's in Honeyford too? That is dope! Have you seen him?'

'No, and I don't intend to, if I can help it.'

'What is the big deal between the two of you?' sighs Sarah, annoyed that I've never properly told her why our fledgling romantic relationship came to such an abrupt halt.

I did think of telling her at the time, but she'd already left for university and would only have marched round in the holidays to have it out with him – and shouting makes everything worse. So I kept my mouth shut about the details, and determined never to think of Noah again.

And it was all going so well until Finn decided to snap up a prime piece of Honeyford real estate.

'There's no "big deal" and it's all ancient history,' I tell Sarah, flicking a fly off my corned beef sandwich. 'We just fell out, that's all.'

'But you don't fall out with anyone, and you and Noah were so close.' She pouts at the screen.

'I'm worried my gramp might be showing signs of dementia,' I blurt out, keen to move Sarah on from my long-lost love life.

'Why? Because he's started saying what he thinks and going out and enjoying himself?'

Hhmm, it sounds far less worrying when Sarah puts it like that.

'I don't know. He's just not himself these days.'

'He's fine, but talk to him about it if you're worried. Oh, and nice change of subject, but I want to hear more about the sexy Shawleys. Like what you're going to do when you bump into Noah, which is bound to happen in such a small town.'

'It's not bound to happen but, if it does, I'll be my usual cool self, obviously.'

'Obviously,' says Sarah, before laughing like a drain. 'Oops, gotta go 'cos Mrs Chivers needs to pay for her perm. But we'll catch up on this later, babe. The subject is not closed. Bye.'

I put my phone away and eat my lunch, but the bread sticks in my throat and I feel jittery; nervous that Noah might walk at any moment through the yellow-stone arches of the market house, and then I'd have to act cool.

Usually at lunchtimes, I have a wander round the town to clear my head. Sometimes I walk down to the river and watch the water tumbling over stones and lapping against the banks. But I give all that a miss today and scurry back to work instead.

Chapter Four

Fortunately, Flora doesn't ask any more questions about Sorrell and Julia, and the next two hours pass in a blur of replenishing stock, serving customers, and trying very, *very* hard not to think about Noah. Which is impossible because, for some reason, he gets under my skin.

Snatches of long-forgotten conversations keep dropping into my mind, along with images of the two of us together – sitting in the school canteen with our heads bent together, paddling in the river where it shallows near Honeyford Bridge, his hand in mine at Blenheim Palace during a sixth-form history trip. We initially bonded over our shared love of local history. So maybe Julia wasn't too off-beam with her nerd comment.

I keep busy, busy, busy but sometimes it's hard to keep the past in its place. And the images keep coming, like an old film, until my head begins to ache.

The pain ramps up big-time just before half-three, when a young woman pushes a pram into the shop, with a screaming baby inside it. The baby's *really* going for it.

Honeyford Bookshop is only small and the space is soon chock-a-block with ear-piercing yells. A couple of tourists put down the book of local walks they were flicking through and beat a hasty retreat.

Flora grimaces and stays behind the counter while I wander up to the mum, who I recognise from yesterday. Then, she looked pretty knackered. Now, she looks on her last legs.

'Can I help you?'

The woman stares at me with glassy, red-rimmed eyes. 'So sorry,' she shouts above the screaming. 'Do you want me to leave? Everyone wants me to leave places because he won't stop crying. But he can't possibly be hungry – he's draining me dry. And I'm really trying to be a good mother. Do you have any books on stopping babies from crying?'

She sniffs as the words stop tumbling from her tired mouth and leans against a high stack of women's commercial fiction titles that Flora's just ordered in.

'I'm sure we do. And we can always order anything you think might help,' I say, putting my hand on her elbow and leading her away from the tottering book pile.

It's going to take more than advice in a baby manual to stop this one from yelling, but I guide her towards a shelf near the window. She wheels the baby over and stamps her foot down on the pram brake.

The baby's still wailing and fat tears roll down the woman's cheeks as she runs her fingers along the small section of parenting books that we have in stock.

'Is she your first baby?' I raise my voice above the din.

'He,' she shouts, nodding at me. 'First and last. It's been awful. My husband says he wants another but I'd rather have a divorce.'

She gulps and brushes tears from her cheeks.

'Does he sleep at night?'

She shakes her head and greasy brown hair sweeps across her pale face.

'He hardly sleeps at all. He's like super-human or something.'

'Do you have any support? Anyone to give you a break?'

'Not really. We've not been here for long and Pete, my partner, is at work all day. And I'm breastfeeding so he can't help at night with Callum.' She bites her lip and scrubs her cheeks with her hands. 'Sorry, sorry. It's all a bit overwhelming. He was IVF and so wanted but now I'd be quite glad if he just disappeared. Oh God, what an awful thing to say. I'm such a terrible mother.'

When she gulps and swallows a sob, I'm tempted to give her a hug. But I make do with an empathetic pat on the arm instead, in case Flora frowns on me cuddling customers.

'You're just tired and human. I'm Callie, by the way. What's your name?'

'Um…' She gazes at me blankly for a second and gives her head a slight shake. 'Mary. My name's Mary.'

'Look, Mary, do you want me to take Callum for a walk around the block while you're searching for a book?'

She peers at me and frowns. 'I'd be a really bad mother to let a stranger walk off with my baby. Wouldn't I?'

'I work here and I'm not a baby stealer or anything. I'll have to bring him back or I'll lose my job.'

As Callum's screams reach a crescendo, Mary makes a decision. 'Take him!' she yells. 'Please. For as long as you like.'

Flora's mouth drops open when I push the pram towards her. 'I'm taking him round the block so his mum can shop in peace. Is that OK?'

Then she shrugs. 'Anything. Just get him out of here.' She winces and shoves her fingers in her ears.

The temperature's dropped since lunchtime and a brisk breeze is blowing down from the hills. I pull the covers up round Callum's chin and tuck him in. His tiny face is bright red with rage and his little fists are drumming on the covers.

I'm sure he's sweet but, boy, is he hard work. I walk briskly up the High Street and do a loop along narrow Sheep Street and Weavers Lane – twice – but he carries on screaming.

Callum would make an ideal contraceptive – put him in the same room as a broody teenager and she'd be in Boots buying condoms before his next nappy change.

While I'm walking past the pub for the second time, I wonder if Flora has children. She's never mentioned any, and her clothes are immaculate, with no Weetabix stains or crayon marks. When I know her better, I'll ask.

After three times around the block, Callum's screaming turns into sniffles and short sucks of breath, and then all goes blessedly quiet. When I peep into the pram, he's lying on his back with his arms stretched out, like an angel. A puce, sweaty cherub with a dribble-slicked chin. Result!

I'm heading back towards the shop, enjoying the peace, when a tall figure turns into the High Street and starts walking towards me. It can't be! My heart starts pounding in my ears because, even from this distance, the loping stride is familiar.

This is so typical of my luck! The last thing I want is to bump into Noah Shawley, so what's the first thing that happens? He appears around the corner, like he's been magicked up by the god of incompetent matchmakers. And if I don't get a move on, we're going to have a horribly awkward encounter.

The pram bumps up and down as I push Callum towards the bookshop and gather speed. I'm covering lots of ground and the doorway's in sight, but Noah is walking quickly with his head down and bound to reach me before I get there.

I stop, ready to turn the pram around and hurtle off in a different direction, but he chooses that very moment to glance up and look directly at me. His stride falters for a moment and then he carries on walking my way. Great! My mouth suddenly feels parched.

It's over eight years since I last laid eyes on Noah Shawley, and bitchy Julia is right; he's changed. At eighteen, he was tall and rangy with round glasses and flyaway fair hair that curled around his neck.

Now, the unruly hair I once ran my fingers through is cut short, he's wearing trendy, horn-rimmed glasses and has swapped his faded jeans for a smart navy-blue suit. And he's definitely filled out in all the right places. Back then, he was a skinny adolescent who was all arms and legs. But he's been working out, if his broad shoulders and the hint of muscles beneath his fitted shirt are anything to go by.

He might look different, but when he stops in front of me, shrugs his shoulders and wrinkles his nose, there's no mistaking who he is.

'Callie!' He says my name like it's an accusation. 'What are you doing here?'

'I live here,' I squeak, in a very uncool voice.

'What, still?'

I feel my body stiffen. *Yes, Noah, I'm still in Honeyford because I love it here and, guess what? I'm still living on the 'rough' Berry Estate.*

I take in a gulp of air and try to smile. 'Yes, I'm still here. Um, where are you living now?'

Best not let on that I know exactly where he's living now or he'll think I've been stalking him.

'New York. I'm working there as an architect.'

'Wow, congratulations. That's pretty impressive.'

'Yeah, thanks.' He shuffles from foot to foot while passers-by tut at us for blocking the pavement. 'Have you ever been? To New York, I mean.'

I shake my head because, though New York is on my bucket list, heaven knows when I'll have saved enough to go. Certainly not while Gramp's spending his pension on parachute jumps and swimming gear, rather than household bills.

'It's a great place to visit. I work close to Central Park, and live on the Lower East Side in a brownstone and…' Noah tails off and pushes his glasses up his nose. 'Not that you need to know all that. So are you still living with your mum?'

'What? No, definitely not,' I huff, as though that's the most ridiculous suggestion ever.

'No, of course not,' says Noah, colouring slightly and glancing at my left hand. 'It looks like congratulations are in order.'

'For what?'

'Becoming a mum.' Noah sticks his head into the pram and gives a tight smile. 'She's very…' He does a double-take at Callum's bright red face and swallows; '… cute.'

'She's a he and he isn't mine.'

An emotion I can't read flits across Noah's face. 'Ah, I thought you must be married or living with a boyfriend, after all this time.'

He waits for me to say something but instead I channel my inner Mona Lisa, smile enigmatically, and stay schtum.

There's no way I'm telling New-York Noah that I'm bunked up with my gramp, only a stone's throw from my childhood home. I could be living in a gorgeous honey-hued cottage with a thatched roof, an Aga and a golden retriever, for all he knows.

Noah shoves his hands into his trouser pockets as the silence between us stretches out, and I start to feel flustered. The man in front of me is all grown-up and different, and not the Noah I once knew. Not that I ever really knew him at all.

A pang of sorrow from the past tightens my throat while cars trundle past and Callum, all cried out, releases a rumbling fart beneath his covers.

'How's Finn?' I say at last, desperate to ease the tension.

Noah hesitates for a moment and then crosses his arms. 'He's doing really well, thank you.'

'And your parents?'

'Ah, you know Mum and Dad. Still moving house every couple of years and still wrapped up in their own lives. Finn and I try to attract their attention every now and then but it's pretty much a lost cause.'

He shrugs while I remember how I envied Noah and Finn. Their peaceful, hands-off parents were very different from mine, who, if they weren't bickering, were trying to micro-manage my life – but maybe the Shawley family set-up wasn't so perfect after all.

'What about your mum?' he asks.

'Mum's living in Spain now. Did you know that my dad died a few years ago?'

'I heard about his death at the time and sent a condolence card to your gramp. I'm so sorry, Callie. That must have been awful.'

Noah stares at me with pale blue eyes the colour of the dawn sky, and briefly touches my arm.

'It's OK,' I say, taking a step back. I'm surprised that Noah sent a card. I don't remember seeing it, but the first few weeks after Dad's death passed in a blur of grief. 'It was hard at the time because his death was so sudden but life has to go on, doesn't it.' I start rocking the pram, hoping that Callum will stay asleep. 'So what about Finn then?' I ask, keen to change the subject. 'I hear he's turning the manor house into a boutique hotel.'

'That's right. Finn wanted it to be hush-hush but nothing stays quiet in Honeyford for long. If I remember rightly, this place is a seething hotbed of gossip and intrigue.'

When Noah grins and runs his fingers through his fringe, my stomach does a weird flip, which is annoying. It's not right that he still has an effect on me. Not after he stood in his posh house and mocked where I come from and told his brother I was nothing special.

Callum squawks and stirs as my pram-rocking becomes more frantic.

'I'd better be getting back,' I blurt out. 'Do give your brother my very best regards when you see him.'

My very best regards? I sound like a maiden aunt passing on her best wishes, rather than a super-cool twenty-something who's living life to the full. I mean, I'm a nerdy twenty-something whose life can be pretty *meh* at times – but Noah Shawley certainly doesn't need to know that.

He's standing directly in front of me and doesn't move.

'Look, I've got to get back to work or I'll be in trouble.'

I tap my watch, like a total idiot, to emphasise the point.

'Of course. Do you work round here?'

He tilts his head at the muddle of stone and half-timbered buildings lining the wide street ahead of us. Some are so old, their top floors seem to be leaning towards the road.

'I work over there,' I tell him, waving my arm in the general direction of the bookshop and the deli, and Mr Fawcett's gift shop which sells Cotswolds honey and knick-knacks to tourists.

There's also a two-man firm of solicitors nearby so maybe New-York Noah will think I've become a hot-shot lawyer. Thought I doubt

Honeyford's answer to Amal Clooney would be heading for work in a cheap T-shirt with a random baby.

'I see. Well, I wouldn't want to keep you,' says Noah, a hint of coldness in his deep voice. He holds out his hand. 'Goodbye, Callie. It was good to see you again.'

'You too,' I say as cheerfully as I can muster, but I hesitate before slipping my hand into his. I vowed never to have anything more to do with Noah Shawley, yet here we are, shaking hands like grown-ups.

His skin is warm but his fingers don't tighten around mine, and the handshake is brief. As it should be, I suppose, between two people who are now almost strangers.

He walks on, and I watch him go for a few moments. My stomach's still churning because I am – to use Gran's favourite phrase – utterly discombobulated.

That's how she liked to describe herself when something unexpected happened and she needed a nip of Gramp's emergency brandy. A friend being taken into hospital, a large bill dropping through the letterbox, a death on *The Archers* – they all warranted a quick slug from the brandy bottle. And right now I could do with a few ginormous gulps myself.

When I get back to the shop, Flora's serving a young man who looks like a student from one of Oxford's colleges. He's wearing a long stripy scarf and buying a biography of Karl Marx which he tucks under his arm.

Flora says goodbye to him before peeping into the pram.

'Thank goodness for that. There's nothing wrong with his lungs, is there? Where's his mum, by the way?'

For one horrible moment, I think Callum's mum has done a runner and I'm now stuck with him. But gentle snoring greets us when Flora and I walk towards the back of the store. There in the shop's sole armchair is stressed-out Mary, splayed back against the cushions and totally out for the count.

Her chest, polka-dotted with milk stains, gently rises and falls. The parenting book she was looking at has fallen into her lap and I carefully place it back on the shelf.

'What shall we do?'

I glance at Flora for guidance, seeing as it's her shop. I know what Ruben would have done – wake the poor woman up, insist she buy a book, and escort her and her sleeping infant out of the store. He wasn't the most empathetic of people.

Flora sighs softly. 'Oh, just let her sleep. How was your walk?'

'Fine. Dead boring.'

'Really?' Flora's mouth twitches in the corner and I wonder if she was watching me from the window. But she doesn't ask about the mystery man I was talking to and I keep busy and out of her way while Mary sleeps soundly in the corner.

Chapter Five

I don't get a chance to have a word with Gramp until the weekend. He's out of the house a lot more these days and I'm totally exhausted from work. It's not that I'm doing anything different in the shop – it's just that I'm not doing anything different in an intense way.

I feel under pressure to prove I work hard and know my stuff – and I'm still getting the measure of my new boss. She was kind to knackered Mary and let her sleep. But she watches me when regulars come in just for a chat, and I get the feeling that not much passes her by.

Avoiding Noah has also become a Big Thing which is taking over my life. Our awkward encounter in the street has left me feeling confused, sad and annoyed – all emotions I like to ignore whenever possible. So I scurry through Honeyford with my head down, avoid Church Lane like the plague, and try not to listen when customers talk about the Shawleys being back in town. And boy, do they talk!

The brothers' reappearance has caused great excitement in everyone except me. Emotions are bubbling beneath my calm exterior, but excitement isn't among them. And the whole thing is extra annoying because there's no good reason why Noah is spooking me quite so much. That was then. This is now. And I've moved on – at least I thought I had.

All I pray is that Noah will do his 'architect and supportive brother' bit and then bugger off back to New York, pronto. And hopefully he's got an eReader jam-packed with bestsellers so won't need to buy any reading material before he leaves.

'Penny for your thoughts,' says Gramp, coming into the hall with a backpack over his shoulders and a bum bag clipped around his waist. 'You're in a world of your own these days and I can't get any sense out of you.'

He prods my foot with the wooden walking stick he's carrying.

'We're only going for a walk in the woods,' I remind him. 'Do you need all that stuff?'

'Ah, you never know what might happen, Callie. And I'm like an elderly Cub Scout – always prepared. Look.' He pulls a slab of Kendal mint cake from the pocket of his bright red cagoule. 'Provisions, just in case we get lost.'

'Lost, in the woods you've walked in since you were a boy?'

'There might be a snowstorm that obliterates the way,' he says, pointing out of the hall window at a bright blue sky. 'It happened to Philip who lives near Marigold Hill. He ended up in hospital with hypothermia.'

'That was because he went climbing in the Cairngorms without a jacket.'

'Same principle,' he insists, pulling open the front door and ushering me outside.

He follows me along the concrete path and closes the rusting metal gate behind us. Tall grass is curling around the gate post and daisies are scattered across the overgrown lawn. The whole garden is in need of a tidy, and it strikes me that the house is looking shabby these days.

It's built of light stone that matches the pretty cottages in the centre of town. But that's where the similarity ends.

Even the smallest cottages in Honeyford have age-old character and style. Roofs are thatched or stone-tiled, gables are pointed and colourful plants climb the walls. Our house is a 1960s council estate box that screams functionality.

Many houses on the small estate are now privately owned and most are well-maintained. But their functional air persists, along with a slight 'us and them' feeling. It's eased over the years, but I was ribbed at school for coming from the Berry Estate, which sits on the very edge of the town as though it's not quite part of Honeyford at all. Kids from the estate tended to stick together, and I have happy memories of playing in the street before heading to Gran and Gramp's for fizzy pop and cake.

'How did you and Gran end up buying this house?' I ask, as we start walking up the lane.

'Penny-pinching,' says Gramp, grinning.

I've heard the story a million times but know he enjoys telling it.

'She was thrifty, my Moira, and put money by from the housekeeping for years without telling me. Then, when I said we should buy the house, she presented me with a tidy chunk of the deposit from under the mattress. Ta-dah! Literally, from under the mattress I'd been sleeping on for years. She was a formidable woman.'

He pulls a white handkerchief from his cagoule pocket and dabs at his eyes. Talking about his beloved wife often brings him to tears and makes me sniffly too. We both still miss her so much.

I link my arm through his and we walk in silence for several minutes to the small beech wood that rises behind the estate. This is where I spent hours when I was growing up – catching beetles, making 'perfume' from flower petals, and scratching my initials on tree trunks.

All around us, vibrant green countryside seems to roll on for ever, splashed here and there with crops of vibrant yellow rape. Flocks of sheep are white dots in the distance and below us, in the hollow of the hill, lies Honeyford and the pale spire of St Cuthbert's church.

I love this place. The gentle beauty of the Cotswolds is soothing during life's ups and downs, and I'm content here – or I was until the Shawleys rolled back into town.

'I've got some news,' I say, lightly, as we pass under the trees.

Beams of sunlight are cutting through the canopy of branches and dappling the soft, springy earth. Gramp stops swishing his stick as though he's hacking his way through the Amazon rainforest.

'What sort of news? Have you got a boyfriend at long last?'

'No I haven't. And it's not that long since Liam and I broke up anyway.'

'It was months ago.' He splutters when a fly lands on his lower lip and brushes it away. 'You should never have dumped that boy. You're far too picky for your own good, if you ask me.'

Hhmm. Liam, a surveyor from Gloucester who had asked me out after coming into the shop, actually dumped me. He said, and I quote, 'You're far too busy looking after the older generation to maintain a proper relationship with someone your own age.' What a pompous idiot! Anyone who can't accept that my gramp means the world to me isn't worth dating.

But I didn't want Gramp to know that he had, inadvertently, helped put the kybosh on my relationship so I told him I did the dumping. It was only a white lie, and I wasn't broken-hearted because my heart's never really been in any of my relationships, apart from the one with Noah.

'A pretty young girl like you should have a boyfriend, especially one with lots of prospects like a surveyor,' grumps Gramp, trudging on along the muddy path. 'Why did you dump him again?'

'I've told you. We decided that our relationship wasn't working.'

'Huh, no sticking power,' he huffs, whacking a low-lying branch out of the way. 'You're lucky me and your gran stuck at it and made it work or you wouldn't be here at all.'

'I'm extremely grateful to the both of you.'

'Anyway, what's your news? Don't keep me in suspense.'

Gramp bats away the fly that's still buzzing around his head.

'I bumped into Noah Shawley the other day.'

Even saying his name makes my stomach go all fluttery, which is utterly ridiculous after all this time.

'Did you indeed? I thought you said the other one with the daft name – Finn, is it? – had bought the old manor house?'

'He has, but Noah's here to give Finn a hand. He's an architect now and has come over from New York where he's living. You don't sound very surprised, Gramp. Did you know already?'

'Dick told me yesterday, though he didn't mention the most important piece of news – that Noah's an architect now. Prospects, girl!' He smudges dirt across his temple when he taps his head.

'You didn't say you knew he was back in town.'

'Neither did you, which is interesting.' Gramp raises his straggly eyebrows and gives a little nod, as though he's very wise.

'Well, I'm telling you now. And it makes no difference to me if he's in Honeyford or New York.'

Gramp comes to an abrupt stop and fixes his grey eyes on me. 'How long is it since you last saw Noah, before you bumped into him the other day?'

'I dunno. Eight years? Just before we went off to university and his parents moved out of town.'

'And how's young Noah doing these days?'

'Fine, I think. I don't know. We didn't speak much. He looked all right.'

He looked more than all right but my grandfather doesn't need to know that.

'He always was a good-looking boy – different from his brother but handsome just the same. So is he married then?'

'You what?'

'You know, married, hitched, hooked up with a life partner, off the market?'

It's daft but I hadn't even considered that Noah might be married. I guess he might have a wife waiting for him in cosmopolitan New York. A glamorous wife who wears designer dresses and goes to early morning yoga classes in Central Park. Ugh.

Gramp's looking at me very oddly. 'I always liked young Noah when he used to come round for tea. He was such a nice boy. No airs and graces, unlike his uppity snob of a brother.'

Hhmm. He wouldn't think so highly of Noah if he knew what I'd overheard him saying about where we live. He'd be so hurt.

A musty smell of rotting wood hits my nose as the sun disappears, and I shudder.

'Are you cold, love?' Gramp puts his arm around me and pats my shoulder. 'Young people today don't wear enough clothes. Your great-grandmother always made sure I had my vest on before I went out.'

'Times have changed.'

'Tell me about it, and not always for the better either.'

I glance at him sideways and run my fingers across the trunk of a tree that's smothered in ivy. Is now a good time to raise my concerns about his recent behaviour? He does worry me.

'You seem to have changed recently,' I say, gently.

'What do you mean? I've always worn a vest.'

'It's nothing to do with vests. I just mean that you seem a bit different these days. A bit more' – I search for the right word – 'difficult.'

Oops, his downturned mouth tells me that's definitely not the right word.

'Uninhibited. That's what I mean. You seem more uninhibited. As though you've had a few.' A thought suddenly strikes me. 'You're not hitting the emergency brandy while I'm at work, are you?'

Gramp frowns. 'I might have a pale ale with my lunch, Callista, but I've not suddenly turned into a raging alky. You're chatting breeze.'

'I'm chatting what?'

'Breeze, Callie. It's youth slang, for talking rubbish. I'd have thought you'd know that, what with you being young. And I don't have a clue what you mean about me being difficult.'

'I just mean different, really. There's the swimming and the jogging, and the youth slang, and what you said to Dick about his car.'

'Oh, for goodness' sake. He's not still banging on about that, is he?' Gramp swishes wildly at the undergrowth with his stick. 'Dick asked me what I thought about his new car, so I told him. Don't ask, if you can't handle the unvarnished truth.'

'It's just that Dick's got used to you varnishing the truth a little bit.'

Which is an understatement. My grandfather usually chucks a whole tin of varnish over everything he says. Like me, he worries about upsetting people and causing arguments – or at least he did, before he hit eighty and went mega-weird.

'Who's on the throne at the moment?' I ask.

'You what?' Gramp puts his hands on his hips and laughs. 'Queen Elizabeth the Second, of course. God bless Her Majesty.'

'And what did you have for tea last night?'

'Steak and kidney pie which was a bit dry, to be honest. I'm going to complain next time I'm passing the butcher's.'

'And where were you born?'

'Cheltenham, why? Oh!' He opens his eyes wide and tuts. 'You think I'm getting dementia because I've started doing things differently. Well, I've got news for you, my girl. I'm perfectly fine and nothing's changed, apart from me having a long overdue change of heart. I want to live a little before I die. And telling the truth is good. You ought to try it sometimes.'

'I do tell the truth.'

'The truth you think people want to hear. You're a people-pleaser, Callie, and so was I. But life is slipping away so it's time to grasp your balls by the nettle and speak out.'

Mixed metaphor notwithstanding, I don't think Gramp has ever before used the word 'balls' in that context. He rarely uses even mild bad language – though, thinking about it, he did call a contestant on *Pointless* a 'daft dickhead' yesterday.

'Anyway, ponder on what I've said, and don't be over-picky when it comes to men with prospects. Oh, and don't be surprised if a sail arrives this week, because I've decided to take up windsurfing.'

With that latest bombshell, he stomps off through the densest part of the wood, his scarlet cagoule a splash of colour in the gloom.

Honestly, he's a nightmare. But I must admit to a grudging admiration for his newly discovered nerve. Fancy having the courage to say and do whatever you want; to show the real you, warts and all, beneath the polite façade. Though it could get you into all sorts of trouble.

I tread the path that Gramp has forged through the undergrowth and wonder, with a sigh, just how much grasping his balls by the nettle my grandfather is planning to do.

Chapter Six

Flora's in a flurry when I get into work on Wednesday. I've scurried in, glancing left and right for any sightings of Noah. None so far, thank goodness.

'Is everything OK?'

My boss is on her knees with a cloth in her hand, wiping imaginary dust from the bottom shelf of 'Fiction: K–M'. She glances up, a pink flush spreading across her cheeks.

'I'm fine. I just want to make sure everything's shipshape because Malcolm might call in later.'

That'll be her husband, Malcolm, who thinks the shop is failing and a foolish investment. Flora brushes a strand of black hair from her forehead and takes a deep breath.

'He didn't say for sure that he'd come but he's over this way later, so you never know.' She shrugs. 'He might want to see how we're doing and I'd like him to see the business at its best. It means a lot to me.'

Flora's not 'done' flustered before and it doesn't seem right. I've grown used to her polished poise. Plus, the shop is clean as a new pin – we haven't had lots of customers this week so there's been plenty of time for cleaning up. But I grab another duster and start wiping over the shelves, anyway.

In the event, Malcolm doesn't show all morning though Flora jumps every time the bell dings over the front door.

But a young girl I recognise comes in just before lunchtime. She often visits the shop for a browse and actually buys the occasional paperback, though she avoids catching my eye and blushes furiously if I ever try to chat.

She's one customer who's hard to miss because her green hair is cut into a severe geometric shape, with such an incredibly short fringe she looks like Mr Spock after he's hit the hair-dye counter.

The girl is puffing when she comes into the shop and heads for the self-help section. But, rather than searching for a book, she stands with both hands on the shelf and her eyes closed. Poor thing. I can sense anxiety coming off her in waves.

'Is there anything I can help you with?'

She doesn't react. Her eyes are still screwed tightly shut and she's biting her lip like she's in pain.

'Are you all right? Are you unwell?'

When I gently touch the girl's arm, her eyes fly open. They're the most gorgeous shade of green, perfectly complementing her emerald hair.

'Sorry,' she gasps. 'I'll leave.'

She goes to dart past me but I move to block her way. 'You don't have to leave. I just wondered if you're all right.'

'I'm fine,' she declares, her body trembling.

'Really? You don't look fine.'

The girl wobbles from foot to foot and takes in a deep whoosh of air.

'It's just a panic attack. My therapist says I need to breathe more slowly. But sometimes I forget.'

When tears start spilling down her cheeks, I take her arm and lead her to the chair that Knackered Mary fell asleep in last week.

'What's your name?'

'Becca.' Her breath is coming in strange little gulps.

'Well, sit there, Becca, keep breathing slowly and I'll get you a cup of tea. I won't be a minute.'

Flora's in the kitchen so I shouldn't leave the store unattended. That's the first rule of retail. But if Becca's a shoplifter, she deserves all the stock she can shove up her jumper for an Oscar-worthy performance.

Flora flattens herself against the counter when I bowl in and reach past her for the PG Tips.

'Malcolm's not here, is he? He only drinks lapsang souchong.'

'No, it's a customer who's having a bit of a turn and could do with a cuppa. You don't mind, do you?'

Flora stares at me for a moment and then shrugs. 'Of course not. You'd better bung in a few extra sugars.'

By the time I come back into the shop, Becca is sitting with her head almost on her knees. She jumps when I gently touch her on the shoulder.

'Are you doing OK?'

I pass her the cup and she folds her hands around it. Steam drifts in front of her face which is pale and ghostly next to her bright green hair.

'Yeah, I'm all right now,' she gulps. 'Sorry. I shouldn't have come out this morning.'

'Come out from where?'

I kneel on the hard flagstones so I'm not towering above her.

'I've just moved in with a friend in Sheep Street because I've been a bit… you know.' She grimaces and takes a tiny sip of her sickly sweet tea. 'I was working in Birmingham and living on my own but couldn't cope. I've always been a bit of a wimp.'

She shakes her head and wipes the back of her hand across her nose.

I lean closer. 'Don't tell anyone but I live with my gramp.'

'Really?' Becca gives me a shaky smile. 'I thought you'd have your own place and be very together, 'cos you work in here and seem so calm.'

'You'd be surprised. Do you get a lot of these panic attacks?'

She shrugs and traces the rim of the mug with her finger. Her nails are painted deep purple and bitten to the quick.

'Not really. I'm just having a bad day, which is why I'm looking for a book. When things get a bit much, I read and it makes me feel better.'

I nod, knowing exactly what she means. With Noah back in town, I'm re-reading *Vanity Fair*. I know I'm feeling antsy when I reach for it. Feisty Becky Sharp, so different from me, is my comfort blanket.

'I'm really sorry.' Becca blinks at me from behind her heavy, black-rimmed glasses. 'Do you know what it's like having a panic attack?'

I shake my head. 'Not really but I'm not the most confident of people and I don't always find life easy.'

'It's never easy,' says Becca with a sigh. She looks around to make sure the shop's still empty. 'You feel like the world's going dark and closing in and crushing you, until you can't breathe. And there's nowhere to go because you can't escape from yourself. Though I wish I could.'

'It sounds horrible.'

'It is.' Becca starts picking nervously at her ragged cuticles. 'That's why I can't work at the moment. Because of my anxiety. My brother says I'm batshit crazy.'

'Brothers, huh?'

'He's OK. And it's fair enough because I can't cope with anything except living with Zac in Honeyford. He's a good friend from university. My mum's stressy like me and is convinced I'm going to be murdered in my bed now I live in the country – *Midsomer Murders* hasn't helped. But I like it here.'

She bends her head and there's a gentle splosh as the silver pendant dangling around her neck drops into the steaming tea. Tiny drips of liquid fall onto her jeans and I have to stop myself from brushing them away. Becca seems brittle, as though she might break if anyone touches her.

'I like it here too. Honeyford's peaceful and permanent and the beauty all around us is soothing, somehow. It helped to heal me when I lost my dad and gran.'

I stop talking, embarrassed at baring my soul, but Becca lifts her head and properly looks me in the eye for the first time ever. 'That's it exactly. And being around books always calms me down. That's why I came in here when I started feeling bad.'

'What sort of books do you like?'

'Books I can lose myself in. Books that take me away from my boring life.'

I pull down the newly arrived Philip Pullman from the shelf in front of me.

'Books like this?'

Becca turns the book over and reads the blurb on the back. 'Yeah, just like this. I read all three of the His Dark Materials books.' But her shoulders drop when she spots the price. 'Maybe I'll buy it another day.'

She self-consciously runs a hand over her tatty jeans and pulls down her baggy sweatshirt.

'There's always the library in Burford,' I mutter quietly, because Flora's back on the shop floor and at the computer, ordering a book for a customer who's just come in. 'I'm sure they'd have this title available or could get it for you.'

'Maybe. I find the library a bit overwhelming and can't always go in if there are too many people about.' She shrugs. 'I told you – batshit crazy. But it's a good idea.'

'Callie,' calls Flora, as the doorbell tings and another customer wanders into the shop. 'I could do with your help, please.'

Uh-oh, she's not happy with me counselling customers rather than flogging books. And I really hope she didn't hear me suggesting that Becca should go to the library. That's got to be a definite no-no for a bookseller.

Becca stands up and hands over the almost-full mug.

'Thanks for everything.' She's almost reached the door when she turns and says quietly, 'You know, you're a very soothing person. I don't normally talk to anyone.'

What a lovely thing to say! Though I'm not sure Gramp would agree with her when I'm nagging him to pick his pants up off the bedroom floor and put them in the washing basket.

Flora watches Becca go and folds her arms. 'You've got a gift, Callie. If only we could charge for counselling and coffee, we'd make a fortune.'

'Do you think?' I say, glowing at two compliments within the space of a minute. 'I did suggest it once.'

'What? Providing a counselling service in the shop for non book-buying customers?'

The way Flora tilts her head to one side and narrows her eyes makes me laugh. She doesn't look particularly cross.

'No, providing coffee. I suggested to Ruben a few times that we could sell drinks to customers but he didn't go for the idea. I think he made some enquiries about it, just after the café in Weavers Lane closed. But then he said we were a small-town bookshop and not flamin' Starbucks and I'd best get back to stacking shelves.'

'The more I hear about the past owner of this place, the more I think…' Flora shakes her head. 'Well, it doesn't matter what I think. Tell me more about your idea.'

'I thought Ruben could put a coffee machine in the old storeroom at the back. And some chairs so people could sit and have a drink and think about what book they wanted to buy.'

'I'm not sure the old storeroom would work.'

'Not at the moment because it's all dark and dusty. It hasn't been used to store books since before I joined the shop. But we could clear it out and whitewash the walls, and there's a door to the back garden so customers could sit outside on sunny days.'

Flora scrunches up her nose at the thought, which is fair enough. The bookshop garden currently consists of a grimy, ancient patio and a scrubby patch of earth covered with weeds.

'We could clear the space and clean the patio and plant tubs of flowering plants to pretty everything up,' I say, eager to convince her of my plan.

Although I'm not sure who the 'we' is because I can't imagine sophisticated Flora on her knees in the weed patch, but I'd be willing to give it a go.

I grin, happy to share my ideas that were pooh-poohed by Ruben. It was frustrating to have them slapped down with hardly any consideration at all.

'How many cafés has Honeyford got now?' Flora starts tapping her pencil against the side of the till.

'Only one, but that's focused more on tourists and the Markhams, who run it, get narky if people sit over a coffee for ages.'

'That's because they're thinking of their profits. We're not running a community project here, Callie, even though it sometimes feels like we are. Any new venture we set up would need to profit the business.'

Flora sounds stern, like a school teacher, and she's got a point. It's daft to think she could run a café when she's only just getting to grips with running a flagging bookstore. My excitement starts to drain away.

'You're right.' I shrug. 'It's stupid.'

'Oh, I didn't say that.'

Flora breathes out slowly and starts sucking the end of her pencil.

'Let me have a think about it. In fact, why don't I take you out for lunch on Sunday to discuss it? I can take you to The Briar Patch – that's the name of my husband's restaurant in Oxford. And you can meet Malcolm, seeing as he doesn't appear to be calling in today. I'd like to meet your family too. You've mentioned your granddad. Why don't you bring him along?'

Oh, heavens! I've spent the last week trying to make a good impression on my new boss and Gramp could undo all that in minutes. So it's the most fabulous piece of good luck that he hates eating out in 'posh' places and will decline Flora's offer with a scowl.

'I'm not sure Gramp's free on Sunday,' I tell Flora, with a confident smile. 'But I'd love to come on my own, if that's OK. Thank you so much.'

Eating out with my new boss is a bit scary. What if I drop gravy down my top or get spinach stuck in my teeth? I walked round with a green tooth for hours once, before Sarah spotted it. But a meal out will give me the chance to talk more about my café idea and maybe even impress Flora. It'll just be like having a business meeting, I tell myself. Plus I'll be able to check out Flora's elusive husband who can't be bothered to even poke his head around the shop door and support his wife.

Chapter Seven

Oxford is my second favourite place in the world. I love its dreaming spires and medieval streets, the wide array of shops, people punting serenely past college gardens. And there's always the chance you might bump into Inspector Morse.

OK, that last one isn't going to happen. But the city's special and I head there for a few hours whenever I can.

However, I have a horrible feeling that this particular visit to Oxford is a very bad idea indeed.

I was confident Gramp would turn down Flora's invitation because he's never liked going to potentially 'posh' places or eating in front of people he doesn't know. But – silly me! – that was Old Stanley. New Stanley loves the excitement of new environments and is totally up for shovelling food into his gob in front of perfect strangers.

At the moment, he's sitting in the back of Flora's car and behaving himself as we drive along a wide street of stunningly ancient buildings. I was going to drive to the restaurant in my clapped-out Mini, but Flora had to nip into the shop this morning to sort out a couple of things, and kindly offered us a lift.

'Have you been married for a long time?' I ask, as Flora negotiates a sharp bend and curses a slow driver under her breath.

'Absolutely ages.' She spots a parking space and reverses into it at speed. 'What about your mum and dad?'

'They were married for over two decades until my dad died of a heart attack a few years ago.'

'How awful for your mother to lose her partner like that. They must have been devoted to each other after all that time. Real soulmates.'

'They were, I think.'

It was hard to tell sometimes, what with all the bickering and door-slamming. They could pick a fight over nothing, and often did. But they loved each other, in their own weird way.

'Mind you,' says a little voice from the back of the car. 'She's found herself another soulmate now – a Spanish toy boy in Alicante who's seeing to her needs. I blame the menopause for sending her round the twist and making her come over all Shirley Valentine.'

'Gosh,' says Flora, turning off the engine. And the surprise in her voice makes me cringe.

I don't want her thinking we're some strange, deadbeat family living on the edge of town. She already did a double-take when Gramp came down the stairs wearing skinny jeans and a Taylor Swift T-shirt.

She pulls the key from the ignition and twists in her seat towards me. 'I don't think age gaps really matter if you're good together. Maybe your mum's boyfriend will end up as your stepdad one day.'

'Over my dead body,' mutters Gramp, pushing his door open into the path of a cyclist who swerves round it and drops the C-bomb as he cycles off. 'Where's this restaurant then? I'm starving.'

He clambers out of the car and adjusts the crotch of his jeans, which are far too tight and probably doing terrible things to his nether regions.

I steer him onto the pavement, out of the path of oncoming traffic, and we all walk together through the city towards The Briar Patch. March sun is peeping from the edges of white cloud, trees are budding with blossom, and there are students everywhere. They amble along in little groups, reminding me of my university days.

I didn't go to Oxford University. I went to a university in London to study English and psychology but Dad died suddenly after I'd been there almost two terms – and my plans for the future went with him. It was hard to care about Renaissance poetry and the Victorian novel when it felt as though my world had been ripped apart.

So I abandoned my degree and came back to Honeyford to support my mum and grandparents, who were devastated. But my return was for me as much as them. When your life's turned upside down, you cling to what's soothing and familiar. London seemed a lonely place, full of noise and strangers, and I craved the peace of home.

Two years later, I left for university again and got a fairly decent degree. But Honeyford was in my bones by then and I missed the place. So I jumped at the chance of moving in with Gramp when Gran died just after my finals.

Everyone said I was selfless to give up my dreams for my grandfather, which made me feel like a right hypocrite. Because the truth was, I loved being back where I belonged.

Gramp is wandering along beside me and takes hold of my arm. We're following Flora, who's striding ahead.

'Your new boss is quite, well… bossy,' he mutters, stumbling slightly over a raised paving stone. His trainers are new and thicker-soled than he's used to.

'Shush! It's very kind of Flora to take us out for lunch, but why are you dressed like that? I thought you were going to wear your best trousers and the green jumper from Marks and Spencer.'

He shrugs. 'Dressed like what? Denim is a very versatile material, I'll have you know, and the shop assistant said these suited me. I could have gone for the low-slung variety of jean, but didn't.'

'For which I will be eternally grateful.' A vision of my grandfather, denim crotch at knee level and Tesco underpants showing, has lodged itself firmly in my head. 'It's just that you've never worn jeans and a T-shirt before.'

'I've never done lots of things before. But *never say never* is my new mantra.'

When Flora glances over her shoulder and grins, I wonder what she thinks of us. And hate myself for caring.

She marches on through town, past the Ashmolean Museum that reminds me of a Roman temple, and along narrow side streets until we come to The Briar Patch. The restaurant frontage is all dark wood and gleaming windows, with tall olive trees in huge chrome pots flanking the front door.

'This is it,' declares Flora, holding the door open and ushering Gramp and me ahead of her. My jaw drops. This is much posher than I'd imagined.

Ferns in green and cream planters line the deep-red walls of the restaurant. Diners are eating at round tables covered in snow-white cloths. And next to a polished-wood bar at the side of the room is a plush, buttoned banquette where two men in suits are nursing drinks.

The whole place has a genteel, Victoriana vibe going on and I'm suddenly acutely aware of my simple blue cotton dress and cream cardi. And as for Gramp's jeans... I glance at my grandfather, who gives a cheery thumbs-up.

A portly man hurries over and bends to give Flora a brief kiss on the lips. He's wearing a well-cut grey suit and his face is flushed, as though he's been drinking.

'This is my husband, Malcolm,' says Flora, brushing a hair from his lapel. 'And this is Callie, who I've told you about, and her granddad, Stanley.'

'So this is Callie from the little bookshop,' purrs Malcolm, amusement sparking in his brown eyes. He's good-looking in spite of his ruddy face, with short dark hair that glints silver under the lights. He grabs my hand and holds it for a fraction too long.

Then he gives Gramp's hand a cursory shake before beckoning over a young waitress whose blonde hair is cascading down her back in corkscrew ringlets.

'Marina will show you to your table and I'll come over and chat later, when we're not so busy.' He turns to Flora and says quietly: 'Pierre is having a hissy fit about the mackerel so I'd better go and calm things down.'

'Pierre?' I ask, as we follow Marina, weaving our way between the tables.

'Our chef. He's worked in Michelin-starred restaurants and is incredibly talented, but he's rather high maintenance. Malcolm will sort things out so let's sit down and relax.'

The table Marina shows us to is beautifully laid with white linen napkins, silver cutlery and sparkling wine glasses. It's all very *Downton Abbey* and Gran would have loved it. She always insisted on cloth serviettes at her kitchen table.

Black menus, embossed in silver with the restaurant's name, stand at each place setting, and I take a peek. Wowzers! The food sounds amazing but the prices here are crazy.

Flora spots my expression and smiles. 'It's all on the house so choose whatever you'd like.'

Gramp has forgotten his glasses so he's holding his menu extra-close to read the small print.

'Nineteen pounds and seventy-five pence for pepper-baked sea cod with a lemon *jus* and triple-fried shards of *pommes de terre*,' he snorts. 'That's basically twenty quid for fish and chips. And the peas – sorry, *petits pois* – are extra.'

'Behave!' I hiss at him, pulling the menu from his hands and placing it on the pristine cloth. 'Remember, we're in company and stop saying whatever comes into your head.'

'I'm only being my true self. Like it says I should be in that magazine article,' he pouts, tucking his napkin into the neck of his T-shirt.

Not for the first time, I imagine chucking the article in the dustbin, covering it with leftovers, and getting my normal grandfather back. I give Flora an *I'm so sorry* smile and she grins.

'Your granddad's a character,' she whispers close to my ear.

That's certainly one word for him.

The food sounds lovely and very fancy – what is 'essence of micro-greens' anyway? – so it takes a while to choose. But Gramp goes for the costly fish and chips, in the end, while I plump for pan-fried duck breast and Flora settles on chicken chasseur. She also asks Marina for a bottle of mineral water and a bottle of Chablis, which makes me chuckle. I had guessed that would be her drink of choice on the very first morning we worked together.

Then we chat about nothing in particular for ages while an old-fashioned fan turns slowly above our heads and a low hum of conversation thrums around us. Talking to Flora outside work is easier than I thought it might be, and I start to relax as she tells me about helping her husband to run his restaurant up north.

Gramp's just started nudging me to complain that he's light-headed with hunger when Malcolm and Marina appear with our food.

They place steaming plates in front of us, and Gramp wrinkles his nose when he clocks the size of the nouvelle cuisine portions. But, blessedly, he picks up his knife and fork and gets stuck in without a word.

'I do hope you'll enjoy the duck, Callie,' says Malcolm, giving my shoulder a squeeze before heading back to the kitchen. Eew! I feel a little uncomfortable, and Flora watches him go with an unreadable look on her face.

'So exactly how long *have* you two been married?' I ask, spearing a slice of duck drizzled in thick soy sauce.

'Yonks! I was only eighteen when we met and we were married less than two years later. Malcolm's a fair bit older than me so he seemed terribly worldly wise. I was bowled over by his drive and ambition.'

'Well, this place seems very popular so he's done very well. You both have, in fact.'

Flora picks up her glass of sparkling water and stares at the bubbles.

'Yes, though it's come at a cost.'

She doesn't offer any further information, which is frustrating, and she only makes small talk while we eat – about the weather, the shops in Oxford, and a brief foray into the pros and cons of Brexit. Gramp always has a lot to say on that particular issue.

Finally, when Flora's polished off her meal, she sits back in her chair.

'Look, Callie – I asked you here because I'd like to talk business. I've been doing some research into what you suggested, and I think it could work.'

'Having a coffee machine in the shop?'

I grin, delighted that my idea's being taken seriously at last, and pop the last piece of sweet, crispy duck skin into my mouth. Mmm, it's cooked to perfection.

'A bit more than that, actually.' Flora smiles. 'I'm talking about opening a proper café in the old storeroom. That room is wasted space at the moment but we can clean it up and put in chairs and tables and a counter for serving drinks and snacks. It's going to cost a bit. The main outlay will be on a decent coffee machine. But we need another income stream for the shop, and it's worth a try.'

'Wow, that sounds amazing. But what about planning permission?'

'I've had a word with the council and they don't foresee any problems.' She dabs at the corners of her mouth with her thick, white napkin. 'So, basically, you're all systems go.'

'*We're* all systems go, you mean.'

'Oh, I'll help, of course, and provide the funding but this is your baby, Callie. It'll be your job to get it up and running while I'm focused on improving the bookshop. What do you reckon?'

I reckon my original idea is expanding big-time and Flora may not have properly thought this through.

'It's brilliant that you think a café might work. That's really exciting, but I'm not sure I'm the right person to be in *charge* of a project like this. I'm a shop assistant with no proper business experience.'

Flora folds her napkin and places it on the table in front of her.

'Callie, I've only known you a short while but I can already tell you're an intelligent, resourceful woman who has great empathy with people. You draw people into the shop. So who better to run the café and entice even more people in to have a coffee and a chat, and maybe buy a book or two on the way out?'

'That's so kind of you to say, but I still have some misgivings about this.'

'Why?'

Flora taps lightly on the table with her nails while I wonder how to explain the butterflies in my chest. It's fantastic that she's listened to my ideas and believes in me. But this is outside my comfort zone. Yes, I've got a degree but, unlike Noah, I've never properly used it. I just chat to people who come into the shop and sell them books, and my confidence levels are pretty low.

'Because I might mess up with your money,' I say, at last.

Inside, I'm kicking myself for not biting Flora's hand off, but a vision of the future is playing out in my head: the café has flopped due to my mismanagement, and Flora, now penniless, is shouting at me that the shop will have to close. And she's shouting very, *very* loudly.

Flora shrugs. 'Malcolm thinks *I've* messed up with my money. But I can see potential in your café idea, and in you. So what do you say?'

Before I can say anything, Gramp drops his cutlery with a deafening clatter. White flakes of cod have fallen from his fork and scattered across Taylor Swift's face.

'Callie, this is it!' he announces to the whole restaurant. 'Your moment of authenticity and the opportunity to be your true self. Your moment to show the world what you can achieve, and to soar free from your self-imposed shackles. Today, a café in a bookshop; tomorrow, prime minister.'

How running a café could lead to running the country is a mystery, but he grabs hold of my hand and presses it to his heart. 'Don't let this moment pass you by, Callie. I beg you. Follow my example and be the best possible you that you can be.'

I swear there are tears in his eyes.

'What he said,' says Flora with a grin, taking a sip of her water.

'Gramp, it's lovely that you think I can do this. I'm really touched, but I'm worried about getting it wrong when Flora's risking her money.'

'Oh, everything's a risk. There's no guarantee I'll wake up tomorrow. But just remember…' he taps the side of his nose, 'living a timid, safe life is no life at all.'

'Is that from the article too?'

'Yep. But the point is, I have every faith in you,' he insists, pressing my hand so hard into his chest I can feel his ribs.

'Me too,' chips in Flora, 'and I've already taken a risk on the bookshop, so what the hell.'

'Yeah, we'll all be dead soon. Nice one, Flora. She'll do it.'

With that, Gramp picks up his last triple-fried shard of *pomme de terre*, drags it through the sticky sauce on my plate, and shoves it into his mouth.

'That's sorted, then. And the cafe's only the first of your ideas that I'm taking on board,' says Flora. 'I'm also going to set up some events to promote local authors, with book signings and the like, and… talk of the devil.' She nods toward the door. 'The first event will be with him.'

She has got to be kidding me.

Finn has just walked into the restaurant and is standing by the bar. The young waitress is making a beeline for him and every woman in the place is eyeing him up.

Gramp shifts in his seat beside me. 'So Finn Shawley is an author now, is he? Huh!'

'Do you know him, Stanley? I suppose you would, if you've lived in Honeyford for years. And didn't you say you knew him too, Callie? Finn's back in Honeyford to set up a new hotel and he's recently written his autobiography.'

'Really?'

I sound sceptical but Finn can't be more than twenty-eight so what's he done that would fill a book? More than me, I suppose. If my autobiography was the size of a pamphlet, readers would still want their money back. Not enough excitement, no intrigue and very little sex.

'Apparently and it's very good. Or so he tells me.' Flora grins. 'I bumped into him in the Pheasant and Fox and he told me all about his self-published book that he's trying to promote. It seems he's quite a draw around here so we agreed he could bring some books into the shop and do a signing. It might create a buzz with the locals.'

She waves at Finn and beckons him over while I nudge Gramp, who's eyeing his empty plate like a Labrador that hasn't been fed for a week.

'Best behaviour, please,' I whisper.

His reply of 'always' doesn't fill me with confidence.

Finn wanders towards us, moving between the tables like a slim-hipped Adonis. His jeans are even skinnier than Gramp's and his tight purple jumper shows the outline of his pecs.

'Flora! This place is amazing. Thank you so much for recommending it. I'll definitely bring some of my business clients here.'

Thick strands of dark hair flop across his forehead as he leans and kisses her on the cheek.

'Would you like to join us for a while? Marina, can you find us another chair, please.'

'That would be absolutely lovely of you, Marina.'

Finn winks at the waitress, who blushes fuchsia-pink and puffs over with a heavy wooden chair. He doesn't offer to help her.

'I was just telling Callie here that you'll be signing your book in the shop. And it turns out that you know each other,' says Flora, as Finn sits down.

Here we go. He'll remember I'm the 'bit of rough' who wasn't good enough for his brother and make some embarrassing comment.

But it seems I've severely overestimated my own importance in Finn's life because he turns to me and frowns. 'Do we know each other? I'm sure I'd remember a babe like you.'

Then he gives his best twinkly smile which was always wasted on me because I found Noah more appealing. He might not have been as classically handsome as Finn but he was good-looking and kinder than his brother. Or so I thought.

'Give me a clue,' says Finn, rubbing at his dark smudge of sexy stubble.

'We kind of knew each other years ago, in the sixth form.'

'Did we? Were we in the same class?'

'You were a year ahead of me.'

We ended up going to the same university too, but there seems little point in reminding him.

'Nope, it's still not coming to me,' says Finn, with a frown.

'Oh, for goodness' sake.' Gramp pushes his plate into the middle of the table. 'Her name's Callie and she was soft on your brother. They went out for a while.'

'Really?' Finn laughs, as though anyone preferring his brother is unlikely. 'Well, if that's the case, you can rekindle your romance any minute. Noah's just parking the car.'

He stretches his long legs under the table while the restaurant hubbub around me fades away. This is not good. This is not good at all. We could just up and leave, now we've finished eating. But Flora's started chatting to Finn about his hotel and I can hardly do a runner, leaving my grandfather behind.

'Are you OK, love?'

Gramp's discovered specks of soy sauce caught in the white bristles on his chin and is busy wiping them into his napkin.

'Uh-huh.'

I nod as the door swings open and Noah steps out of the rain that's splattering the windows. He brushes water droplets from his fair hair and hangs up his damp jacket. Then he scans the restaurant and starts walking towards Finn, but stops when his eyes meet mine. *Awkward* is written all over his face.

'Come on,' calls Finn. 'What are you doing? We're over here. Marina, love, get us another chair, will you?'

By the time Noah's taken the chair from Marina and carried it to our table, I've pulled myself together. It's just one more nails-down-a-blackboard meeting with someone I knew a long time ago. Someone who'll soon be far away in New York and out of my life.

'This is Flora from the bookshop,' says Finn, 'and this is – what was your name again? My memory's shocking. Too much business stuff to remember.'

'It's Callie,' says Noah, sitting down opposite me and taking off his rain-smeared glasses. He doesn't much resemble his brother at all, when the two of them are sitting side by side. Finn is all dishevelled, in-your-face smoulder, with a bad boy vibe that seems to send most women wild. Whereas Noah, with his chiselled jaw, fair colouring and quieter nature, is more like your traditional boy next door – your geeky, unremarkable neighbour who blossoms overnight into a handsome hunk.

Crikey. I take a swig of my wine and cough when it goes down the wrong way.

'It's good to meet you, Flora,' says Noah, wiping his glasses with a clean napkin before putting them back on. 'Finn said he'd met you in the pub. And Stanley, how lovely to see you again, after all this time!'

He beams at my grandfather and shakes his hand across the table.

'You too, young man. It's a long time since you came round to our house for chips.'

'It's been ages. Eight and a half years.'

'So you and Callie *do* know each other.' Finn's still looking confused.

Noah picks up a menu and runs his finger down the list of starters.

'Callie and I were friends a long time ago, in sixth form,' he says, without looking up. 'She used to come round to our house so we could revise together for exams.'

That's true enough. What he doesn't add is that, as summer kicked in and the temperature soared, we walked hand-in-hand beneath weeping willows on the river bank and stole tentative kisses.

'Nope,' says Finn, shaking his head. 'Still can't place you. Did you live locally?'

Noah closes the menu with a snap. 'Callie lived on the edge of Honeyford, on the Berry Estate.'

'Really?'

Finn looks taken aback because he didn't mix much with people from the rougher end of town. The Shawley boys lived in one of Honeyford's posher houses, and Finn was a bit of a social climber, even then.

'So, Noah, are you here to see Finn's new house out of curiosity or are you in business together?' asks Flora, waving at Malcolm, who's strutting his stuff by the bar. He waves back but doesn't come over.

'We're sort of in business together. I work as an architect in New York and got involved with some of the plans for Finn's latest venture, so I'm here to see how things are going.'

Finn chips in. 'He's on extended leave and keeping an eye on me so I don't mess up. He's always been far more serious than me. In fact, I sometimes wonder if he knows how to have fun at all!'

He gives Noah's arm a none too gentle shove.

Flora smiles. 'I'm sure you have lots of fun in New York. Have you got family there, Noah?'

'No family. Just a full in-tray, but my boss has been understanding about giving me time off. And it's good to see what Finn's doing with the house.'

'Well, I walked past the place for the first time yesterday and think it's a fabulous venue for a hotel. It's such a grand and beautifully proportioned house, and that orangey stone makes the whole building glow.'

Finn nods. 'It's perfect for what we've got planned. We want to attract a certain type of clientele so we're going for a top-end, boutiquey vibe.'

'Which is so important if you want to keep the plebs out.' Oops, did I say that out loud? Gramp snorts beside me, but Noah tilts his head to one side and gives me a 'does not compute' stare. He really has no idea how his casual snobbery broke my heart.

Flora frowns and starts talking about project management while I sink back in my chair and let the conversation go on around me.

I say conversation, though it's more a monologue from Finn, who's keen to impress us with his business successes. He's a whizz at doing up properties and selling them on at a huge profit, apparently.

He talks and talks and I listen and smile, but the details of this amazing deal and that multi-thousand-pound mark-up go over my head. I'm too busy kicking myself for my plebs comment to concentrate.

At long last, when the food Noah and Finn ordered arrives, Flora suggests it's time for us to head off.

She's hardly finished her sentence before Gramp's out of his chair like a whippet out of a trap. He's been restless for the last ten minutes. But I take longer to gather my things together. We don't want to seem too keen to escape.

Finn stays seated, carving into his rare ribeye, but Noah stands and kisses Flora on the cheek as we're saying our goodbyes. Am I next? It's been eight years since his lips last touched my skin and I'm not sure how I'll react if he kisses me now. The thought of him being so close scares and excites me at the same time. Jeez, my emotions are all over the place!

But in the end he doesn't touch me at all. He vigorously shakes Gramp's hand, nods in my general direction and doesn't look up from his turbot in white pepper sauce as we slip outside into the rain.

Flora drops us back home but doesn't come in for a coffee, which is just as well. The wetsuit Gramp bought off eBay is draped across the sofa, and he's drying a pair of pants on the radiator near the telly. I don't dare ask why.

'Well, that was an interesting if slightly tense outing,' declares Gramp, waving to Flora from the doorstep. 'Those Shawley boys haven't changed one jot over the years. That Finn's still full of himself and Noah's in his shadow.'

He shuts the door behind us, ambles into the front room and plonks himself down in his favourite chair. 'What did you think of the afternoon, then?'

'It was nice to do something different. The restaurant's lovely and the food was amazing.'

I shrug off my cardigan and move away from the wetsuit, which smells like damp dog.

'It was OK if you like over-priced French grub,' says Gramp, who can be very ungrateful sometimes. 'It got a bit weird when the Shawley boys turned up, though. And you went a right funny colour when Flora was asking about Noah's family situation. There was no mention of a wife so you're all right.'

'He can have an American wife and a bevy of American kids for all I care,' I say defiantly, feeling my face flush.

Gramp clicks his false teeth because he knows it makes me wince.

'You know, Callie, you're going to have to start saying what you really think one day.'

'I just said what I really think. And anyway, there's a lot to be said for white lies. If everyone only told the truth, the world would implode.'

Gramp looks unconvinced, but can you imagine?

'What do you think of my new baby?'

'He looks like Winston Churchill.'

'Does my bum look big in this?'

'It looks absolutely fecking ginormous.'

World War Three would break out in days.

Gramp huffs and goes to speak but I hold up my hand.

'So I'm absolutely fine about Noah Shawley's romantic situation, thank you. Nothing really happened between me and Noah, it was a long time ago and we've gone our separate ways very happily.' *Very happily* is pushing it. Actually, everything I've just said is pushing it. I quickly change the subject. 'Do you fancy a cup of tea?'

The prospect of a brew often distracts Gramp when he's straying into unwanted territory. It's a trick learned from Gran, and it works a treat.

'That would be great, love.' He kicks off his shoes, adjusts his strangled crotch, and settles back against the cushions. 'Bring me a fondant fancy, while you're at it, will you? You couldn't keep a cat alive on the portions at your boss's place.'

I bite into a pink fancy while I'm waiting for the kettle to boil and stare out at the back garden. My oval face surrounded by waves of blonde hair is reflected back at me, like a ghost.

Beyond the garden, thin sunlight is breaking through cloud and there's the faintest hint of a rainbow arcing over the hill that rises above Honeyford. This place probably seems very dull and provincial to Finn and Noah, but I think it's beautiful.

Next door's cat is circling a stout pigeon in our plum tree, and I knock on the glass to disturb it.

'Front door!' yells Gramp from his armchair.

'Just me,' I shout back. 'Stopping Fifi from attacking the local birdlife.'

'That cat's a damn menace. Where's my cup of tea?'

'Just coming.'

I fetch Gran's old china teapot from the cupboard and find the teabags as wisps of steam start curling from the kettle spout. Gran inherited this pot from her mother and she'd love that it's still being used to make Gramp's cuppas.

Quite what she'd make of her husband's new gung-ho attitude to life, I dread to think.

She always had her feet firmly on the ground and I'm the same – except when Noah's about. There's something about him that shifts my centre of gravity and makes me feel I might career off emotionally at any minute.

You're overthinking things, love, and being a bit of a prat. That's what Gran would say. And she was usually right.

I shove the rest of the cake into my mouth and let the sugar hit work its soothing magic.

Chapter Eight

Flora is a woman of her word. Over the next week, she helps me empty out the storeroom, gives me a budget, and backs off to focus on the bookshop. The café really is going to be my project – and, now I've got used to the idea, I'm getting excited. The faith shown in me by Flora and Gramp seems to be catching.

I still have dark moments, of course, when I imagine making a total cock-up of the whole thing – humiliation, bailiffs, Flora yelling at me in the street; the whole caboodle. But my confidence grows as the storeroom empties and I start making plans.

On Sunday, Gramp's spending the afternoon with Dick, who drives up with the car roof down and his big bald head sticking out. And as soon as I've waved them off, I head for the shop because Sarah's agreed to give me a hand.

She owes me a few favours so I've roped her in to help me spruce up the storeroom while the shop's closed. Giving it a makeover in work time is tricky – Flora's ordered new books following early results from her customer survey, and the whole shop needs reorganising to accommodate them.

Sarah rocks up, looking fabulous as always, in jeans and a fitted T-shirt that shows off her curves. Her coral eyeshadow complements the olive complexion she inherited from her Italian grandmother.

'Wow, this place looks different,' she says, carefully negotiating a tower of paperbacks near the window display. There are stacks of books everywhere now. We don't have enough shelving to hold them all.

'It really smells in here,' she sniffs.

'Smells? What sort of *smells*?'

Sarah wrinkles her snub nose and gives an extra-deep, snotty sniff. 'I dunno – paper, ink, dust.'

'It smells like a bookshop, then.'

'I guess.' Sarah shrugs. 'It used to smell like a toilet in here. A really clean, disinfected to within an inch of its life toilet.' She runs her hand along a shelf of historical fiction and grins. 'Come on then, Callie. What's this Flora like? Give me the goss.'

'She's fine.'

'Fine? What sort of fine? "*Gosh, Callie, you're wonderful, take the afternoon off*" fine or slave-driver, up her own backside fine? I'm assuming the latter, seeing as we're here on a Sunday afternoon. Do you need me to be your champion and beat her up?'

Bless her! Sarah was my Rottweiler guardian at school and, though she's never actually thumped anyone for me, she relishes a good row and enjoys wading in on my behalf. Even when I don't want her to.

'Nah, you're all right. Thanks, though. Flora's OK, actually. Very composed and sophisticated and willing to take a chance on this place.'

'She looks sophisticated, all right,' says Sarah. 'I found a photo of her on her husband's restaurant website. She looked very understated – quite Audrey-esque really.'

Which is praise indeed from Sarah, who reckons she's Audrey Hepburn's number one fan. We initially bonded in Year Eleven over our shared love of *Breakfast at Tiffany's*.

'Where's this café, then, that you need a hand with?'

'Follow me and I'll show you.'

I lead her through the shop and fling open the door to the store-room. 'Ta-dah!'

'Crikey!' Sarah pokes her head through the door and peers around the room. 'You're optimistic, Call, I'll give you that.'

'It's good to have vision and imagination,' I say, parroting Flora's words and trying to see past the dark, empty room with its low ceiling and grubby concrete floor.

'If you say so.' Sarah grabs hold of the whitewash I'm carrying, walks into the room and dumps it in the middle. 'Let's get on then because Gemma will be back from her dad's this evening. Did I mention that I'm engaged to Gemma?'

'Only a few hundred times.'

I laugh, delighted for my friend that she's finally found the woman of her dreams. They only started going out eight months ago but she's already moved into Gemma's Cheltenham flat and her lovely mum is picking out wedding hats.

Over the next few hours, we sweep the floor, wash the uneven walls and apply a light, bright coat of whitewash. The window in the back wall is covered in grime but light floods into the room when it's washed off, and there's a view of the tiny garden outside.

Describing it as a garden is generous, to be honest. We step outside to take a look. Tall plants with gnarled stems are fighting for space as they climb the stone wall enclosing the courtyard. There's a scraggy apple tree in the corner. And I can just make out the leg of a slimy garden chair and a rusty watering can peeping out from the jungle.

'Those are all weeds,' declares Sarah, who's splattered with pinpricks of white paint. 'Whew, let's catch our breath for a minute.'

She drags up a rackety wooden crate that's standing on its side against the wall, and we sit on it, gingerly.

'So how are you doing, then, Callie? Really doing, I mean.'

'I'm fine.'

'Seen Noah recently?'

'Not since last Sunday at Flora's restaurant.'

'Hhmm. Still dreaming about him?'

'Not since I was eighteen.'

Which is a bit of a lie because I dreamed about him two nights ago. He was standing on top of the Empire State Building, throwing books at me.

'Did he go all weird when he saw you in the restaurant?'

'Not really.'

I sigh because I'd rather not be talking about this. Sorting out my feelings now that Noah is back on the scene is hard enough without Sarah gearing up to give me advice on what I should do. She only wants to help but her fierce approach to life is so different from mine.

'How did he look?' she asks. 'And don't say fine.'

'He looked OK.'

'Urgh, you're hopeless and such a liar.' Sarah pulls her phone from her back pocket. 'I've Googled him so I know he looks more than OK. Here!'

'No, don't.'

I make a grab for the phone but Sarah jumps to her feet and turns her back on me. She stabs at the screen a few times and then waves the phone in my face.

'Phwoar! Formerly nerdy Noah is featured on his company website and looks absolutely fabulous, darling! Even I might be tempted.' She laughs and strokes the small diamond ring on her fourth finger. 'Have you seen this?'

'No, I'm not interested enough in Noah to look him up online.'

Sarah shakes her head. 'Such a *bad* liar, too. Look!'

She's almost shoved the phone into my face so looking at anything other than the screen is not an option. And she's right – Noah does look *phwoar!*

There's something about a handsome man sitting at a huge desk in front of floor-to-ceiling windows that's very appealing. Especially when he's doing a crinkly-eyed smile, with a spectacular city skyline behind him.

My first reaction to the photo is *Oh! My! God!*, and the second is a strange bitter-sweet feeling that lodges in my chest and refuses to move. I'm proud of him for doing so well in New York.

'So did you two part on good terms last Sunday?' Sarah asks.

'We did. Everything between us is absolutely fi… um, good,' I say, giving her a beaming smile as proof.

'You're lying. Again!'

Sarah yanks the phone away and shoves it into her jeans. Then she marches to the back door, locks it from the outside and pockets the key.

'OK. You're not going anywhere until you tell me what happened between you and Noah before you went to uni. I know there's more than you're telling me.'

'Really? You're holding me hostage until I tell you all my secrets? I could scale the wall, you know.'

'Try it!'

Sarah folds her arms as drops of rain start splatting onto the grimy patio stones. A thick black cloud has blotted out the sun and is heading straight for us.

'We're going to get soaked out here.'

'Then you'd better talk fast.'

I sigh because I haven't talked about what happened, ever – not to Noah, not to my family, and definitely not to Sarah, even though she knows lots of other stuff about me.

'What's the point?' I ask her. 'It was ages ago and it doesn't matter now. Yes, things are a bit awkward between me and Noah but he'll be back in New York soon so it's not a problem.'

'It obviously is a problem because you've been weird since he came back to town. And the two of you used to be so good together. You were love's young dream when I went off to uni. But by the time I came back at Christmas his family had moved to Scotland and you told me the relationship had just fizzled out, though you wouldn't mention his name after that.'

I wrap my arms around my waist and shiver.

'Noah wasn't who I thought he was, and I definitely wasn't what he wanted.'

'Too cryptic. I want details.' Sarah sits back down beside me on the crate. 'You've got to remember that I'm almost married now and boring so I need to live vicariously through the love lives of others. I reckon it's about time you told me the whole story.'

I sigh loudly and consider wrestling the key from Sarah's pocket, but she's stronger than she looks.

'All right. Noah and I were going to different universities, do you remember? I was going to the same one that Finn was already at. Anyway, Noah and I were planning to meet at weekends and continue our relationship, if you can call it that. We'd only been going out properly for a few weeks. But then I overhead him talking about me to Finn.'

'And…?' Sarah raises her eyebrows and waits.

'And… do I really need to go into all of this? It was embarrassing and humiliating and disappointing enough at the time.'

'Yes, you do. It'll be cleansing for the soul.'

'I'm not sure my soul needs cleansing.'

'Oh, believe me, it does.' Sarah leans forward with her chin in her hands. 'You keep far too much bottled up, Callie, and it's not healthy. So, continue.'

I shield my face against the spitting rain with an upturned hand.

'It was the night before I left for university and Noah and I had already said our goodbyes but I had a small present I'd forgotten to give him. Just something stupid. So I went back to his house and he and Finn were laughing in the garden.'

'And?'

'And I was round the side of the house so they didn't see me but I heard Noah say' – I swallow because I've never said the words out loud before – '"Of course it's nothing special or serious with me and Callie. How could it be? You know she lives on the Berry Estate, right? She's pretty rough."'

'What the…?' Sarah's jaw has dropped. 'That's a horrible thing to say, and the man's mad because you're gorgeous. Your big brown Bambi eyes are to die for.'

'No, he meant "rough" as in the house and area where my family come from. It was the shabbiest bit of the village back then. Still is. At least, I think that's what he meant.'

Bloody hell. Perhaps I misinterpreted what he said all those years ago and he *was* talking about my face. I'm not sure which is worse – Noah being a crashing snob or Noah thinking I'm gross. Either way, it broke my adolescent heart, and thinking about Noah now makes me feel fizzy inside with little bubbles of an emotion I don't quite recognise. It might be anger, sadness, or desire.

'So what did you do?'

'Nothing.'

'Nothing? You are totally hopeless, Callie!'

'I know, but I was so gutted and humiliated I crept away and went to university and tried to forget about the Shawley brothers. The first thing I did when I got there was text Noah and tell him the relationship was off, before he got the chance to dump me.'

'Didn't he ask why?'

'When he tried to call me, I texted back that I'd found someone else and blocked his number. That did the trick and he never contacted me again. I needed some dignity, Sarah, so I made out it was my decision to break up.'

Plus, I couldn't bear the thought of arguing with him. Not after listening to my parents bicker on endlessly. Slinking away seemed preferable at the time.

'So you never spoke about him to Finn?'

I shake my head. 'Nope. Finn moved in far more exalted circles than I did, even back then. I spotted him on campus a couple of times but he never acknowledged me and had probably forgotten who I was. He hasn't got a clue who I am now.'

'And their parents moved away from Honeyford. Ah, it's all making sense now.'

'His parents moved to Scotland for some business venture, so he went there in the holidays and never came back here.'

'Until now.'

'Yeah, until now. Um, can we discuss this inside, please?'

The rain's getting harder and Sarah's usually bouncy curls are starting to stick to her head.

'You should have told me. I know you like to keep things close to your chest but for goodness' sake!' Sarah's on her feet and pacing up and down the tiny patio. 'What that man said is outrageous. Aren't you angry?'

'No, not really. I don't think so. It was a long time ago.'

I ignore the bubbles that are starting to make my heart ache.

'Right!' Sarah fishes the key from her pocket and heads for the door. A vein is throbbing above her left temple.

'Where are you going?'

'To Honeyford Manor to tell Noah exactly what I think of him. If I can get this stupid key into this stupid lock.'

She's so furious, she jabs the key into the door frame once, twice, three times, as she misses the lock.

'Please don't. You'll make everything worse.'

I stand between her and the door. It's really pouring now and water is running in rivulets down my cheeks.

'This is why I've never told you exactly what happened – because I knew you'd go off the deep end and it wouldn't help. I'm dealing with this in my own way and what I just said was in confidence so you're never to mention it again. Promise me.'

'You can't expect me not to say anything. Jeez, this weather!'

'You're my friend and I'm asking you. So promise me! I mean it, Sarah.'

'Oh, I s'pose so.' She pouts, wincing as thunder grumbles around the hills. 'So what's your way, then, that's better than giving him a right mouthful?'

'My way is leaving the past in the past and having a civilised relationship with Noah, like the two adults we are.'

'In other words, letting him get away with it.'

'There's nothing to get away with. Noah and I were over a long time ago and my feelings for him are now gone. I'll always remember what he said and feel awkward when he's around but arguments that rake over the past aren't my thing.'

'That's true enough.' Sarah twists her lip and bites the inside of her mouth. 'You've always been a kinder person than me.'

She very kindly doesn't add, *and more of a wimp*. But I'm fine with wimp-dom. If keeping quiet and letting things lie gets me through until Noah goes back to New York and leaves me and my heart in peace, then bring it on!

Chapter Nine

'This looks amazing!'

Becca's green eyes open wide as she stands in the middle of the floor and takes in the newly painted walls and cobweb-free corners. Light is streaming through the open back door and the room's transformed from the dark, musty space it was just a few days ago.

'I can't believe you're opening a café. That's such a good idea and it's bound to be a brilliant success,' says Becca, whose over-the-top enthusiasm makes me grin. It's so good to see her with some colour back in her pale cheeks.

She dips her head when Honeyford carpenter Charlie gives her a wave from the back wall where he's putting together a counter. He grins and goes back to tunelessly whistling the chorus of 'Havana' over and over again.

'Come and see the garden, if you've got time.' I nabbed Becca as she was walking past the shop so she might be on her way somewhere. But I couldn't resist showing her the fledgling café, and checking that she's OK. She hasn't been into the shop since her panic attack and I worry that she might be feeling uncomfortable about what happened.

She shrugs and says, 'Sure, I'm never busy,' before following me into the back yard, where a stray ginger cat is sunning itself on the warm patio stones.

'This area needs a little more work,' I say, then laugh because what this garden needs is a flame-thrower. The weed patch hasn't improved since Sarah and I were out here. In fact, the plants appear to have grown a good few centimetres overnight and tangled into even more tortuous shapes.

'It just needs a clear-up,' Becca says, 'and I can help if you'd like.'

She bends down and strokes the cat, which stretches its body in delight. But she straightens up quickly when Flora steps into the courtyard behind us.

'Hi, Becca. What do you think of Callie's café, then? Isn't she doing a fabulous job?'

'It's good,' mumbles Becca, nervously playing with her ultra-short fringe.

'Actually, Becca was just saying that the garden needs clearing.'

'You think? It's like a jungle out here,' snorts Flora, but she bites her lip when Becca's face falls. 'It is rather overgrown and in need of some attention.'

'Actually, Becca has offered to help.' Though it was only a casual offer, I get the feeling that having this project to work on might help Becca as much as the café.

'Really? That's kind of you, Becca, though I'm not sure...' Flora takes a deep breath. 'But it's Callie's project and budget so any decisions are up to her.'

'I could certainly do with some help in the garden because I'm clueless when it comes to plants.' A thought strikes me. 'The problem is I couldn't afford to pay you much.'

Becca shrugs. 'That's all right. I've got nothing else on so I don't need paying.'

'We can't let you do it for nothing. It's going to be hard work.'

'I don't mind and it'll get me out of the house. My friend Zac says I need to get out more to help my mental health. Anyway, you can always pay me a bit in books.' Panic suddenly ricochets across her face. 'You don't have to, of course. I totally understand if you don't want me around.'

Her bottom lip wobbles and that clinches it. 'It'll be lovely having you here to help out in the garden.'

'Looks like you're hired, then, Becca,' says Flora. 'And I'm sure Callie will pay you a little bit.'

When Becca grins, dimples appear in the curves of her cheeks. I've never noticed them before because this is the first time I've seen her properly smile.

'Is it all right if I bring a friend along to help me? She knows lots about gardens, and she's quite lonely.'

Ooh, that's a bit of a curveball. I open my eyes wide at Flora, who hesitates before giving a tight nod.

'I can start now, or tomorrow morning.'

Becca's anxiously twisting the hem of her T-shirt out of shape.

'Let's say tomorrow morning, as long as it's not tipping it down.'

Becca smiles again. 'I don't mind a bit of rain.'

When Becca's gone, Flora turns to me and sighs. 'Why am I starting to feel that we're setting up a community project for the lost and lonely rather than a bookshop café?'

'The shop *is* part of the community, and Becca and her friend just want to help out for a short while. Do you think it's a terrible idea?'

'I guess not. It's not really what I had in mind for the shop but we'll see how it goes.' She shrugs. 'Oh, by the way, please don't mention it to Malcolm if he comes in.'

'OK. Wouldn't he approve?'

'He'd say it doesn't make good business sense. He already thinks the café idea is a non-starter and he wouldn't get the *giving back to the community* thing.'

The more I hear about Malcolm, the more I think he's a bit of an ass. Though I'd never say as much, obviously.

My heart sinks when Becca shows up the next morning pushing an elderly lady in a wheelchair. The woman has a tight grey perm and is wearing thick stockings even though the sun's shining and casting shadows across the High Street.

'I was expecting a younger, female version of Monty Don,' hisses Flora. 'Not Miss Marple on wheels.'

But she plasters on a smile and greets the woman, who declares her name is 'Phyllis, like the plant'. Though whether that's what she'd usually say or simply to prove she knows something about gardening, I'm not sure.

'Phyllis knows everything there is to know about plants and stuff,' says Becca, quickly. She's picked up on our unease. 'So she can tell me what to do and I can do it. I'll be her legs.'

'Then let me take you through,' says Flora. 'And we'll see how you get on.'

Thirty minutes later, after ordering six second-hand tables online, I head outside with steaming cups of coffee and a packet of digestives.

'Wow, this is brilliant!'

A cleared patch of scrubby ground is already visible, next to a pile of uprooted weeds. Phyllis, now wearing a wide-brimmed hat, has a flowerpot on the tray of her wheelchair and is pushing soil into it with long, gnarled fingers. A thin gold band on her fourth finger looks shiny-bright against her chalk-white skin.

Becca stops digging and wipes a grubby hand across her forehead.

'Do you think it's looking better already? Phyllis is telling me which plants to dig out and which to leave.'

'It's going to look great. Where did you find the flowerpot?'

'Under the old wheelbarrow,' says Phyllis, pointing at a heap of rusting metal that's now propped up against the wall.

I place a mug on her tray. 'Here you go, Phyllis. Did you want any sugar, or a biscuit?'

'No thanks. I'm trying to lose weight.'

She brushes soil from her fingers and picks up the mug with both hands. But it still shakes when she raises it to her lips and takes a slurpy sip.

I perch on the wooden crate with my coffee and we watch as Becca goes back to digging.

'Do you live nearby, Phyllis?'

'In the bungalows, near the old bridge. Do you know them?'

I nod. There's a row of four bungalows that back onto the river, just a stone's throw from the manor house.

'Do you live there on your own?' I ask, taking a bite of biscuit and wiping crumbs off my lap.

'Yes, it's just me. I lost my husband a while ago and my daughter lives in Australia with her family.'

'Do you ever visit?'

'No, the flight's too expensive. Elaine suggested me moving there, after Tommy died, and I sometimes wish I had. I'd be near my grandchildren. But I'm not well enough to move now and, to be honest, my daughter doesn't need an oldie like me, holding her back. She's always off out, doing something or other. But we speak on the phone every week and Becca's setting up something called Pike.'

'Skype, Phyllis,' calls Becca from the jungle patch. She puts down her spade, steps over the weed pile and sits on the patio stones with her coffee. The sun has caught her cheekbones so she looks less like a ghost.

'How come you two know each other?'

'I saw Phyllis sitting by the river and was worried her chair was going to roll into the water.'

'Becca gets anxious about stuff and imagines bad things happening. I was never in any danger – I had the brakes on. But it was kind of her to check, and we just got chatting. Or rather, I chatted to her because she's quite shy.'

'Phyllis reminds me of my dead grandma,' Becca suddenly blurts out.

'Nice,' mutters Phyllis, but she gives me a grin. 'So I kind of lost two grandchildren to Australia but gained a new adopted granddaughter here in Honeyford. Do you have children, Callie?'

'Me?' I splutter. 'No.'

'Ah, well. Give it time. What about a boyfriend? Are you courting at the moment?'

Becca shakes her head and shoots me an apologetic look. 'Phyllis, you're not supposed to ask questions like that.'

'Why not? I thought youngsters these days were all for baring their souls on social media.'

'Not all of us,' I tell her. 'And no, I don't have a boyfriend.'

'Really? I can't understand why not, and what about you, Becca? You're both pretty, dynamic women in the prime of life and you're both alone, which is not all it's cracked up to be, I can tell you. You need to get yourselves boyfriends, pronto.'

'And now you're reminding *me* of my gramp, Phyllis, who's very much alive.'

I laugh to cover my dismay that talk of boyfriends immediately made me picture Noah. Not as he is now, all sophisticated and distant in a suit, but eight years ago, in cut-off jeans, as we sat beside the river and he put his hand in mine – a lost memory filed away that's suddenly so vivid.

'Anyway.' As I stand up quickly, the crate wobbles back and forth on the uneven flagstones. 'I'd better get back to work and I'll come and see how you're getting on in a while. Thank you for all your hard work.'

Then I dart back into the storeroom before Phyllis can quiz me further on my love life. And I sweep the floor with hard, brisk strokes, and listen to Charlie, who's still whistling 'Havana'– the only tune he seems to know – until the memory starts to fade and is filed away under 'Best Forgotten'.

The next couple of weeks are crazy busy, which suits me just fine because frantic activity keeps the Filing Cabinet of Unsettling Memories locked.

One exciting highlight is the arrival of a gleaming, stainless steel espresso machine with a steam arm, hot water tap and solid legs that anchor it to the counter top.

Of course, I turn into a beverage geek immediately and spend ages learning how to make the perfect cup of coffee. Flora eventually declines taste-testing yet another treacly espresso or frothy latte because caffeine overload is making her twitchy. But Becca and Phyllis never say no to yet another cup.

Another highlight is Knackered Mary turning up in the garden one morning and announcing that she's here to help while Callum's snoozing in his pram. And no, she doesn't expect payment because, one, it's to thank us for letting her snooze in the shop, and two, it's better than trading sore nipple stories with the local mums and babies group, thank you very much.

It turns out she's a whizz with a hoe, and the garden starts to look less like a battleground and more like somewhere you might actually choose to visit. It's still a bit scrubby and bare – Becca seems to be operating a scorched earth policy and nothing except a few shrubs remain. But Phyllis has potted up some crocuses and pansies which provide a cheerful splash of spring colour.

There's no sign of the tables and chairs I've ordered for the café and I have to make several phone calls to chase them up. But they arrive at last in a huge lorry which parks outside the shop, causing traffic chaos.

They're unloaded by two grumpy blokes in sweaty T-shirts who give V-signs to beeping motorists. And they're more battered than I expected, which is disappointing. But Phyllis offers to run up half a dozen pink tablecloths on her sewing machine and I start painting the chairs white to hide the scratches.

Flora uses her culinary connections and arranges for a local business to supply us with cakes and pastries each day. I make sure we're registered with the right people at the local authority and swot up on food safety and allergens. And soon all that's needed are the finishing touches and we'll be ready for the official opening.

Usually, I keep my head down and avoid the limelight. But having a celebratory 'do' to launch the café in the local community and attract customers seems a good idea. However, there's another event to get out of the way before the café opens, and it's one I'm rather dreading – our first official book-signing by Finn.

He's already emailed Flora a list of demands including a table next to the door, a large bottle of sparkling water, a supply of chocolate digestives and, bizarrely, four cans of energy drink. I mean, how much energy does it take to sign his own name? But I can cope with Finn being a pain for a couple of hours. All I hope is that he won't drag his brother along to help him flog a few copies. I'm not sure my confused heart could take it.

Chapter Ten

Finn arrives half an hour before the signing's due to begin with two large boxes of books and an adoring gaggle of women. They troop into the shop and start piling his books on the table.

'Heavens! Finn's brought a harem with him,' says Flora, making me giggle.

'He's always been rather popular with the ladies.'

'I'm not surprised.'

Uh-oh. I give Flora a sideways glance. She's not falling under Finn's spell as well, is she? Am I the only woman in Honeyford who's immune to Finn's charismatic charm? But Flora folds her arms and grins.

'You'd better get yourself over there, Callie, and give the author's groupies a hand.'

Everyone around him is working hard but Finn's just sitting at the table, pen in hand, all poised to sign his masterpiece.

'Cathy!' he says, giving me his best smile when I pick up one of the paperbacks.

'It's Callie. And hello, Finn. Congratulations on your book.'

There's a very large photo of Finn's face on the front cover. Has he digitally whitened his teeth? His real-life smile is unfeasibly bright anyway but in this picture it's blinding. I blink and read the title picked out in large red letters across the top of his head: *Business Balls!*

'You've chosen an unusual title.'

'Catchy though, don't you think? That's what you need these days to be as successful in business as I am – balls of steel.'

A middle-aged woman behind him, who quite frankly should know better, starts to titter.

'Is it a how-to book about succeeding in business or an autobiography?'

'A bit of both,' says Finn, airily. 'My life's been pretty fascinating, really, and I've become a bit of a role model for up-and-coming entrepreneurs.'

Flicking through the paperback, I come to the index and see what's listed. Honeyford's mentioned once, the Cotswolds twice, and Noah's there under 'S' – *Shawley: Noah*. He appears on pages eight, sixty-five and one hundred and twenty-three.

I resist the urge to turn to them immediately and scan on down the list. The largest entry seems to be for Finn's dad, Robert, who's mentioned numerous times throughout the book. It's a shame he's not here to support his son today.

Finn's busy talking with a fan so I wander back to Flora, who's wedging the front door open. A warm breeze curls in and blows strands of dark hair across her perfectly made-up face.

'Will Noah be along too?' she asks.

'I have no idea.'

'Didn't you ask Finn?'

'Why would I?' I can feel my cheeks starting to burn. 'It doesn't matter to me one way or the other.'

'Ah, only I thought that might be why you've put on a dress.'

Damn Flora and her attention to detail!

'I always ditch the jeans when we have book signings. More professional,' I mumble, picking up a copy of Lee Child's latest and studying it intently.

'I thought you said this was the first one.'

'Yeah, kind of,' I say, though this is definitely the first signing since I've worked here.

When I suggested to Ruben that we should organise one, he said he didn't want J.K. Rowling causing chaos in the store. The fact that we'd never get J.K. in a month of Sundays passed him by.

Flora bites her lip as though she's stifling a grin, which is disconcerting. But the market house clock is striking midday and Finn's book event is about to begin. His harem forms an orderly queue and he starts signing his name in big, loopy handwriting.

A lot of people call in over the next thirty minutes. But not all of them buy books. Some just nip into the shop during their lunch-hour, have a good gawp at Finn and then push off.

Interest has been drummed up by an article in the local newspaper which focused on Finn's 'property empire' and painted him as Honeyford's golden boy making a triumphant return to the town. Noah didn't get a mention.

I've just relaxed because Noah's clearly going to be a no-show when a shadow falls across me. I glance up from the toppled pile of thrillers I'm sorting out, and my mouth goes dry.

Noah is standing there, in faded jeans and a royal-blue sweatshirt with 'New York Mets' picked out in orange letters. The faintest trace of stubble is shadowed across his square jaw, and my fingers itch to push back a curl of fair hair that's grazing his forehead.

'Do you need a hand?' he asks.

'No, thanks. It's all done.' I straighten up and wipe my hands down the skirt of my yellow cotton dress. 'How are you?'

'Fine, thanks.' Noah hesitates. 'And you?'

'Yeah, fine.' I nod, desperately trying to think of something else to say. 'I've got a bit of a headache but, you know...'

I trail off because why would Noah give a monkey's about my headache?

'Drinking more water might help, or so I've heard.'

'Good idea. It is pretty hot today.'

'Yeah, it's quite close,' he says, panic flickering across his face.

'Absolutely. The weather's been unseasonably warm lately and the river is low.'

Now it's me that's panicking. The river is low? I sound like a spy parroting codewords before handing over vital microfilm. This is the worst small talk ever.

Noah blinks, grabs a copy of *War and Peace* from the shelf behind me and starts leafing through it. Can I just wander off or would that appear rude?

There's a sudden loud 'ooh' from the locals gathered around Finn, and Noah glances up from his book.

'I see he's still got it. He's no doubt regaling them with tales of his property business prowess. He'll be boasting he's on first-name terms with the presenters of *Location, Location, Location* next.'

On cue, the name 'Kirstie' wafts across the store, and Noah laughs. He looks younger when he laughs, and more like the Noah I used to know. The Noah who whispered next to me in class, and watched *Will & Grace* at my house, and let me study in his peaceful kitchen.

God, I loved his huge, posh kitchen with its shiny black Aga and marble-topped counters completely devoid of 'stuff'. Our tiny kitchen was crammed with higgledy-piggledy pans and boxes of breakfast cereal.

The first time Noah ever kissed me, in fact, was in his kitchen. We were sitting at the breakfast bar, cramming for A level History, and I'd just asked him when the industrial revolution began.

Rather than admit he didn't know, Noah leaned forward and pressed his lips against mine. He kissed me on impulse. Or at least that's what he claimed afterwards, once we'd done a fair bit more kissing.

But I have my doubts because his lips tasted of mint, even though he hates the taste. I reckon he was planning to kiss me all along and sneaked a Polo for fresh-breath courage.

'It was good to see Stanley the other day,' says Noah, interrupting my thoughts.

Oops, I realise I'm staring at his full mouth and thinking back to how soft and warm his lips felt on mine. How he pulled me close and ran his fingers along the back of my neck.

'He hasn't changed at all,' continues Noah, sucking his bottom lip between his teeth as though he can read my mind.

'You'd be surprised,' I gulp.

'Neither have you. Changed, I mean.'

I don't suppose he means that in a negative way but, as he stands there all New-York cosmopolitan and composed, my heart sinks. Flora was right – I put on a dress to look grown-up and sophisticated if Noah called in. But a pretty dress from ASOS doesn't disguise the fact that I'm still living with my family and selling books a stone's throw from the pub we went to as teenagers. I've hardly changed at all.

'Yep, that's me. Still in Honeyford, planning my great escape to the big city.'

Noah shakes his head. 'No, what I mean is you still look…' He breathes out slowly. '… amazing. Even more amazing than you used to back when we were…' His face is only inches from mine, and I can feel his warm breath on my skin. If I just lean forward the tiniest bit…

Then he stops, rakes his fingers through his short hair and takes a step back. 'That's what I meant. You look the same.'

He clamps his mouth shut and goes back to leafing through *War and Peace.*

OK, I'm properly confused. Noah leaned close and paid me a fabulous compliment which made my legs feel shaky. It was kind of a *moment,* wasn't it? But now there's a frosty edge to his voice and he's acting as though nothing just happened.

He must have remembered, I suddenly realise. He remembered that Callie Fulbright is a bit rough and nothing special. Damn my stupid legs for getting the shakes over a man who was so rude about me in the past.

'Are you a reader, Noah?'

Flora has wandered over from the till and gives my arm a quick squeeze.

Noah shrugs his broad shoulders. 'I enjoy a good book, though I've never read this one. Would you recommend it?'

'Definitely, especially as Callie mentioned that you enjoy history. Did she tell you about her new business?'

My new business. That's pushing it, when Flora's coming up with the cash. But she smiles when I raise my eyebrows.

'It's calmed down in here a bit now so why don't you take Noah out back and show him?'

Panic flutters in my stomach at the thought of being alone with him. 'I'm sure Noah's not interested.'

'I'm sure he is, aren't you?'

'Um.' Flora's brooking-no-argument tone takes Noah by surprise, but he obediently puts his book back on the shelf. 'Sure. I've got five minutes.'

'That's all you'll need,' says Flora, looking mighty pleased with herself. 'Off you go, Callie.'

Reluctantly, I lead Noah through the shop and stand back when we get to the storeroom so he can go in first. The doorway is narrow and I shiver when his hand brushes my thigh as he steps inside. He looks around him at the transformed room.

Phyllis has made four bright pink tablecloths so far and they stand out against the bumpy whitewashed walls. She's also made a row of red and blue bunting which I've pinned up over the wooden counter. It all looks very jaunty.

At the back of the room stands my pride and joy: the coffee machine I've nicknamed Charlie, in honour of its glorious silver sheen.

Charlie is wonderful. Not only does he make a delicious cuppa, he also wafts the rich aroma of coffee beans through the whole shop. Sometimes I stand next to Charlie, breathing in the smell. Sometimes I polish off all his finger marks until he gleams. And sometimes I worry that I'm developing an unhealthy obsession.

'Wow! This place is going to be great.' Noah sounds genuinely impressed and is acting as though the *moment* in the shop didn't happen. He walks into the centre of the room and turns slowly on the spot. 'When's it opening?'

'Next weekend. It just needs a few finishing touches.'

'Those look familiar.' Noah points at my gran's copper kettles, lined up on a shelf near the back door. They're glowing burnished gold in the sunbeams streaming through the window.

'They belonged to Gran and she was very proud of them. You must have seen them on display at her house.'

'Must have, when we were watching the telly and she was force-feeding me Battenberg cake. I was always very fond of your gran, and she'd be really proud of you doing this.'

'Do you think so?' I blink back the sudden tears that are threatening to embarrass me. 'I'm not so sure. She always wanted me to be a doctor or a teacher. Or Terry Wogan's PA.'

'Random!'

'She always loved Terry.'

A wave of grief sweeps through me when I remember Gran singing along to Radio 2 and talking to Terry as though he was sitting next to her.

'I know she'd be proud of you running your own business,' says Noah, fishing in his pocket and holding out a clean tissue. 'Even if it wasn't what she expected.'

I take the tissue and dab at my eyes. 'Yeah. Setting up a café wasn't quite what I had in mind when I went to uni, but plans change.'

'All the time. So what happened to yours?'

Well, Noah. My confidence took a battering just before I went to uni – thanks for that – and it disappeared completely when my dad died so I came home where I feel safe. However, you don't have to feel sorry for me living such a provincial life because I love it here.

I could say that, but I keep it simple.

'Life happened. I came back for a while after my dad's death, then went back to uni. After that, my gran died and my mum left, so I came back to Honeyford and stayed.'

'To look after Stanley?'

'Kind of.'

'You were always close in your family; closer than we were.'

'Really? My parents were always bickering.'

'My parents are incredibly polite to each other but quite distant. At least yours were communicating and had a passionate, if rather fiery, relationship. Where's your mum gone now?'

'To Alicante. To find herself.'

'Gosh. How's that going?'

'It's a work in progress. Though her search is aided immensely by input from a sexy Spaniard who's ten years younger than she is.'

'Crikey. Go, Mrs Fulbright!'

'Yeah, go, Mum!' I say, with rather less enthusiasm, seeing as she left me to sort out Gramp on my own.

A babble of voices drifts in from the shop as I open the back door and gesture for Noah to follow me. 'Come and see what we've done out here.'

It's daft but I still get a jolt of surprise every time I step into the garden. As though my brain's expecting jungle chaos and can't quite compute the changes made by Becca, Phyllis and Knackered Mary.

'What do you think of our outdoor dining area?'

Noah steps over the sleeping ginger cat that's adopted us and sits at the black filigree table I found in Argos. The garden looks particularly lovely at this time of day. Sunlight is filtering through the branches of the apple tree and casting dappled shadows across the patio.

'It's great, Callie. The perfect place to sit and enjoy a drink.'

'That's the plan.'

I hesitate, but Noah's being so normal now – as though we're just old friends catching up – I drag over another metal chair and sit down.

'How's the boutique hotel going?'

'OK,' says Noah, wrinkling his nose. 'It'll look great when it's finished and I dare say Finn will make a success of it. I just wish he'd taken on the project with a clear head and for the right reasons.'

'What reasons does he have, then?'

'Just one – impressing our father. Do you remember him?'

'Of course, though I hardly ever saw him.'

He always seemed to be abroad, brokering one hugely successful business deal after another. Which is why the Shawley family were so loaded and lived in one of the best houses in town.

Noah gives a rueful grin. 'None of us saw him much which was partly a blessing 'cos he's not the easiest of men to get on with. He expected a lot from us, particularly Finn, who was always trying to impress him. But Dad was never impressed or satisfied with what he had – still isn't. He always wanted to move when we lived here because he didn't like our house.'

'You're kidding!' I splutter. 'Your house was amazing. You had that huge hallway and a gravel drive… and a utility room.'

Oh, how I coveted a utility room when I was growing up. Having a separate room to house your washing machine seemed the epitome of poshness when ours filled most of the tiny kitchen.

'It wasn't grand enough, so he wasn't satisfied with it.'

'You never told me that.'

Noah shrugs. 'I liked where we lived and had teenage stuff to sort out so my dad's discontent didn't register much.'

'Where did he want to live?'

'In the manor house, only it wasn't for sale and Mr Jacob couldn't be bribed to move out.'

'Oh!' The penny drops. 'So that's why Finn's bought it now.'

'Absolutely. It's all to impress Dad. That's why he's spending a small fortune on setting up a business outside his comfort zone. Mind you, it's a fascinating house. Guess what the builders found when they were restoring one of the fireplaces?'

'Mice? Gold bullion? The body of Mr Jacob's first wife?'

Noah grins. 'No bodies. Just a child's leather shoe that's about 200 years old.'

'No way!'

'Yeah way!' Noah puts his elbows on the table and leans forward, eyes shining. 'What would old Baldwin think of that?'

'He'd be totes emosh.'

He really would. Mr Baldwin, our history teacher, cried at the drop of a hat. Anything could set him off – the Tolpuddle Martyrs, the French Revolution, the flaming red-gold of a Cotswolds sunset.

It was Mr Baldwin who told us about the custom of hiding shoes to protect a household from evil spirits. And he turned a blind eye after spotting me and Noah snogging on a school trip to Blenheim Palace.

When Noah bites his lip and gazes over my shoulder, I wonder whether his mind's on Mr Baldwin or the kissing.

'Do you want to see it?' he says, slowly. 'The shoe.'

'That would be great. Maybe you could drop it into the shop some time.'

'Or you could come to the manor house and I could show you around. The place is jam-packed with original features. You'd love it.'

He's right. I've longed to explore the manor house for years. Ever since I pressed my nose to the railings as a child and imagined living there. But I'm not sure Noah as my tour guide would be a good idea. He wants to be friends, it seems, but that moment in the shop – whatever it was – shows we have too much shared history to be totally at ease with one another.

'I couldn't come next week because I'm getting ready for the café opening,' I tell him.

'That's OK. Maybe we can organise some time after that so you can look round and see if the place will do the trick with Dad. It better had so I can bask a little in Finn's reflected glory.'

'Your dad *must* be impressed with you already because you've done so well.'

'Not bad, I suppose.'

'Not bad? You've got a good job in New York, the city that never sleeps.'

The cat snoozing at Noah's feet stirs, and he leans forward to stroke its sun-warmed back.

'New York has full-blown insomnia. There's always something loud happening, whatever time it is. And there are people everywhere – the subway's totally rammed.'

'It sounds like a very vibrant place.'

'It's vibrant and amazing, but it's quite nice to be back in the peace of Honeyford. I missed the calm and the countryside and the wide open spaces.'

'Not enough to come back before, though.'

'I thought about it, but my parents had moved away and there was nothing else to come back for.'

He looks up and stares at me with his pale blue eyes that see into my soul. Or that's what I thought as a smitten teenager. Now I can't read what he's thinking at all.

He opens his mouth to say more but turns away when Finn bowls into the garden with an armful of his autobiographies. He trudges around us and dumps them on the table.

'There you are, Noah. Come on, mate. I've flogged all the books I'm going to and could do with a hand getting my stuff back in the car. I'll leave a few books here for people who missed the signing session. What are you two doing out here anyway?'

'Callie was showing me her new café business.'

Finn bares his improbably white teeth.

'This is going to be a café? Good luck with that. I wouldn't touch a small café business with a bargepole.'

'Come on, Finn,' says Noah, sounding embarrassed. 'A café will be a lovely addition to the bookshop.'

'But you don't make money from "lovely", do you? This place has been done on the cheap and will be an economic disaster. Sorry to be blunt, Callie, but I know what I'm talking about and you're wasting your time with this. People pay a fortune for my business advice, but you can have that nugget for free.'

He gives me a wink as I press my lips together, not trusting myself to speak.

Finn's verdict on the café is upsetting, but mostly I'm infuriated by his unsolicited opinion. Who the hell does he think he is? Red hot anger is pulsing through me like lightning strikes.

Noah frowns and the cat bolts when he pushes himself to his feet.

'That's not on, Finn,' he says in a tight, low voice. 'Sometimes you remind me too much of Dad, the way you always think you're right about everything.'

An ugly red flush spreads across his brother's cheeks but, before he can bite back, Flora pipes up from behind me:

'Finn, I think your adoring public is missing you.'

She's snaked into the garden, without making a sound. Just like she suddenly, noiselessly, appears standing behind me in the kitchen, or looking over my shoulder in the shop. She'd make a fabulous assassin.

'It's such a curse always being in demand,' huffs Finn, gathering up his books and stalking off.

Noah follows him but murmurs to me as he passes by, 'Take no notice. He can be a dick sometimes.'

'Did you hear what Finn said?' I demand, when both men are out of earshot.

'I did, and he reminds me of my husband, who's also full of constant encouragement. At least Noah stood up for you.' Flora beckons me back into the café and forces a smile. 'Look, I suggest we follow Noah's advice and take no notice of Finn. He's a successful businessman but that doesn't make him a café guru. Are you OK?'

I nod, less jittery now the anger is dissipating. Where does all this strong emotion go, I wonder? Does it evaporate into nothingness or is twenty-six years of acid anger bubbling like molten lava in the dark recesses of my soul?

'Callie? Don't let it upset you. I know you've poured your heart into this project and I'm sure it will be a great success.'

'I hope so.'

'Quite honestly, it's hard to believe those two are brothers. Finn seems pretty tactless and hard-hearted, but Noah's different.'

'Hhmm.'

I wander over to my beloved coffee machine and stroke the smooth stainless steel.

'Are you saying he's not different?'

'I'm saying the Shawleys are more alike than you'd think, or at least they used to be.'

'People can change, you know,' says Flora, giving my arm a reassuring pat as she brushes past me.

When she's gone, I stand for a while in the empty café that's going to be a disaster, according to Finn, and I worry.

I worry that Flora will lose her money, and the shop will close, and Gramp will be destitute and die in a ditch, and it will all be my fault.

I worry that I'm the least confrontational person in the world but still wanted to punch Finn's lights out.

And I worry that Gramp's right and being your 'true self' is important. Which means I'm screwed because the only person I've ever felt fully comfortable being my true self with was Noah – but, ironically, I now feel distinctly uncomfortable whenever he's around. I can't forgive the way he broke my heart and, even if I could somehow get past it, he'll soon be on the other side of the Atlantic, anyway.

Chapter Eleven

The house is eerily quiet when I let myself in after work. I kick my shoes off in the hall and yawn loudly because today's been never-ending.

Only a handful of customers came in after Finn's book-signing so I spent the afternoon making a selection of signs for the café: *Toilet, Garden Seating This Way* and *Browse Through Our Fabulous Selection Of Books On Your Way Out.*

Will there be any customers to read them? And where is my gramp? It's quarter to six so the telly should be blaring through the house. He never misses *Pointless*; he hero-worships Richard Osman.

'Gramp?'

I burst into the front room, expecting to find his lifeless body stretched out on the rug, TV remote clasped in his hand. But the room is chilly and empty.

'Where are you?' I call, going from room to room until I find him sitting still as a statue on the bed he shared with Gran.

Photos of her are scattered around the room – a wedding picture in a silver frame on the chest of drawers, Gran with my dad just a babe in arms, Gran and Gramp on their ruby wedding anniversary and, next to his bed, white-haired Gran smiling at the camera shortly before she died.

'Are you all right? You're missing *Pointless*, you know.'

I sit down close to him on the high, lumpy bed.

'It can't be helped. This is too important.'

'More important than Osman cracking jokes?'

When I nudge my shoulder against his, Gramp shuffles his backside round until he's facing me.

'What I'm dealing with is far more important, Callie. Today, I discovered something very upsetting.'

'What's the matter?' I fold my fingers over his wrinkled hand. 'Tell me what's happened.'

'It's dreadful news,' he murmurs, shaking his head.

'Has one of your friends died?' I ask, gently.

'Most of my friends are dead already.' He sniffs. 'No, this is worse.'

Panic starts to bubble through my chest and tighten my throat. 'Have you had bad news about your health? Are you ill?'

'It's much worse than that.'

'Oh God, you're not going to die, are you?'

Gramp wrinkles his broad nose and snorts.

'We're all going to die, Callie. Some of us sooner rather than later – I'm specifically referring to Dick, who reckons he's Nigel Mansell behind the wheel of his late-life-crisis car. But no, it's even worse than that.'

OK. I'm officially stumped. When I raise my palms to the ceiling, Gramp draws in a deep breath of air which whistles through his false teeth.

'He's cutting down the trees.'

What the what? When I gaze blankly at him, he sighs.

'Finn Shawley is cutting down three trees at the edge of the meadow that backs onto the manor house's garden. He wants to put down tarmac and extend his car park.'

Gramp's eyelids are half-closed, as though this news is too heavy a burden to bear, but my panic starts to fade.

'Cutting down trees isn't great, but there are more trees at the top of that meadow, so it's not the end of the world. And it's certainly not worth missing *Pointless* over.'

'Osman would understand me missing an episode if he was au fait with the full gravity of the situation.'

Nope, I'm still baffled. 'Which is?'

Gramp utters a faint moan and the muscles in his jaw tighten. 'The trees Finn Shawley's going to murder are your Gran's.'

'Nope, you've lost me.'

'Moira and I did our courting in that meadow in the 1950s. Our parents were very strict and kept an eye on us, so we'd say we were going for a walk and escape outdoors for some unfettered canoodling.'

Eek. Imagining even fettered canoodling between my grandparents is unsettling. I breathe deeply and catch a faint whiff of Gran's perfume, which Gramp likes to spray on his pillow.

'I can see how upsetting this is but the meadow and the other trees will still be there. What's so special about those particular trees?'

Gramp picks up the bedside photo of his wife and runs his finger across her lovely face.

'They're special because it was underneath those very trees that Moira and I first made love and your father was conceived.'

I stare at my grandfather, not sure how to respond to this piece of information. His true-self policy of 'saying it like it is' is totally pants.

He shrugs. 'Don't look so shocked, Callie. Did you think your dad was the result of an immaculate conception?'

'To be honest, I've done my best never to think about Dad's conception at all.'

He ignores me. 'And my Moira's still there beneath the trees.'

'She's there in spirit.'

'No, she's there physically. That's where her ashes are scattered.'

'We scattered Gran's ashes at the top of Cranwick Hill. Mum and I were there with you.'

'Not all of her. I put some of her ashes in a coffee jar and went to the meadow on my own to scatter them under the trees and remember her.'

'You put Gran in a coffee jar?'

'An empty Maxwell House one. She was addicted to caffeine so I didn't think she'd mind, and I washed it out first.'

'But why didn't you tell us so we could come with you?'

'I thought your mother might not approve. But now you know the truth, and that's why Finn will cut down those trees over my dead body.'

I lie back on the bed and stare at the ceiling. My head's reeling with information I was far better off not knowing.

'Finn doesn't own that land.'

'You what?' says Gramp, drumming his fingers on the patchwork bedspread.

I sit up and brush hair from my face.

'The meadow doesn't belong to Finn.'

'It does now.' Gramp scowls. 'He bought the bottom bit of it from Bill Fairburn, who took his thirty pieces of silver. That's the last time I buy him a pint in the Pheasant.'

'And is Finn allowed to cut down the trees?'

'Bill says he is because the trees are diseased.'

'In that case, I'm sorry, Gramp, but I'm afraid there's not a lot you can do. I'm sure Gran would understand and wouldn't want you to be so upset about it.'

He lifts his chin and stares out of the window at distant hills outlined on the horizon.

'Don't sit up here on your own. Why don't you come and watch the news while I make tea? It's lasagne tonight.'

But even the prospect of stuffing his face with stodge isn't enough to tempt my grandfather downstairs. He folds his arms and puffs out his skinny chest.

'There might not be a lot that Old Stanley could do about it but that Stanley is gone. That's why I'm up here, working out my plan of action.'

The words 'plan of action' strike fear into my heart.

'What sort of action do you mean?' I ask, nervously.

'That has yet to be decided. But mark my words, Callie. I, very much like Moira's trees, won't go down without a fight.'

By the time I come downstairs next morning, Gramp's already been out and come home again. I managed to doze through the front door banging but my planned lie-in vanished when the hammering began.

Loud thuds reverberate through the house as I stumble downstairs, bleary-eyed in my dressing gown.

The first thing that hits me when I push open the kitchen door is the smell of paint, swiftly followed by the realisation that the kitchen is a mess. Ragged bits of cardboard and thick chunks of wood are scattered across the floor and I can't see the table. It's covered in sheets of newspaper, loose nails, rolls of brown parcel tape and a soggy paintbrush.

'Morning, Callie,' says Gramp, hammer in hand. 'Mind your feet. Oops, too late.'

I yelp in pain when a splinter pierces the arch of my foot. Ouch, that really hurts. I limp over to the table, leaving spots of blood on the vinyl tiles.

'Gramp, what exactly are you doing?'

'Enacting my plan of action.'

'Which is?'

'This!'

He turns around a large square of cardboard which has been hammered, very badly, onto a long strip of wood. It's a placard – a very big placard which has *Shawleys: Tree Murderers!* scrawled across it in thick red paint.

'I've done two so I can mix and match when I get there.'

He pulls one he prepared earlier from beneath the table. This one is even bigger, and has *Shawleys: EnvironMental Criminals!* daubed across it.

I sink onto a chair, feeling sick.

'Mix and match when you get where?'

'To Honeyford Manor. I'm going to stage a dirty protest outside the main gate.'

Jeez, I certainly hope not!

'I don't think you mean dirty protest, Gramp. You don't, do you?'

He screws up his face and pouts. 'I'm going to protest and I'll use dirty tactics if required. Why, what does dirty protest mean?'

There's no way I'm going into detail this early in the morning.

'Why don't you write to the paper instead, or contact your Honeyford councillor? I'm sure Joe would take up the issue on your behalf.'

'Huh,' he snorts. 'Joe is the most shite local councillor this side of Oxford.'

'He's your friend!'

'And he's a very good friend, but he's a shite local councillor. He admits it himself. He only does it for the expenses.'

Setting down his hammer, Gramp picks up a dripping paintbrush and adds another exclamation mark after *Murderers!*

'I know you're annoyed at Finn but why do your placards say "Shawleys"? Why are you including Noah?'

'They're in this hotel thing together so they both have to take responsibility for their actions,' says Gramp, firmly. 'Noah's a good lad but he's fallen in with the wrong crowd.'

'The wrong crowd? He's here helping his brother.'

'Exactly. I rest my case.'

When he bangs on the table for emphasis, the paintbrush flies out of his hand and arcs red paint across the kitchen before splatting onto the tiles.

'Is there anything I can say that will stop you going?' I ask, desperately. 'What about if I make you a lamb stew for lunch? Or nip down the shop and buy some florentines?'

'Nope,' says Gramp cheerfully. 'I'm on a mission and I've got my whole morning planned. An hour marching up and down outside the manor house gate, a quick pint and toilet break at the Pheasant, and then back to the gate for round two.'

You've got to give him top marks for determination, innovation and general bloody-mindedness. I'm quite impressed, really, but worried he'll end up either collapsing in a heap or being carted off by the police.

'You'll be exhausted,' I tell him. 'And the BBC weatherman said it's going to rain later.'

'Then I'll take my coat. I might get soaked, but at least I'll be saying what I truly think and protecting Moira's legacy.' He points at a mug that's half-hidden under a pile of cardboard cut-offs. 'I made you a cup of tea, by the way.'

I take a swig of the stone-cold tea while he gathers his placards together, and I consider my options. I could go back to bed and let him stage his protest on his own. Alternatively, I could go with him in case he starts throwing stones through Finn's windows – Finn seems the litigious type. The final option is to lock my grandfather in the toilet and refuse to let him out.

Sadly, imprisoning senior citizens – even bonkers ones – is frowned upon, so I have little choice.

'I understand that you're upset, Gramp, and I'm sorry about the trees but I don't think this will help. However, if you insist on going through with it, I'll come with you. Not to march,' I add quickly, when he thrusts a placard my way. 'Just to keep an eye on you.'

'I'm not ten,' he mutters, but then he smiles. 'If you're coming with me, you'd better get dressed because I told Frank I'd be at his place before ten to pick up his megaphone.'

Oh, Lordy. I slowly lower my forehead onto the table. Bits of cardboard and sticky tape dig into my skin and, where the newspaper's rucked up, I spot dent marks in the table where Gramp's missed the placard with his hammer. I have a very bad feeling about this. All I can hope is that Finn's gone out for the day, and taken his brother with him.

Chapter Twelve

I try talking my grandfather out of his protest plan again. I even threaten a culinary strike so he'll have to cook his own tea. But it's no use, and by half past ten we're approaching the manor house.

Its wrought-iron gate is gleaming black in the sunshine and behind it, along the sweeping gravel drive, is the house with its tall chimney pots and stone-tiled roof.

'Here we are, then.'

Gramp leans his placards against the wall that surrounds the house, places his megaphone on the ground, and takes off his backpack.

People passing by smile at us and wave. Lots of them have known Stanley for years and don't realise he's morphed into someone else entirely.

'Are you going to march with me?'

Gramp chooses the *Tree Murderers* placard, which is dribbled with red paint, like blood spatters. He balances the placard in one hand and picks up the megaphone with the other.

'There's no way I'm joining in with this. I'm not here to support you. I'm here to stop you from wearing yourself out or getting arrested.'

'It's a free country, the last time I looked. And I've got a right to free speech.'

'Not if that free speech is slagging off someone else.'

'Oh, you're far too serious and sensible, Callie. You always were, even as a child, with the weight of the world on your shoulders, biting your little lip so you wouldn't upset anyone. Why don't you live a little and let it all out? You'll be dead soon, like me.'

Urgh, he's impossible. *Though he's got a point,* says the little voice in my brain.

I sigh. 'You're right that I don't like getting on the wrong side of people, and I admire that you're standing up for what you believe in. But there are other reasons why I'm against this protest.'

'Which are?'

He folds his arms across his skinny body and waits. But how can I tell him the Shawleys look down on our family enough already, or that a tiny part of me wants to keep in with Noah, now we appear to be sort of friends again?

'Well? I need to get this protest started or I'll never get my pint in the Pheasant.'

'Just… have a bit of a march then, but take it easy,' I implore him.

When Gramp starts pacing up and down outside the gates, I skedaddle pronto to a wooden bench nearby. A bench which has the distinct advantage of being almost completely hidden from the house by a huge beech tree.

Peering around the tree trunk, like Honeyford's resident spy, I take stock of what's happening at the manor house. It's Saturday morning but the house is a hive of activity. Builders and craftsmen are going in and out of the open front door, and two men are erecting what looks like a flagpole in the garden – for the Shawley family crest, no doubt.

No one has noticed Gramp, thank goodness. And there's no sign of Finn, or Noah. Perhaps this won't be so bad after all.

'Save our trees from Shawley slaughter!' suddenly booms into the still April air and echoes across town.

I slump on the bench and put my head in my hands as the verbal onslaught continues.

Here I am, young, free and single, but currently babysitting an eighty-year-old eco warrior in a tiny Cotswold town.

My café has to be ready to launch in seven short days, long-stifled emotions are threatening to overwhelm me, my love life is non-existent, and the man who broke my heart eight years ago – the man I never truly forgot – is at this very moment being slandered by my grandfather. It's funny how life turns out.

Hopefully, once the novelty of protesting wears off, Gramp will give it a rest. But he keeps on marching and he keeps on shouting.

At first, the only people taking any notice are passers-by who giggle nervously and cross to the other side of the road. But gradually, a little huddle of workmen gathers on the other side of the manor house gate. And they start pointing and laughing at him.

I shift about on the wooden bench because making fun of Gramp isn't on. He doesn't seem that bothered but the mockery is making me uncomfortable.

'Hey, mate,' yells one man, 'speak up a bit 'cos I can't hear you. Has your carer gone walkabout?'

OK, that's it. I'm going to have to intervene, even though it means confrontation.

But as I'm walking briskly over, the sea of workmen parts, the gates swing open and out walk Finn and Noah.

It's too late to scurry back behind the tree because I've been seen. So the only option is brazening it out – if only I was better at brazening.

'What the hell is going on?' huffs Finn. 'I can't hear myself think with all this racket.' He reads the placard that's being waved in his face and his mouth drops open. 'What's going on, Danny?'

'Stanley,' murmurs Noah behind him. I try to catch his eye and give him a *what is he like?* look, but Noah's reading the placard too.

'You're tree murderers, both of you,' yells Gramp through the megaphone.

Jeez, that's loud! I've gone deaf in one ear and Noah, who copped the full force, is wincing with pain. Finn snatches the megaphone and drops it onto the floor with a clang.

'Hey, be careful! That's Frank's and he needs it for football practice with the Cubs.' Gramp picks it up and examines it closely. 'You've cracked it now, so the sound will come out all funny.'

'I don't give a monkey's what the sound comes out like. Did I hear you yell that all this madness is about trees?' Finn does a double-take at the spare placard propped up against the wall. 'What the hell? Have you forgotten to take your medication, old timer?'

Noah steps forward and places a steadying hand on Finn's arm. 'Stay calm. What's this all about, Stanley?'

'You and your brother,' blusters Gramp, who's looking less sure of himself now a group of onlookers has started gathering behind him.

When Finn plays to the crowd by rolling his eyes, I step in front of him.

'It seems you're cutting down some trees to extend your car park and my grandfather's upset because the trees are important to him.'

'But they're just trees. This town's got loads of them. Look, there's one over there, and there.' Finn's lip curls. 'Is that what this ridiculousness is all about? A few unhealthy trees on my land that I've got every right to cut down?'

'You might have the legal right but you don't have the moral one,' says Gramp, swallowing loudly. 'You and your brother are both morally bankrupt.'

I wish with all my heart that he'd keep Noah out of this.

'We're morally what?' Finn's handsome face is going puce. Used to people fawning over him, being spoken to in this way must be a whole new experience.

He ferrets about in the pocket of his tight black jeans and pulls out a mobile phone. 'I'm going to call the police and see what they think about me being harassed and slandered in my own home.'

'I'm not in your home. I'm on the pavement,' retorts Gramp, unhelpfully.

Finn frowns and starts jabbing at the phone with his finger.

'Please don't involve the police! He's already… um…'

'He's already what?' barks Finn. 'Slandered and deafened other people in the town? Does he make a habit of behaving like this?'

'No, it's not that.'

'Well?'

Finn's waiting for an explanation, but I can hardly say the police know all about Stanley Fulbright already. I doubt mentioning he was brought home in a cop car for swimming in his underpants would help the situation.

'For goodness' sake, Finn. Just leave it.' Noah grabs the phone from his brother, clicks it off and pushes it into his pocket. 'This protest is an overreaction by Stanley, but so is ringing the police.'

He turns and addresses Gramp directly. 'You've had your say so just go home now. I'm not sure what this is all about but we'll look into it. I promise.'

Then, as Finn and Gramp lock eyes in a scowl-off, Noah moves close to me and says softly, out of the corner of his mouth, 'I'm surprised at you, Callie, for making a fuss like this. I didn't think this kind of thing was your style.'

'I'm not making a fuss,' I hiss. 'Not really. I only came along to keep an eye on him.'

'You should have talked him out of it.'

'Don't you think I tried? You should try living with a barmy eighty-year-old and see how that goes.'

'Oi, I can hear you,' says Gramp, poking me in the back with a placard post.

'Just ring the police,' huffs Finn. 'What's wrong with that?'

Noah sighs. 'It's unnecessary.' He turns his back on me and murmurs to his brother, 'You can't afford to antagonise these people if you want your hotel to be a success.'

These people?

'Is that how you see us provincial types now you're some fancy, hot-shot architect living in New York?'

Ooh, that's got to be worse than my plebs comment. It just popped out of my mouth.

'You go, girl,' murmurs Gramp, behind me.

'I'm a very ordinary architect who happens to work in America.' A flush is spreading across Noah's high cheekbones. 'And I think that comment says more about you than me, Callie. You always did have a chip on your shoulder about where you come from.'

'And that's hardly surprising, is it? You should know that more than most.'

Emotion ricochets across Noah's face, but Finn grabs hold of his arm and starts pulling him towards the gate.

'Come on. Forget the lovers' tiff and let's get back to what we were doing. But if it carries on,' he calls over his shoulder, 'I'll be ringing 999.'

'My grandfather has every right to make his views known,' I shout after them. 'Though, not necessarily in this way. Anyway, he's going home now.'

'I'm not going any—' splutters Gramp. But I cut him off with a wave of my hand.

'Yes, you are. You've made your point so let's leave before you're arrested.'

'I'm not scared of the filth,' he blurts out, as though he's spent half his life in the nick.

'You might not be scared of being arrested. But I am.'

I gather up the second placard and backpack while Gramp shuffles from foot to foot in the morning sunshine. Now his bravado has started evaporating, he just looks like an old man with a dented megaphone.

Linking my arm through his, I pull him away from the manor house. Finn and Noah are walking up the gravel drive, deep in conversation. But as they get to the front door, Noah suddenly looks back and catches my eye.

'Keep going!' I hiss to Gramp, putting my head down and almost hitting myself in the face with the placard. 'God, I've never been so embarrassed.'

'Really? You need to get out more, though I was proud of you for standing up for yourself.'

'I did, didn't I?'

Faint stirrings of pride ripple through me. That was the closest I've ever come to confronting Noah about his snobbery.

'You went a bit over the top, mind, but, hey, you said what you really thought so it's a start.'

'*Me* over the top? You just accused the Shawleys of being murderers, very loudly. I expect the whole town heard you.'

'I hope so. It's time I stood up for what I believe in. I'm being my true self at last.'

'It's just a shame that your true self is a cussed old whatsit.'

That came out more sharply than I intended and Gramp's shoulders drop. We trudge on past the war memorial and the park, which is crammed full of trees swaying gently in the breeze.

Before long, I can't stand the strained silence between us.

'Don't worry. It'll all blow over,' I tell him, noticing a red splodge of paint above his left eyebrow. 'I really am sorry about the trees but you did your best.'

'Is that it as far as you're concerned?'

Gramp stops dead in the street and spreads more paint when he wipes a hand over his face. He looks like he's been in some terrible placard-related accident.

'That's the trouble with us, Callie. We've always been the sort of people who sweep a problem under the carpet rather than encountering it head-on. The sort who give up far too easily.'

'I'm not sure that's true. All I'm saying is, this is one argument I don't think you can win. But you tried, so don't feel badly about it.'

'Oh, I don't feel bad at all. That was only the first shot across the bows, and though the Shawley brothers might have won the battle, they haven't won the war. Mark my words.'

He marches off, the spring back in his step, while I follow behind with my placard trailing in the dust.

Chapter Thirteen

It's the day of the café opening and my stomach is doing somersaults. Not only because my new 'wouldn't touch with a bargepole' business (thanks, Finn) is about to be launched on Honeyford. But also because I've been feeling pretty icky since Gramp went all eco-crazy and Noah and I ended up having words.

It's daft because our clash was pretty mild and he'll be heading back to New York soon, anyway. But I'm feeling destabilised these days.

Usually I'm a pretty level kind of person, with highs that aren't too high and lows that aren't too low. I muddle along with my emotions at seventy-five per cent and well under control.

But everything seems to be ramping up to a hundred per cent since Noah came back to town: I'm much more worried about Gramp and his mad schemes; anxiety about the launch has killed my appetite; and yesterday I cried with joy when I saw the café, all complete with pretty tablecloths, jaunty mismatched crockery and pictures by local artists on the walls.

But most disturbing are the dreams that stay with me long after I've woken up. Weird and disjointed dreams in which Noah, a nebulous figure in the distance, is telling me something really important but I can't hear a single word.

'Callie, a woman from the paper's here,' says Flora, smoothing down her dress. She's looking stunning today in emerald green silk and high heels that would cripple me.

'Don't you want to speak to her?'

'It should be you really, and anyway, she wants to take your photo.'

Oh dear! I steal a glance at my reflection in the shop window while Flora's bringing the journalist over. My tan trousers and lilac top are plain and made of cotton. And, although my blonde hair is pinned into a messy bun and I'm wearing more make-up than usual, I don't measure up to my super-sophisticated boss.

'Callie, this is Chelsea from *The Cotswolds Courier.*'

Chelsea, who's in shorts and a bright pink T-shirt, shakes my hand and pokes her nose into the café when I lead her to the back of the shop.

'Is this it then?' she sniffs. 'Yeah, looks good. Let's get the pics done and then we can have a chat.'

She poses me by the coffee machine with a couple of mugs in my hands, and then leaning against the doorway with the garden behind me. I feel like a right plonker and insist that Flora, Phyllis and Mary join me.

Becca is a no-show which isn't surprising. She warned me that she might stay away, as too many people make her anxious. It's a shame because she's worked so hard to help me set up the café.

After the pics have been taken, Chelsea asks a few general questions about me and the café and plans for the future. She's finished and put her notebook away when I raise the subject of the trees.

Getting involved in Tree-Gate is not a good idea, but I promised Gramp.

'Have you heard much about the manor house being turned into a hotel?' I ask, casually, showing Chelsea to the shop door.

'I have! That's such an exciting project and Finn reckons we'll have all sorts of celebrities staying over. He's so inspiring,' she gushes. Clearly another female who's fallen under Finn's spell.

'Has there been anything said about the trees he's cutting down at the back of the premises?'

Chelsea scrunches her button nose. 'Funny you should ask because we had a tip-off about that – a note came in the post, all in capital letters. But there's nothing in it. The trees are diseased and Finn needs parking for all his celebrity guests. His hotel is going to be such a boost for the town.'

She shakes my hand and heads off, passing Malcolm, who's just parked his shiny blue Mercedes opposite Amy's sweet shop.

'Callie! How marvellous to see you again. You're looking lovely today.'

My nostrils flood with his musky aftershave when he kisses me on both cheeks. He's dressed more casually than the last time I saw him, in grey cords and a white polo shirt.

'Gosh, you've been busy in here by the looks of things.' He narrows his eyes at the piles of books everywhere and runs his hand along a display of small clip-on reading lights near the till. They're a new addition to the shop, along with a range of bookmarks, arty greetings cards and china mugs bearing literary quotes.

'Flora's been working very hard to improve the shop and boost sales,' I say, pointedly.

'Talking of which, where's this café that's going to keep everything afloat?'

No pressure, then. I take Malcolm through to the café and he strides around the room, looking thoughtful.

'Malcolm, you came! What do you think of the café?' asks Flora, who's brandishing a very large knife for cutting the celebratory cake.

Malcolm puts his hands on his hips and breathes out through pursed lips. 'It's been done quite well but I'm still worried it'll be like the shop and a case of throwing our good money after bad.'

'It's *my* money,' says Flora, quietly, her face falling. 'Money that my parents left me.'

But Malcolm ignores her and heads for Knackered Mary, who's bouncing Callum in one arm and unwrapping paper plates with her free hand. Thankfully, Callum is quiet, because he's fast asleep.

'Wow, this all looks very snazzy,' declares Gramp, wandering into the café with Dick beside him. 'Did you do all of this yourself, Callie?'

'Absolutely not. I had loads of help from Flora, Sarah, Mary – who's over there – Becca, who's not here, and Phyllis, who's by the cakes.'

'That woman in the wheelchair? I think I know her.'

Gramp waves at Phyllis, who gives him a tentative wave back.

'Are you OK, Dick?' I ask. 'You don't normally come into the shop and you seem a bit uncomfortable.'

'Too many books in one place. It's not right,' huffs Dick, loosening the collar of his smart blue shirt. 'But Stanley insisted I should come in to support you.'

'I'm so glad you did.' I give his arm a squeeze. 'I'm really pleased that you're both here.'

And so grateful that Gramp's ditched the combat trousers he's taken to wearing lately. He found them in a charity shop and they're a bit tatty. But today he's in a suit which is lovely, even though it's his 'funeral suit', which has been getting quite an airing recently.

'Friends are dropping like flies,' he announced over tea last night. 'And I'll probably be next.'

'Don't be daft, Gramp. You'll go on for ever,' I said, patting his hand while one hundred per cent emotions whooshed through me – overwhelming sadness at the thought of losing him, guilt because once he's gone I'll be more free, and fear at the thought of being alone.

'I want to know what's under this.' Gramp leads me back into the shop and points at a swathe of blue fabric draped above the café door.

'It's covering the name of the café. Flora's going to unveil it when she does her speech.'

'Speech? I hope she's not going to witter on for ages. I only came for the cake. So what's the name of this place, then?'

'You'll find out.' I tap the side of my nose and try to look mysterious as a group of people starts to gather behind me.

Not a lot happens in Honeyford on Saturday mornings so a sign outside the shop offering free coffee and cake has attracted a few locals.

Two arms suddenly snake around my waist. 'Hey, Callie, where's the free stuff? The journey from Cheltenham was a bitch and I need carbs.'

'I didn't realise you were coming!'

When I give Sarah a hug, she pats me on the back like I'm a child in need of comfort.

'I thought you'd welcome some moral support, plus… free stuff! Hey, Stanley! You're looking very dapper.'

She's giving him a hug when Flora taps me on the shoulder. 'It's almost midday so let's get this café open. I'll kick things off.'

Flora steps in front of the little huddle of people and Malcolm bangs loudly on the shop counter for everyone to be quiet.

'Thank you, Malcolm,' says Flora with a frown, 'and thanks to all of you for coming along to the opening of our wonderful new café. We thought it was about time Honeyford's only bookshop had a place where you can relax, enjoy some delicious coffee and browse books, which you'll be desperate to buy, of course.'

She laughs and nods to someone in the crowd. When I follow her gaze, I spot Noah, right at the back as though he's trying to be incognito. Sarah's seen him too and gives me an almighty nudge with her elbow.

'We look forward to welcoming you to the café and we'll also be setting up a book club in the not too distant future and hope some of you will come along to that.' There's a hum of interest from the crowd. 'Anyway, that's enough from me. This has been Callie's baby from the start, so she should unveil the name before we all get stuck into coffee and cake.'

A small cheer goes up and now, oh God, everyone's looking at me, including Noah. He's staring at me with a strange look on his face and then he gives me a wide smile that crinkles the skin around his eyes. My throat feels constricted and I appear to have forgotten how to breathe.

'Thank you again for being here this afternoon.'

My wavering voice makes me sound nervous. I bet Noah never sounds nervous when he's presenting his architectural projects to clients. I suck in as much air as my tight chest will allow. A lot of people have supported me to get this café open and I don't want to let them down.

'This café has been a labour of love and a real joint effort,' I continue, my voice sounding stronger. 'I'd like to thank Flora for being such a supportive boss and four women who've helped to get this café off the ground – Phyllis and Mary over there, my good friend Sarah, and Becca, who can't be here, sadly. I couldn't have done any of this without their brilliant help.'

There's a ripple of polite applause and Mary stops rocking Callum to give me a thumbs-up.

'So, let's get this café named and open without further ado.'

When was the last time a twenty-six-year-old used the archaic phrase 'without further ado', I wonder, as I grab the edge of the blue fabric. It's only Blu-Tacked on so one tug should do it.

'I now declare this café well and truly open,' I say, pulling at the fabric and mentally kicking myself for being so cheesy.

The cheap fabric floats to the floor and people around me clap when the painted wooden sign is revealed.

'Oh,' says Gramp, behind me. 'Well, I say.' He gulps and tears shine in his rheumy eyes.

'What do you think?' I ask him. 'I wanted Gran to feel a part of my new business. Would she be pleased?'

He stares at the large black sign which has 'The Cosy Kettle Café' picked out in swirly white letters. It took me ages to get the letters all the same size, but it was worth it. Gran loved her collection of copper kettles and I know she'd have loved the café too.

'Your gran would be honoured, love,' he sniffs.

It's over an hour later and the café's doing a roaring trade. Cakes have been eaten, coffee's been drunk, books have been bought – and my stomach's stopped churning.

We stopped giving out free coffee half an hour ago but people have stayed, sitting at the tables and in the garden. And they've bought refills. The café has made its first few sales and customers are full of praise for the coffee and the décor, and say they'll be back. So put that in your pipe and smoke it, Finn Shawley!

'I'm really proud of you,' says Sarah, who's slipped behind the café counter during a quiet patch. 'Who knew there was a kick-ass businesswoman lurking beneath that eager-to-please exterior?'

'Yeah, that's me. Sheryl Sandberg in a pinny.'

I do a little twirl in my Cath Kidston apron that almost matches the tablecloths.

'And your helpers are brilliant, especially the old bloke in a suit.'

She grins at Gramp, who, along with Phyllis, has insisted on being waiting staff for a while.

Phyllis is zooming up to tables with soft drinks balanced on her wheelchair table, and Gramp is carrying coffees, one at a time. Mary had to leave to feed a fractious Callum but I was delighted when Becca turned up. She's sitting in a corner of the café on her own at the moment, nursing a cappuccino.

'Where's Noah, then?' asks Sarah. 'Have you buried him in the garden?'

'You know very well that he left as soon as the unveiling was done.'

'I don't know how he dares show his face here.'

'Sarah, let it go. My break-up with Noah was ages ago. I'm over it and over him.'

'Not if the way you were both eyeing each other up during the speeches is anything to go by. You've still got feelings for him, haven't you?'

'Absolutely not.'

'So you're telling me you're not tempted to rip his clothes off and make him pay for being so horrible about you.'

'That's exactly what I'm telling you.'

Sarah sighs, unties my apron and yanks it over my head.

'OK, that's it. I've had enough of this obfuscating. And now you've made me use a stupid word like *obfuscating*! Is that scared girl called Becca? The one who helped you set this place up?'

'Yes, why?'

'Hey, Becca,' yells Sarah across the café. 'Can you come here a minute?'

Becca's eyes open wide, but she jumps up and hurries over.

'Here you go.' Sarah thrusts the apron into Becca's hands. 'You're in charge for a bit.'

Becca and I both start protesting but Sarah's unstoppable when she's in full flow.

'Do you know how to use the coffee machine thingy?' she demands.

Becca nods. She and I figured it out together one afternoon, using YouTube videos.

'That's great. There's the price list and, if you run into any problems, Callie will be with me, spilling the beans. We're off to buy sherbet lemons.'

With that, she grabs hold of my arm, marches me through the shop and out into the High Street.

'Off to buy what?' I ask, being pulled along beside her.

'Sherbet lemons. They're your favourite, aren't they?'

'Yes, but—'

'You could do with a treat after your hard work getting that café open, and I need to talk to you. In private.'

She pulls me into Amy's sweet shop which smells of dark chocolate and boiled sugar, and waves her arm. 'There you go. Take your pick.'

Large glass jars line the wooden shelves that run along the walls, and each jar is jam-packed with old-fashioned sweets: chunks of peanut brittle, rainbow jelly beans, mint humbugs, chocolate limes and garishly coloured flying saucers that taste of cardboard to me. So much choice. So many calories.

'Many congratulations on your new café, Callie,' says Amy, shovelling my chosen sherbet lemons into a small paper bag. She's dressed retro-style today in a red 1950s style skirt and white blouse, with her greying hair sculpted into waves. 'It's what this town needs – somewhere for people to gather together and chat, that doesn't involve alcohol.'

Amy purses her lips, a keen advocate of sobriety following her disastrous marriage to a man who could always be found in The Pheasant. She fills another bag with rhubarb and custard sweets for Sarah and rings up our purchases before moving on to another customer.

'Come on,' says Sarah, opening the shop door. 'Let's head to the bench for a bit before you go back to work. Flora won't miss you for five minutes.'

Flora probably won't but Becca will, I think. Glancing at my watch, I follow Sarah to the town's medieval church and we park our backsides on a weathered wooden bench in the graveyard. It's not the most glamorous of locations, but we spent hours here as teenagers, eating sweets and discussing the important things in life – including the boys I fancied, how my parents' bickering was driving me mad, and the best way for Sarah to come out to her grandparents.

'Right, Callie,' says Sarah, shifting round so she's looking at me. 'Time is short so I'll just come out with it. You're one of the nicest people I've ever met. In fact, you are *the* nicest person I've ever met. And that's not a compliment. You never say what you truly think, even to me half the time. You let people get away with stuff, you don't argue, and, quite frankly, you do my head in. So, for the love of all that's holy, tell me the truth for once. How do you honestly feel about Noah?'

OK, that's direct – even for Sarah. I carefully place the sherbet lemon I'm holding back into the bag and open my mouth, but no words come out. The truth is, I've been repressing my feelings about everything for so long, I honestly don't know how I feel.

'Speak to me, Callie.'

Sarah pops a sweet into her mouth and closes her eyes to savour the taste.

'I don't know what to tell you,' I say eventually. 'It's thrown me, him being back in town. It's brought up a lot of feelings that I thought I'd got rid of.'

'Repressed, you mean,' mutters Sarah, opening her eyes. 'What sort of feelings? Love, lust, murderous anger? Ooh, I can't speak with a gob full of rhubarb and custard.' She spits the sweet into her palm.

'Sadness,' I whisper. 'And maybe a little bit of annoyance.'

'Good. Annoyance is a start. So what are you two going to do – ignore each other, fight, make up? Maybe a brief fling with an ex is what you need to shake your life up.'

'Really? You were ready to floor him a while ago. What changed your mind?'

'Gemma did. You know how she always thinks the best of people? Well, she agrees that what he said was awful but reckons he might have had a change of heart and regret it now.'

'You told Gemma about it?'

'Don't look so disappointed. Of course I'm going to talk to Gemma about it. She's my fiancée.'

'And I'm your friend.'

'Which is why I wanted Gemma's opinion.' Sarah drops the sucked sweet into the bag, leans forward and grabs my hands. Her skin is warm and sticky. 'Look, we both just want you to be happy. So what would you like to happen between you and Noah? What do you want from him?'

A sudden breeze swirls through the long grass curling around the ancient gravestones.

I take a deep breath. 'I don't want anything from Noah. I'd just like him to go back to New York and my life to go back to normal so I can concentrate on getting the café up and running.'

Which is all true. Though the thought of Noah leaving makes me feel low sometimes, because America is so far away. For some reason, I'd feel happier if he was staying in the UK – even though it really makes no difference if he's in Manhattan or Melton Mowbray. His location won't change the fact that he thinks I'm not good enough for him.

'OK,' says Sarah, wrinkling her snub nose and letting go of my hands. 'Then all you have to do is avoid any rendezvous with him for the next couple of weeks, he'll head back to New York and you can go back to your comfortable life of people-pleasing repression. Simple.'

'Is that how you see me? A repressed people-pleaser? That sounds awful!'

Sarah shrugs. 'It's not *awful*. It's quite sweet, really. But sometimes all that frantic *not upsetting anyone ever* messes up your life. Maybe just think about it and start being a teensy bit more of a bitch sometimes?'

She puts her arm around my shoulders and grins. 'Anyway, I'm incredibly proud of you for setting up this café and taking care of Stanley. And I'm so glad you've told me everything, at last.'

Oops, not quite everything. Would Noah showing me an ancient shoe at the manor house count as a rendezvous? I felt sure the whole thing was off following our spat at Gramp's protest. But maybe him turning up for the café opening means the invitation still stands. Truth be told, I'd love to see inside that amazing house at last, and I don't suppose a brief visit would hurt. Would it? I sigh, because life's far too confusing right now.

*

Back in the café, Becca's pressed against the coffee machine, as far away from the front counter as she can get. And her eyes light up with relief when she spots us.

'All OK, Becca? Any problems?' I ask, taking the apron she thrusts back at me.

'No, I made a couple of coffees and sold some sponge.'

She watches as Sarah helps herself to an orange juice from the fridge and drops coins into the till. 'If you've got a minute, can I tell you about an idea I've had? It's probably stupid but I'd like to help you.'

'You already have. You and Phyllis sorted out the garden and you've been helping me to get organised. You've been brilliant.'

'Thanks. I enjoy organising stuff and actually,' she starts gabbling, 'my idea's about organising publicity for the café. It wouldn't cost you anything and it might be useful. Though you might have things in mind already and I don't want to intrude if…' She trails off and stares at the floor.

'Now I'm intrigued. Go on, tell me your idea.'

'I thought I could set up Facebook and Twitter accounts for the café – to let people know it's here and get more customers in. My friend Zac could help me 'cos he's better with social media than me. And it would be a shame if the café didn't do well and the shop had to close.'

She stops and blinks rapidly. 'I heard you and Flora talking about how important the café is. I wasn't spying or anything. But I'd like to help. Coming here is good 'cos it gets me out of my own head, if you know what I mean.'

'I do know what you mean. Who would keep the social media accounts updated?'

'You and Flora, and I could too, if you like. We could post pictures of the coffee and the garden and some of the customers, if they didn't mind, and position ourselves better from a marketing perspective in the local market.'

'Wow! Get you with your marketing perspective in the local market!'

Becca giggles. 'But I don't want to tread on your toes if you already had all that planned.'

'To be honest, I've been so busy getting the café up and running, I haven't had time to sort out social media. I'll need to run it by Flora, but that's a great idea. Thanks, Becca.'

Becca beams. But Flora has reservations when I mention the idea at closing time.

She pauses from re-doing the window display, which went flying when two youngsters had a bust-up near the Young Readers' section. She had to wade in as they scuffled on the floor.

'Malcolm has a website and Facebook page for the restaurant, and we definitely need the same for the shop. People were surprised in the survey that we didn't have them already but I'm assuming Ruben wasn't terribly au fait with IT.'

'He wasn't what you'd call technologically savvy.'

Flora grins. 'I can imagine. Anyway, I'll be sorting out the shop's online presence in the near future, so maybe we should wait while the café beds in and set up its social media accounts at the same time.'

'We *could* wait.'

'But you don't think we should?'

'I think it's good to publicise the café as soon as we can, and social media could help us with that straightaway.'

'And the rush is nothing to do with giving Becca a project to help boost her self-esteem?'

'Well…'

Flora rolls her eyes but smiles to soften any criticism. 'I thought as much. Actually, I'm a bit old-fashioned about social media. I prefer speaking to people face to face or on the phone, but I can see that it might help get bums on seats. Are you on social media?'

'Not really. I'm on Facebook but only use it to check up on what my friends are doing. I rarely post anything.'

For the very good reason that my posts about doing the weekly shop in Tesco would seem rather boring compared to Sophie's Italian stallion updates.

Flora thinks for a moment and then nods.

'What the hell – if Becca's happy to set it up, let's see how it goes. Just so long as she knows that we have the final say on everything that's posted. What could possibly go wrong?'

Chapter Fourteen

My Sunday morning is all planned – a lovely lie-in, followed by a healthy breakfast and maybe a walk to the top of the hill to clear my head for the busy week to come.

But while I'm stretched out across the bed and sunlight is creeping under the curtains, thoughts of Noah's invitation to the manor house – if it still stands – start running through my head. After that *moment,* or whatever it was, in the shop, would it mess with my head too much to go? Or maybe the *moment* is all in my head, anyway, and a quick tour of the kick-ass house would be fine. Just so long as I remember I'm from the Berry Estate and don't start getting ideas above my station. Huh.

Staring at the ceiling only makes the thoughts louder, so I slip out from under the covers and pull on my dressing gown. One thing I am sure about is not telling Gramp about the invitation. He'd only accuse me of consorting with the enemy and I don't want to stir all that up again. Not now it seems to have died down.

Or so I thought. The first hint that Gramp hasn't let the tree slaughter drop is when I almost break my foot.

'What the hell?' I yell, hopping around our narrow hall which is almost blocked by a large brown box. A brown box full of lead weights, judging by the throbbing in my big toe.

'What's all the racket?' complains Gramp, appearing in the hall in full camouflage combat gear. He's been trawling the charity shops again.

'I stubbed my toe on this box,' I yelp. 'What on earth is it?'

Sitting on the bottom stair, I massage my foot, which has gone bright red.

'I had a delivery before you got up. Though I don't really agree with weekend deliveries. In my day, everything was Monday to Friday, nine to five, and we all knew where we were with that. It was so much better. I was working at—'

'I can see you've had a delivery.' I cut across him before he launches into one of his long reminiscences about the 'good old days'. 'But what is it?'

'Ammunition.'

'What, like bullets and stuff?'

I eye the box with apprehension. With Gramp the way he is at the moment, there could be absolutely anything in there.

'Bullets?' he splutters, folding his arms. 'Don't be ridiculous, Callie. It's flyers.'

When I look at him blankly, he opens the top of the box, pulls out an A5 sheet of paper and shoves it into my hands. 'See! Totally non-shooty flyers.'

Good grief! *Save Honeyford's Trees From Death* is written in big red letters on an acid yellow background and slap bang in the middle of the sheet is a head and shoulders shot of Finn. He's grinning widely and looking demonic, mostly on account of the devil horns that have been superimposed onto his scalp.

That image is seared onto my brain. Forever more, when I close my eyes in the hope of drifting into a peaceful sleep, Finn in full Antichrist mode will float before me.

'Where did you get these… these things?'

'Sean's son, down the road, helped me to make them on his computer. It's amazing what he can do on it. And then I ordered them online. Lots of people do it.'

'Really? Lots of people order millions of defamatory flyers that depict their neighbours as the devil?'

'You're overreacting as usual and being far too tame. You have to grab life by the horns, girl.'

'But not by Finn's horns!' I protest, waving the neon-bright flyer. 'How many did you order?'

Gramp shrugs. 'I meant to order a hundred and fifty but you know I'm not good on the computer. I think I might have accidentally put in too many zeros.'

I rub a hand over my tired face and wish I'd stayed in bed. My grandfather is wonderful and I love him dearly, but he does have his moments.

'So what exactly are you planning to do with these flyers?'

'Distribute them around the town. I wasn't going to tell you because you can be a bit po-faced about stuff like this.'

'If by po-faced you mean sensible rather than barking, and not keen to be sued by Finn, then yes, I am.'

Gramp frowns. 'Is that what you think of me, that I'm barking mad?'

'No, not mad. That's not what I meant.' Jeez! I glance at the clock in the front room. It's not even half past freaking eight and I already have a battered foot and a disgruntled pensioner to contend with. 'I just think you can get carried away when you feel passionately about something.'

Sighing loudly, he shuffles over.

'Budge up.' He parks his camouflaged backside next to mine. His breath smells of PG Tips. 'I get why you're quiet about things and don't want to get involved in arguments. God knows I'd keep my head down if I'd been brought up by parents who could pick a fight over nothing. But sometimes you have to stand up for stuff.'

'I get that, Gramp, but with this?' When I wave the flyer, Finn's demonic face flutters in front of me. 'I'm not convinced this is the right way.'

'Horns too much?' He takes the flyer from me and studies it. 'Sean's son did ask if I was sure. But at least I left Noah out of it, seeing as you're sweet on him.'

'I'm not sweet on…' Oh, what's the point? When I stand up, my toe starts throbbing all over again. 'If you want to carry on protesting about the trees, I can't stop you and making your views known is fine. But please tell me you won't distribute these flyers. They'll just cause a whole heap of trouble.'

'We'll see,' is his final enigmatic comment as I head for the kitchen, suddenly in desperate need of a ginormous bowl of Coco Pops.

Gramp doesn't mention the flyers again, praise the Lord. He puts them in the shed and there they stay, with the spiders and encroaching ivy.

Every now and again, I check that none of the flyers have disappeared, but the box remains full to the brim.

Dumping them in the recycling bin is tempting but there's always the risk that some could escape. And Devil Finns fluttering down the street might be more than Honeyford can take.

Chapter Fifteen

The café's been open for just over a week and, fingers crossed, it's going well. We're not inundated with customers but a steady trickle of people stop by for coffee, and a fair few leave with a book. So Flora's happy – and so am I.

Becca has also started tweeting and updating The Cosy Kettle's Facebook page. And, much to my surprise, it seems to be working, with several people saying they've called in after reading about the café online.

What's also surprising are Becca's posts and tweets, which are really confident. It's like a different person emerges when she can hide behind online anonymity.

'I can be who I want,' she explains, shyly, after an upbeat tweet of Phyllis potting plants in the garden gets dozens of likes. 'In real life I'm Anxious Becca but online I can pretend to be someone else. Does that sound stupid?'

After I've assured her it doesn't sound stupid at all, she pushes her phone in front of my face.

'Have you seen this feedback, by the way?'

I read the comment left below a Facebook post about our range of coffees.

Lovely old-style coffee shop – just what this gem of a Cotswold town needs. Gorgeous small courtyard garden, a cheerful welcome and you can browse books on the way out, says someone called Alison from Gloucester.

'Gorgeous' garden is pushing it but I'll take that. Cheers, Ali!

So the café's going pretty well. And I've also managed to avoid bumping into Noah and Finn, which isn't easy in a small place like Honeyford. But there's no escape from the gossip.

The town is abuzz with talk of the work going on at the manor house and who will stay at the hotel once it's up and running.

'I reckon celebrities like that woman with the funny voice in the car ad will be regular visitors,' says Vernon, who runs the local butcher's and always smells slightly of sausages.

Whereas younger people reckon Kylie and Beyoncé will be spending countless weekends in the middle of nowhere. I can't see it myself but Finn does seem to have connections.

A quick Google search reveals him with his arm draped around the shoulders of B-list soap actresses and minor singing stars. So maybe we will get the odd visiting celeb in Honeyford.

Personally, I wouldn't mind bumping into Zac Efron in the local pub and showing him all that Honeyford has to offer.

But though I listen to gossip about the hotel and say 'really?' and 'gosh!' in the right places, I don't add to the fevered speculation. The hotel will open soon enough, Noah will head back to his bulging New York in-tray, and life will get back to normal.

'Penny for them,' says Flora, who's crept up on me in the café doorway.

'I was just wondering whether I need to up the daily cake order. It's only' – I check my watch – 'just after midday and we're already out of doughnuts and brownies.'

The pastries, delivered to us by a local bakery, are delicious – caramel slices, sweet lemon sponge, moist carrot cake and eclairs topped with a shiny slick of dark chocolate. Our bestsellers are delicious iced cherry tarts in fluted silver cases. But getting the order just right is tricky.

Gramp loves it when we have leftovers and I take a paper bag-full home. He's mostly avoiding sweet stuff at the moment – part of a new health kick that he reckons will take him to his one hundredth birthday. But he's quick to make an exception when I arrive home with choux pastry. 'Life's not worth living without the occasional treat,' he murmurs, peering into the bag like a child at Christmas, seeing what Santa's brought.

'Mind you,' I tell Flora, 'we won't be so busy later on so the few cakes we've got left might keep us going.'

We've already noticed a regular ebb and flow in the café, even though it's early days for The Cosy Kettle. One of our busiest times is late morning when, according to Flora, we attract a certain type of clientele.

'Yep, it's the usual crowd,' she declares, standing in the doorway and scanning round the tables. 'Elderly people on their own, young people without jobs and mums with grouchy babies. You really are catering for the lost and lonely, Callie.'

'Do you think?' I say, bristling slightly in case it's a criticism.

'Absolutely. Tell me who's here.'

'Those people over there with the map are American tourists. They meant to go to Stow-on-the-Wold but ended up in Honeyford instead so I've been telling them which road to take.'

'So they're literally lost.' Flora grins. 'And the rest?'

'That's Julie.' I nod at a young woman in the corner who's breast-feeding her young son. 'She's back to work next week after maternity leave so she's spending some quality time with Hamish.'

I gesture at a man near her who's staring moodily into his steaming coffee.

'Paul over there has just lost his job so he's feeling a bit low and wanted to get out for a while. Behind him is Daphne who lost her husband a couple of months ago and isn't looking after herself properly.'

Flora squints at her. 'What's she eating?'

'A sandwich.'

'We don't sell sandwiches. Did she bring it with her?'

'No. I'm worried she's not eating properly so I gave her my lunch. I can buy myself something else.'

Flora gives a snort of laughter. 'Callie, you are absolutely hopeless. And absolutely wonderful.'

'Hardly. People just come in for somewhere to sit down with a coffee.'

'They come in for you. You're a natural at this. I think you've found your calling.'

'As a café proprietor?'

'As someone who brings people together and makes them feel better. It's a gift.'

My boss thinks I have a gift! My confidence level jumps up a notch.

'What's a gift, ladies?' Malcolm has come up silently behind us – another serial creeper – and I can feel his hot breath on the back of my neck.

'I didn't know you were calling in today!'

Flora turns and kisses her husband on the cheek.

'I was nearby sourcing courgettes for Pierre, who's insisting he use local produce as much as possible. It's a bit of a faff but it looks good on the menu.' Malcolm shrugs. 'Anyway, I thought I'd call in to check on our investment. It's a good job I'm not a shoplifter, with you both back here.'

He's smiling but criticism is more than implied and Flora's mouth pulls into a tight line.

'I'm keeping an eye on things, don't you worry. I was just checking on the café and telling Callie how well she's doing.'

'Hhmm. You do seem pretty busy for a Tuesday morning.' He wrinkles his nose. 'So what's a gift, then?'

'Callie's ability to connect with people, draw them in and provide excellent customer service, including giving that elderly lady her own sandwiches.'

'Just so long as you charged her for them. We're not a charity.' Malcolm laughs. 'Anyway, don't let me disturb you and keep you from your work. I'm just going to have a little wander around to see how our business is doing.'

I'm pretty sure Flora said it was just her money invested in the shop, but I guess it's different when you're married. Malcolm wanders off and Flora settles behind the till, watching him as he runs his finger along the spines on the bookshelves.

Oops. He looks across and catches me staring at him, which is embarrassing. He gives me a slow, deliberate wink and goes back to inspecting our stock. What a sleazeball! Flora deserves so much better.

It's almost half past four, the café's dead as a dodo and I'm wondering what to buy for tea on the way home.

Chicken maybe, from the tiny grocery store near the church. Or eggs to make Gramp an omelette, though that's a right palaver. However I make the damn things, he always complains they're 'not like my Moira's'.

I've just decided on sausage, egg and chips – not overly healthy but a safe Gramp favourite – when my phone pings with a text.

The number's unfamiliar so I almost ignore it. Just how many offers to claim PPI and make gazillions of pounds does one girl need? But curiosity gets the better of me.

Hi Callie. Noah here. I called the shop and Flora gave me your number.

Really? Flora's head is bent over the wholesaler's list so she doesn't clock the look I'm sending her way.

House will be quiet if you have time to call in after work to see the shoe.

Oh, no! The invitation still stands, which means I have to decide once and for all what I'm going to do, rather than flipflopping madly as I've been doing for the last couple of days. Exploring the manor house would be fantastic – it's fascinated me for years. But my visit would mean spending time with a man who gives me goosebumps but lives in New York. Oh yeah, and he thinks I'm common. Ugh, my head is all over the place, and as for my heart…

OK. I make a final decision and my fingers fly across the letters on my cracked phone screen.

Sorry. Can't make it this evening. Have to feed Stanley and then am out on a date x

Oops, a kiss is so not appropriate in the circumstances. I delete the 'x' but my thumb hovers over the 'send' arrow.

Why am I lying about going on a date? It's childish and might sound a bit desperate. I delete the last sentence and suck my bottom lip between my teeth. *Sorry. Can't make it this evening* sounds brusque, and I don't do brusque. Not even to heart-breaker Noah.

Maybe I could add an emoji or two to soften the message? I start scrolling through reams of faces and figures, looking for an image that strikes a balance between frostiness and friendship.

While I'm discounting the shoes emoji (too predictable) and the thumbs down (too disappointed), I start changing my mind yet again and delete the whole text with shaking hands.

'Are you OK, Callie?' calls Flora, tucking her dark hair behind her ears.

'Yes, thanks, I'm fine,' I lie, shoving the phone into my pocket.

'Only I thought you might like to head off early, seeing as Noah's invited you to look round the manor house.'

'He told you about that?'

'Of course. It's not a secret, is it?' She grins. 'I'm sure you'll have a lovely time. The house looks fantastic from the outside.'

'Actually, I don't know whether to go.'

I shrug in a *not sure I can be bothered* kind of way but Flora fixes her violet eyes on me.

'Have you got something better to do?' she asks, closing the customer order book and clicking the top of her silver pen.

'I need to get back and cook Gramp his tea.'

'I don't think Stanley's going to die of starvation if he has to wait an extra hour for his next meal.'

Probably not, if the massive pork chop he wolfed down last night is anything to go by.

When I hesitate, Flora grasps the small diamond around her neck and runs it back and forth along its silver chain. 'You're always looking after other people, Callie,' she says, gently. 'Why don't you think of yourself for once and go and have a look around the house. Didn't you tell me that you love history?'

'I've always been a bit of a history nerd.'

'There you are, then.' Flora drops her diamond and folds her arms. 'You can feed your inner nerd while being fabulously nosy at the same time. Perfect!'

Chapter Sixteen

Twenty minutes later, I'm striding towards the manor house, enjoying the late afternoon sun on my back. It's been a mixed spring so far, with sunny days few and far between. But right now the sky is china-blue and cloudless.

Ahead of me, green fields sweep towards the horizon and halfway up the hill, perched high on the edge of Honeyford, lies the Berry Estate. From this distance, it blends well with the golden-hued town.

The air around me is still with a hint of pollen, and I take a deep breath. Honeyford isn't cutting edge or cosmopolitan – talk of an Indian takeaway in Sheep Street almost drove the parish council to distraction – but it's beautiful and I'm so lucky to live here.

That lovely fuzzy feeling starts to evaporate when I reach the imposing gates of the manor house. A mud-splattered builders' van is parked outside but there's no one about as I push open the gate, which catches on the gravel.

What are you doing? whispers a niggly little voice deep in my brain. *There's still time to change your mind because you never texted Noah back.*

But maybe Flora's enthusiasm or Gramp's new gung-ho nature is rubbing off on me because I curl my hands into fists, crunch up the drive and press the doorbell.

I'm pressing my lips together and wondering if I've overdone the lip gloss when the door swings opens and Noah's in front of me. He has bare feet and damp hair, as though he's just got out of the shower.

'You came then?' His mouth curls into a smile.

'Did you think I wouldn't?'

'I wasn't sure after Stanley's tree protest.'

'He doesn't know I'm here.'

'Ah,' says Noah, ushering me inside. 'That's probably a wise move.'

The door closes with a bang behind me and I take a look around.

Wow! The huge, square hallway I'm standing in has a flagstone floor that's worn over the years into dips and grooves. A rug, three times as long as me, is rolled up against one wall and white dust sheets are draped over what must be a round table.

A muddle of buckets and power tools is cluttering one corner. And lining the back wall is a brand new wooden reception desk. Sawdust is scattered in little piles all around it.

'Excuse the mess,' says Noah, holding out his hand to take my denim jacket and the carrier bag containing Gramp's tea. He places them on the dust-sheet table. 'Work in the house is almost done but there are still a few things to finish off and it can get messy. Have you ever been in here before?'

'No, I've seen the place often enough from the outside but we were never invited to any of Mr Jacob's parties. It's very grand.'

'Yeah, it's a lovely old house, though sticking to all the planning regulations has been a nightmare. It's a good job I'm here to keep Finn in check or he'd have ripped out half the original features and installed a disco on the top floor. He's not one for sticking to the rules.'

'Really?'

'I know it's hard to believe.' Noah raises an eyebrow and grins. 'Did you want to see the shoe?'

For a moment, I'm not sure what he's talking about because his smile is so distracting. Then I remember why I'm here and nod. 'I'd love to.'

'Follow me. It's upstairs.'

Noah leads me up a wide, carpeted staircase at the very back of the hall. The polished-wood banister feels smooth under my hand as I pad along behind him, keeping my eyes focused on the steps rather than his backside in snug blue jeans.

Upstairs, sunshine is flooding through a landing window and a chandelier is reflecting rainbow colours across the pale walls. Ahead of me is another staircase leading to what was once the attic but is now, presumably, more luxury bedrooms for Finn's guests. I dread to think how much he'll charge to stay here.

'The shoe's in here,' says Noah, pushing open one of the doors and standing back so I can walk into the room first.

Jeez, I thought the hallway was grand but it looks like our box-bedroom compared to this magnificent space.

Floor-length curtains of ruby-red silk are rippling onto a thick cream carpet. There's a fabulous old fireplace with a carved stone mantelpiece on the back wall. And in the centre of the room stands the pièce de résistance - a four-poster bed with ruby drapes that match the curtains.

'This is the master bedroom where we – well, one of the workmen – found the shoe.' Noah moves to the fireplace, bends his head and pushes his arm up the chimney. 'It was tucked away behind some bricks,' he says, his voice muffled.

Then he pulls out his hand and opens it wide. Nestling on his palm is a child's boot in dark leather with three worn button-fasteners. The leather's covered in a maze of cracks, like crazy paving.

'What do you think of that?'

'That's awesome and it looks so old. Can I touch it?'

'Of course.'

Noah gently places the shoe in my outstretched hand and stands with his arms folded while I examine it.

'It's so small and delicate.'

I stroke the cracked leather and wonder about the person who last wore this shoe. Was it outgrown by a healthy child or a reminder of a child who died? Who knows how long it's been hidden here with people sleeping nearby?

'I remember old Baldwin telling us that shoes were hidden in houses to chase away bad spirits,' says Noah, perching on the edge of the four-poster bed.

'That was one reason. Sometimes they were fertility symbols and hiding a shoe was supposed to help the woman of the house get pregnant.'

'Is that how it happens?' Noah's mouth twitches in the corner and I suddenly feel very hot. He stretches his long fingers across the brand-new mattress and breathes out slowly.

I swallow and wander over to the window, with the shoe still nestled in my palm. The room looks out over the back of the house, past the stone fountain and the gardens to the fields beyond.

'Are those the trees?'

I wasn't sure about bringing up the trees. They're potentially contentious. But changing the subject seems a very good idea right now.

Noah joins me at the window and peers through the glass. He's so close I can see the faintest trace of stubble on his chin and smell his aftershave. Eight years ago he wore cheap citrus aftershave that made me sneeze, but this one has a subtle tang of ginger and exotic spices.

'It's those three trees there.'

He leans past me and points at a small huddle of trees edging the car park. The cotton of his blue shirt-sleeve grazes my bare arm.

'Finn's hoping he can tarmac that little bit and add a couple more parking spaces.' He shrugs. 'It's not ideal but those trees have to come down anyway because they're unhealthy and unstable. I've seen the report from the tree surgeon.'

'So whatever my gramp does, they'd definitely have to be felled?'

Noah nods. 'Afraid so. That's not going to change, even if he parades naked through the town.'

'Or distributes flyers depicting Finn as the devil.'

'That too. He's not, um…?'

'God, no.' My laugh sounds forced. 'He wouldn't be that daft. That was just an example. It's a shame, though.'

'It is, particularly when they mean so much to Stanley, though I'm not exactly sure why.'

There's no way I'm giving him a potted version of my dad's al fresco conception. So we stand in silence, looking at the doomed trees and the meadow beyond that's scattered with wild flowers.

Noah clears his throat. 'Do you remember that time we were making out in the park and sheltered under a tree when it started thundering? That storm was fierce.'

Where did that come from? I glance at Noah sideways, but he's still staring through the window.

'How could I forget?' I reply, keeping my eyes firmly fixed on the horizon. 'The storm was apocalyptic and I was convinced we were about to be fried by a lightning bolt.'

'You were terrified. You clung onto me so tightly I could hardly breathe.'

'Which totally serves you right for persuading me to ditch my revision in the first place and walk to the park when it was raining.'

When I turn my head, I realise that Noah's mouth is just a few centimetres from mine.

'If I remember rightly, you were easily persuaded,' he says, his eyes on my lips.

'That was before the thunderstorm went nuclear and I thought I was going to die.'

Oh God, my voice has gone all husky. I sound like I'm doing a bad impression of Marge Simpson.

'You were never going to die, Callie,' murmurs Noah, moving so close his thighs are brushing against mine. 'I'd have taken a lightning bolt for you.'

He doesn't say how he'd have managed this superhero feat and I contemplate asking. But then he bends towards me and all thoughts of thunder and physics fly out of my head as his lips gently meet mine.

Ooh, I'm so annoyed. It's outrageous that snobby Noah Shawley thinks he can break my heart and then, eight years later, arrive all posh and grown up, and kiss me. Utterly, completely outrageous.

That's what goes through my mind as he kisses me harder, hooks his arm around my waist and pulls me against him. That, and *Wowzers, he's been practising.*

Back when we were teenagers, Noah's kisses were lovely but adolescently tentative. And though we came close to sleeping together before the break-up, we never quite did. But now, it's like kissing someone else entirely – a passionate grown man who knows exactly what he's doing.

Back then, he was a wiry adolescent whose ribs poked through his skin when he hugged me. Now he's filled out and I can feel the muscles in his arms when he pulls me tighter against him.

Noah's kissing becomes more urgent as he slides his hands into my hair and presses me back against the window-frame. The heat of his body warms mine and I realise I'm tingling all over. Plus, my knees are wobbling. Proper full-on wobbling.

All I want to do is put my arms around his neck and shove him backwards onto the four-poster. Would that be so wrong?

Suddenly, the front door slams with a deafening bang and the floor beneath my feet vibrates.

'Oh, God.' Noah pulls away, his face flushed and eyes bright. 'Finn's back.'

He wipes traces of my lip gloss from his mouth with the back of his hand while I tidy my hair. What the hell just happened?

'Noah! Where are you?' yells Finn.

'Master bedroom!' shouts Noah, turning his back on me and walking to the fireplace.

There's a thundering up the stairs and Finn bowls into the room.

'You'll never guess what my solicitor said about the Holborn deal. He wants to…' He stops dead at the sight of me and grins. 'Well, well, I didn't know you were entertaining guests up here. Hello, Callie. What have you two been up to?'

'Absolutely nothing,' says Noah, a tad too quickly. And he gives the same incredulous laugh that I heard eight years ago in his garden. Is he regretting the kiss already?

Finn wanders to the window and frowns. 'You're not here about the trees, are you? Like an environmental spy.'

'Callie's only here to see the shoe.'

When Finn looks blank, Noah points at the shoe which is lying on the carpet where I dropped it during the kiss.

'You came to see that old thing? Noah reckons I should display it downstairs in Reception. What do you think?'

He bends to pick it up and turns it over roughly in his hands.

'I think your guests would love to see it,' I say, deliberately not looking at Noah.

'Some might. But look at the state of it, after being up a chimney for God knows how long. I might just chuck it out.'

'You could, though bad spirits might descend on your hotel if you do.'

'Fortunately I'm a modern businessman rather than a superstitious local,' says Finn. But a flicker of uncertainty crosses his face and he carefully places the shoe back on the mantelpiece. 'How's your café going, by the way?'

'Really well, thanks. We're getting repeat customers and tourists too, now the weather's picking up. I'm run off my feet all day.'

Which is another white lie, but I'm hardly going to tell businessman extraordinaire Finn that my, in his opinion, tin-pot café is intermittently busy and doing OK.

'Really?' A deep ridge appears between Finn's eyebrows but then he smiles. 'That's excellent news. Good for you. Has my brother shown you around this place yet?'

'Not yet.'

'In that case…' Finn walks to the door and beckons for me to follow him. 'Let me rectify that immediately. We'll give you the grand tour.'

I should get back to feed Gramp and check he's not pushing defamatory flyers through people's letterboxes. But I'm so discombobulated by what's just happened, I follow Finn without a word.

Oh. My. God. How the other half lives! Finn might be full of brash swagger but his hotel is a beacon of luxurious elegance. All the rooms have high ceilings and are painted in soft dove grey, the palest blue or rich cream. Curtains are full swags of opulent silk that cascade to the floor, and the furniture fits beautifully with the age of this magnificent house.

'I absolutely love the cornicing, and that panelling is exquisite. Is it oak? This place has been renovated incredibly tastefully.'

'We've done our best,' says Noah, jauntily. He opens a door that leads into a long, wide kitchen. 'Here we have the hub of the house, if you'd care to take a look.'

With Finn as chaperone, we're both acting as though nothing whatsoever happened in the bedroom. This seems to involve Noah being über jolly and me being über interested in renovation minutiae and using words like *exquisite*.

I gaze around me at deep enamel sinks, a stainless steel range cooker to die for, and floor to ceiling fridges.

'How much of an influence have you had in what's been done to the house, Noah?'

'Quite a lot,' he concedes, running his finger along the top of a black worktop. Tiny silver chips in the granite shine under halogen spotlights. 'I worked with an interior design expert in our office on the layout.'

He lowers his voice as Finn steps away from us: 'Do you want to talk about what just happened?'

Do I? I have no idea what I think about what just happened. My head's too rammed with swirling one hundred per cent emotions to think rationally about anything.

I hesitate, but Finn is wandering back towards us anyway.

'Well, it all looks blummin' marvellous,' I say, cringing because I appear to have morphed into Eliza Doolittle. Noah folds his arms and steps back behind his brother.

'Come with me,' says Finn, leading me out of the kitchen and flinging open a glass door. 'This is the conservatory. Don't you think it's a wonderful space?'

It certainly is.

Golden sunlight is pouring through huge panes of glass overlooking the gardens, and dappling on the tiled floor. Wood-framed French windows are thrown open to catch a breeze, and there are sand-coloured blinds, draped like canopies just below the domed glass roof.

'This room is utterly…'

I've already used the word 'exquisite' too many times but can't think of a better one.

'I know, right? It's gorgeous,' says Finn, standing in the middle of the room and grinning like a Cheshire cat.

'Is this going to be the hotel dining room?'

'Nah, we've already earmarked the room behind the kitchen for dining. My father thinks this room this would be the perfect space to set up a coffee house for hotel guests and visitors, selling drinks and Cotswold cream teas.'

'Really?' says Noah.

'Yeah, I sent him photos and he said that's what he'd do with this room. What do you think, Callie?'

When I catch Noah's eye, he gives the slightest of shrugs.

'I think it would be' – I hesitate – 'a great idea.'

I can't lie, even though my stomach is nose-diving at the thought of this space being turned into an elegant coffee house. Relaxing here over a coffee might be more enticing than sitting in a bookshop's old storeroom.

'It's certainly got a lot of potential,' booms Finn.

'I'm just a bit confused because you implied – quite strongly, actually – that you weren't keen on cafés as business ventures.'

'It depends on the location. Mine would have the hotel as a setting which would be a great advantage. Anyway, nothing's confirmed. I'm just thinking about it, along with a number of other options for this space.'

'Has your father been to see the hotel since the work's been done?'

Finn shifts and loosens the neckline of his T-shirt. 'He's really busy so hasn't had time to visit since I bought this place. But he'll be here soon to see what I've been up to. He's going to be so proud of me, don't you think, Noah?'

Just for a moment, I glimpse teenaged Finn trying to live up to his absent father's high standards.

'He'll visit soon, I'm sure,' says Noah.

'I can always invite him to the hotel opening as guest of honour. He'd like that.'

Noah nods and gives his brother the ghost of a smile.

'Anyway, Callie.' Finn treats me to a sexy wink as he clicks back into smoulder mode. 'Do you want a coffee or is that like coals to Newcastle now you're running a successful café?'

'Thank you but I'd better head off.'

'No time even for a very quick drink?' asks Noah, his pale eyes locking onto mine.

'Afraid not. Gramp will be wanting his tea.'

'I'll show you to the door, then.'

'No need,' I say, brightly. 'I can find my own way. Thanks so much for showing me around, Finn, and for showing me the shoe, Noah, which was… splendiferous.'

What the actual…? I've never used that word before in my entire life. Turbulent emotions obviously turn me into a complete moron.

I'm not sure but I think I give a slight bow as I exit the conservatory backwards, before hightailing it through the kitchen to the front door.

Finn's purple Porsche is parked at an angle on the gravel and I scoot round it before hurrying up the drive.

My brain is a whirling maelstrom of absolute uselessness. I can't think straight at all. Finn's coffee house plans are a bombshell, but it's the kiss with Noah that's totally thrown me. That was most definitely a *moment* – a *moment* with flaming knobs on.

I hurtle through the gate, almost taking out Mr Evans, who's walking past with his Labrador, and scurry along the road, muttering under my breath. Why did Noah stir everything up and kiss me when he's going back to New York soon? Is he willing to overlook my humble origins for a quick fling? And why am I so disappointed that Finn arrived when he did? Sleeping with Noah would have only battered my very confused heart.

I'm tempted to ring Sarah for her advice, but she'd only totally overreact. So I plug earphones into my mobile, do three laps of the town centre at speed to walk off my adrenaline, and let the soothing tones of Ed Sheeran drown out any thoughts at all.

By the time I get back, feeling calmer, Gramp is standing at the hall window.

'Why are you back so late?' he grumbles. 'I'm absolutely starving.'

'You could have got yourself some food,' I say, stopping to kick off my sandals. 'If you're capable of parachuting from a plane, you're perfectly capable of making yourself beans on toast.'

I mentally kick myself for mentioning parachuting because Gramp hasn't for a while, but he ignores me and delves into my carrier bag.

'No leftovers today then?' He tuts with disappointment.

'The cakes were all snapped up, I'm afraid. Araminta from the riding stables had the last Belgian bun this afternoon.'

'Huh, that's the second day in a row of no leftovers and, to be honest, Araminta's backside is padded enough for horse riding as it is,' he moans, striding towards the front room. 'That café of yours is getting far too popular because you keep taking in all the waifs and strays.'

While tea is cooking, I rootle about in the fridge. I thought as much! There's a bowl of Angel Delight at the back that will do for his pudding. In addition to free bakery goods, Gramp's penchant for retro desserts has survived his health kick.

I find a clean teaspoon and dip into the Delight for a sugar fix while sausages spit at me from the frying pan.

What would my grandfather say if he knew where I'd been after work? And what I'd been doing? The heat in my cheeks has nothing to do with my proximity to the hob.

Sinking onto a chair, I try once more to make sense of what happened. One minute, Noah and I were being all adult about the past and distantly friendly. And the next, I was almost having sex with him on a fabulous four-poster. Which is far too spontaneous and exposing – in so many ways – for a buttoned-up person like me who always thinks things through.

Oh no! The smoke alarm on the hall ceiling is beeping. I pull blackening sausages off the hob but it's too late. A high-pitched shriek echoes through the house and drowns out my swear words as I distractedly flap a tea towel at the alarm.

Super-human effort is required to keep my emotions in check at all times. And it works – apart from with Noah, who's still the one person who can get under my skin and make me behave erratically. He's the only man I know who can make me angry, excited, sad, and desperate to tear his clothes off, all at the same time. Basically, I decide, as I flap, flap, flap, Noah Shawley is emotional kryptonite.

Chapter Seventeen

I still feel kryptonited the next day. Thoughts of me and Noah locked in a steamy embrace up against the silk curtains keep popping into my head. Though it's the feelings, rather than images that I recall – the feel of his hand in my hair and his lips against mine. I have to admit that the kiss was amazing – the best I've ever had – and it's brought lots of old feelings for Noah to the surface. But I can't let myself be hurt by him again.

So I deflect Flora's questions about the manor house and reply with a polite *thanks so much for showing me around* when Noah texts to ask if I'm OK. Then I throw myself into work and the first meeting of Honeyford's Afternoon Book Club, which I'm worried will be an almighty flop.

We've ended up with two book clubs: the evening club is due to meet in a month's time, and we're trialling the idea with a daytime one for anyone who'd rather talk books in daylight.

It seemed like a good idea at the time but, fifteen minutes before the afternoon club is due to start, I push two tables together and then pull them apart. I'm convinced no one will turn up and I'll end up talking to myself like Billy No Mates.

Flora watches me with an amused smile on her face.

'It'll be fine.'

'But what if no one comes and we don't end up selling any books?'

Sales have been sluggish so far this week, with rain showers keeping shoppers and café customers away.

'I'm sure some people will turn up, Callie. And if they're anything like our regular callers, they'll be here for a pep talk from you rather than to buy books anyway. Ooh, look. I rest my case.'

Becca and Phyllis have appeared in the café doorway.

'You came! I'm so pleased to see you. I'll get you both a coffee.'

Becca parks Phyllis at the table and follows me to the coffee machine. She can't stay still today. First, she's fidgeting with her nails and then she keeps pulling up the collar of her shirt, as though she's trying to disappear into it.

'Is everything OK?' I call over my shoulder while curls of steam waft through my hair and towards the ceiling.

'Fine,' says Becca. 'There's just something I need to talk to you about after the club.'

'Can it wait until then?'

'Probably. Yeah. That'll be fine.'

I glance at Becca and put down the coffee I'm making. She'd be rubbish as a spy because every emotion she has is immediately played out across her pale face.

'What on earth's the matter? Are you having another panic attack?'

'Something terrible has happened and it's all my fault,' she whispers.

'What, at home?'

'No, with the café.'

'Callie, why don't you take Becca into the garden for a quick coffee and I'll keep an eye on people turning up for the book club,' says Flora, wandering over.

She shakes her head at me, as though I've let her down. Then she mouths, *sort it out.*

Jeez, I'm feeling more like an agony aunt than a café manager these days. And I've got enough emotions of my own to sort out. But whatever Becca's done, it can't be that bad, can it?

I pick up the scalding coffee and follow Becca into the empty courtyard. Dark grey clouds are scudding across the sky and a discarded tissue is dancing across the garden in the chill breeze.

'So what's going on, Becca?'

I put the coffee down in front of her on the table and pull up a chair for myself.

'It's the social media stuff.'

Becca's almost crying, and I pat her fingers as they drum up and down on the ironwork.

'Has one of the sites gone down? Don't worry. We can get it sorted.'

'No, it's worse than that. Your reputation is ruined.'

'I seriously doubt that.' I grin. 'My squeaky-clean reputation remains unsullied.'

It's true. There are no skeletons in my closet. No illicit affairs with charismatic colleagues, no shoplifting in my teens, no backstabbing workmates to climb the corporate ladder, no arguments – with anyone. I even pick up stray crisp packets in the street and drop them into litter bins.

'Not *your* reputation, the café's,' says Becca, thrusting her phone under my nose. 'Look at that!'

I take the phone from her, focus on the screen and my smile freezes. Someone called Jim Jones has posted on the café's shiny new Facebook page: *Poor service and shabby décor. I won't be back and advise you not to waste your money or your time.*

'See?' says Becca, her breath coming in shallow gasps.

'Well, it's upsetting,' I say, racking my brains over who Jim Jones might be. Lots of new people have come in recently and I've chatted to some of them, but I don't remember anyone called Jim.

There's very little info about him when I click on his Facebook profile, and his photo doesn't ring any bells. He looks the sort of unremarkable middle-aged bloke you'd pass in the street without a second glance.

'It's such a horrible thing to say and everyone will see it because it was my stupid idea to set up a Facebook page,' whispers Becca.

'It is horrid but it's not the end of the world and it's definitely not your fault,' I say, shrugging my shoulders. 'It's just one post and maybe we do need to do better. Let's try to view it as valuable customer feedback that we can learn from.'

Becca chews nervously at her lip while I look at the café I've poured my heart and soul into. It's not high-end like Malcolm's restaurant but it's clean as a new pin, cheerful and welcoming, with fresh flowers on every table. We passed our hygiene inspection with flying colours and people often compliment the coffee.

I shrug again and plaster a smile on my face. 'Don't worry about it, Becca. Come and enjoy the book club and I'll speak to Flora about it later.'

'Should I reply to Mr Jones?' Becca looks as if she'd rather stick pins in her eyes.

'No. We'll take care of it so just leave it with us.'

'All OK?' asks Flora, when we wander back into the café. 'You've got people arriving for the book club.'

She nods towards the café doorway which Mary is currently bumping into with her buggy.

'Yeah, I'll tell you once everyone's gone.'

Poor Mary still looks knackered. She's made an effort with her make-up but forgot to blend in her blusher, resulting in a vivid pink streak across her cheeks. And she's also wearing one black shoe and one brown, but who cares? At least she's here.

'Is it OK if I bring Callum to the book club?'

She gestures at the tiny sleeping figure, swaddled in a soft blue blanket.

'Of course. Settle down next to Phyllis and Becca and I'll get you a cappuccino.'

I've just arrived back at the table with a tray of coffees when a tall woman walks purposefully into the café and looks around.

'I take it this is the book club,' she barks. 'Aren't there more people here?'

The newcomer is wearing aubergine cords and a purple gilet, with a beautiful paisley silk scarf around her neck – and she looks familiar.

As she moves closer, my heart sinks. She's the woman who barrelled into me in the street on Flora's first day.

'My name's Millicent,' she says, her eyes narrowing when she recognises me too. 'I live a few miles outside Honeyford but I saw your tweet and thought I'd come along if that's all right. It's not just for Honeyford natives, is it?'

'It's for anyone who'd like to be here.'

'Good.' Millicent winces. 'Is this where you've having the meeting?'

'Yes, I thought we could have a coffee while we chat.'

'Just so long as your coffee range includes a decaffeinated option or I'll be up all night. I thought a book club would be more popular. Did you publicise it at all?'

'We told customers in the shop and mentioned it on social media, but it might be that this time of day isn't great for people. This is just the inaugural meeting so we'll see how it goes. If that's all right with you.'

That sounds a little sarcastic and Millicent stares at me down her long nose, but she stops asking questions, thank goodness. She takes a seat next to Becca, who slinks away from this scary newcomer.

Now what? Flora is beckoning madly at me from the doorway.

'Look who's just arrived,' she calls out, stepping aside so Dick and Gramp can get past her.

At least Gramp's ditched his combat gear and is looking fairly age-appropriate. Though, dear Lord, is that an ear piercing? Yep, a round gold stud is sitting resplendent in the left earlobe of my eighty-year-old grandfather. Dick tilts his head towards Gramp's ear and raises his eyebrows.

'Why are you here? I didn't know you were coming,' I say, as they wander over.

'I've come along, as your grandfather, to provide you with moral support. And I dragged Dick along too now he's marginally less phobic about setting foot in this shop.' Gramp grabs the coffee I've just made for myself. 'Is this it then? Hello, all.'

When he and Dick start pushing two tables together, I lend a hand and lean in close.

'What have you done to your ear?'

'Duh! It's a piercing.'

'I can see that but why have you had it done?'

'Because I could, obviously. Dick took me into Oxford and a nice bloke called Needles did it for me.'

'I gave him a lift under false pretences,' complains Dick, scraping a chair across the floor. 'He told me he had a chiropody appointment but came back to the car park with a stud. I'm only grateful it was in his ear.'

'It hardly hurt at all, but I forgot to check which ear I should have done. Doesn't an earring in your left lobe mean you're gay? Or maybe it's the right.' Gramp smiles. 'Who cares? Anything goes at my age.'

'Um, it's gone two o'clock,' says Millicent, tapping her watch. 'And much as I love listening to your grandfather coming out, a late start isn't a good start.'

Becca pulls a face beside her.

'We'll talk about this later,' I whisper to Gramp, as he and Dick take a seat.

'Happy to talk about it now if you like,' Gramp replies in a booming voice, twiddling his new earring as Phyllis starts tittering and Becca gives him a thumbs-up.

'Later will do fine, thank you. First, I need to get things moving.' I stand up straight and address the small gathering. 'Thank you everyone for coming to the first meeting of Honeyford's Afternoon Book Club!'

'Whoop, whoop!' says Gramp, punching the air. I ignore him.

'We obviously haven't read a book yet so I thought maybe we could talk generally this time about the books we love, and decide on a book to discuss next time.'

Everyone nods in agreement, except Millicent, who's examining her fingernails and looking bored.

'Perhaps we can start by saying a little bit about ourselves, why we're here and what we're hoping to get out of this group. Though,' I add with a quick glance at Becca, 'no one has to say anything if they don't want to. Shall I start?'

I perch on the edge of a chair and take a deep breath.

'Most of you know me already. I'm Callie, I work in the shop and run the café, and I thought this group might be a good place for people who love books to talk about them and enjoy some friendship and company.'

'And boost shop profits,' butts in Millicent, rubbing at a chip in her nail varnish. 'Shall I go next? My name is Millicent and I live in Little Besbridge.'

Ooh, that's very posh. The tiny village is a magnet for tourists with its picture-perfect cottages, winding streets and duck pond. There isn't an ex-council house in sight.

'So why are you here, Millie?' asks Gramp cheerfully.

'It's Millicent. And I'm here because I enjoy reading books and I have some time on my hands now my children have left home. Celeste is working in Toronto after graduating from Oxford University with a first in French, and Benedict is very busy with his banking career in Zurich.'

She pauses, to see if we're impressed with her children's glittering careers. Phyllis gives a loud sniff.

'Anyway,' continues Millicent. 'I had a spare afternoon so thought I'd give the group a try. Next one!'

We all turn to Mary, who's half-slumped across the table.

'Is it me?' She straightens up and yawns. 'My name's Mary and I'm here because I'd rather go to this club than the Baby Babbles group that's meeting in the market house right now. Quite honestly, if I have to hear about one more cracked nipple or the contents of another nappy, I think I might become violent.'

Becca's eyes open wide as Mary slumps back in her chair, even though our new mum looks the least violent person ever. Callum gives a tiny spluttering cough and settles down under his blanket.

'Me next. I'm Stanley, I'm Callie's grandfather and I'm here giving her moral support because she's been very nervous about this afternoon. Like really properly off-her-food anxious. She hardly ate any tea last night and she was up at six o'clock.'

So much for trying to appear confident. Although I'm touched that he noticed, I give Gramp a glare but he carries on, oblivious. 'I've never been to a book club before so it's good to add this to my list of firsts after hitting the big eight-oh.'

'What other firsts do you have in mind?' asks Phyllis, hands cupped around her coffee.

'Skydiving, wild swimming, protesting and – a few decades too late but better late than never – throwing off my shackles and becoming my true self.'

'Gosh!'

Phyllis seems impressed but, next to her, Dick gives a loud sigh.

'What about you, Dick?' I ask quickly, keen to move the conversation on.

Dick strokes his long white beard. 'You know me, Callie. I don't read books. Never have since the teachers at school told me I was stupid.'

'That's terrible,' blurts out Becca. 'Teachers aren't allowed to say that.'

'This was a long time ago, before pupil empowerment. They also said I wouldn't amount to anything, but now I have a sports car.' He lets that non-sequitur hang in the air for a few seconds before continuing. 'So I'm only here to keep Stanley company and to make sure he doesn't do anything daft.'

He gives those last few words some extra welly, but Gramp carries on calmly sipping my caffè latte.

'Phyllis, would you like to say something?'

'OK. I live in the bungalows near the old toll bridge. I'm a widow – my husband died a few years ago and my daughter lives in Australia with my grandchildren. It gets lonely sometimes but I've kind of adopted Becca here and she wanted me to come today.'

Becca nods and twists her hands together underneath the table.

'Thank you and, as Phyllis said, this is Becca, who lives in the town and helps us to run the café's social media accounts,' I explain. 'Is there anything you'd like to add, Becca?'

Becca smiles at me and shakes her head.

'Then let's get started and have a chat about the type of books we love.'

We talk for a while about favourite genres and authors. Who would have guessed that Phyllis is a steampunk fan? But before long the discussion turns to Honeyford and the work going on at the manor house.

'It's going to be rather grand,' says Millicent. 'I understand it's been bought by Finn and Noah Shawley, who are turning it into a boutique hotel. They're very successful men of some standing so I imagine it will be very tasteful – and ideal for when I have a party and can't accommodate visiting family and friends overnight. Obviously, Little Besbridge doesn't have a B&B establishment.'

When she laughs at the very thought, I try very hard not to dislike her. Getting on well with just about everyone is my 'thing', but snobs present me with a particular challenge.

'My Callie used to go out with Noah Shawley,' says Gramp, fiddling with his stud. 'He used to moon about after her.'

'Really?' Millicent screws up her nose as though she can't quite believe it.

'We didn't properly go out together. We were friends at school.'

Millicent nods as though that's easier to believe and takes a sip of her coffee. She grimaces but it's her own fault for letting it go cold.

'Did you know that the Shawleys are killing trees?' adds Gramp, before I can change the subject.

'Here we go,' murmurs Millicent. 'I wondered when this would come up. I had the misfortune of being in Honeyford when he was booming out protest slogans.'

But Becca seems switched on all of a sudden. She sits up straight and pushes her hands through her green hair.

'What do you mean, Stanley?'

'They're cutting down three beautiful trees at the back of the property and covering the area with tarmac to extend their car park.'

'That's terrible!'

'It is, especially seeing as those trees have a special place in my heart. It was underneath those very trees that—'

'Thank you, Gramp,' I cut in quickly. 'But we should really be focusing on books while we're here. Let's decide on which book we'd all like to read and discuss next time.'

Gramp grumbles under his breath about me being a 'Shawley sympathiser' before clamping his mouth shut with a mutinous look on his face.

Flora isn't as sanguine as me about the nasty Facebook comment when I show it to her.

'We can't afford bad reviews, Callie,' she says, worry lines furrowing her forehead. 'I'm only just keeping my head above water and I really need the café to do well. That's the trouble with social media – it's great when it's working in your favour but a potential nightmare when it isn't. You really need to fix it.'

So whether the café sinks or swims will affect the long-term future of the shop – and my job.

I spend ages deliberating over my reply to Jim Jones and eventually post: *We're upset that you were disappointed with your visit, Jim, particularly as yours is the first negative feedback we've received. We try to make all our customers feel special and apologise if we didn't manage that when you visited.*

'Miserable old bugger,' says Flora when I run my wording by her before posting. 'But hopefully that'll do the trick.'

I nod, feeling shaken about the whole thing. It's daft, really, to get upset about one person's opinion, but it feels rather like being shouted at for not being good enough.

Flora notices and gives my arm a squeeze.

'Don't worry, Callie. You'll need a thicker skin if you're going to make it in business. Malcolm's had to cope with far worse over the years.'

I imagine that Malcolm's skin is rhino-tough, but Flora's right. Coping with conflict is just a normal part of business life – and personal life too, I guess. I press 'publish' on my reply to grumpy Jim Jones, and vow to toughen up.

The afternoon book club is due to meet once a fortnight. I was initially thinking monthly but was outvoted. And, as Gramp pointed out during the inaugural meeting, the club is run along democratic lines so I would just have to lump it.

But when I wander into the café just a few days after our first get-together, I do a double-take. It's like *Groundhog Day* in The Cosy Kettle. Millicent, Mary, Phyllis, Becca, Dick and my gramp are sitting around the same table, in the exact same places.

'It's not been a fortnight, has it?' I ask Flora, worried I'm stuck in a space-time vortex after reading too much sci-fi. My reading preference is eclectic – I power through everything from Dickens and Orwell to Barbara Taylor Bradford and Richard Dawkins.

Flora spots my expression and laughs. 'It's not even been a week, and yet your clan has gathered to await your soothing support and pearls of wisdom.'

'Ha, hardly.'

But my denial's shot to pieces when Becca wanders over.

'Hey, Callie,' she mumbles, cheeks paler than ever. 'I brought Phyllis in 'cos she wants your help with a letter to the council. And there's something I need to ask you about, if you don't mind.'

'Your public awaits,' says Flora with a grin, spreading her arms wide. 'Oh, and Callie, do encourage them to at least buy a coffee before they leave.'

As it turns out, they do all buy coffees, and Knackered Mary has two slices of lemon drizzle cake to raise her energy levels. Then they start talking about the thriller they've started reading and will be discussing at the next official book club meeting.

Their views on the novel are already poles apart. Millicent reckons it's too 'low brow', whereas Phyllis is 'can't put it down' hooked. And I get a warm glow, listening to them slug it out.

They only break from their conversation when Becca pulls out her phone and asks to take a photo for the café's Facebook page.

'How are you going to describe us?' asks Millicent, sharply. 'I'm not sure I want all my friends to know I belong to a little group like this.'

'What friends?' murmurs Phyllis.

'What's that supposed to mean?'

'Phyllis just wondered why you're spending time with us if you have so many friends,' says Gramp, who seems to be an almost permanent fixture in the café these days. 'I'd have thought you'd be fighting off offers of days out.'

'Hhmm.' Millicent picks a loose pink thread from the tablecloth and studies it intently. 'My friends are very successful and busy people and, now my children are gone, the house gets a bit' – she pauses, almost whispering the next word as though it's shameful – 'lonely.'

'Ah, tell me about it,' says Phyllis. 'My old man had the gall to up and die on me, and I haven't seen my grandchildren for three years now my daughter's in Australia.'

'Really?' Millicent cautiously gives Phyllis's arm a light pat. 'That seems rather cruel to deprive you of your grandchildren.'

'Yes, well, I want Elaine to do what's best for her and I've got used to it. You will too. And, in the meantime, you can put up with us lot, if you can possibly bear it.'

She folds her arm across her large bosom and settles back in her wheelchair. Millicent picks up her coffee and tiny flecks of foam float across the table when she gently blows on it. She looks around the motley group and nods slightly as she takes a sip.

Chapter Eighteen

'You'll never guess who's just walked in. Don't look! I said don't look!'
Sarah splutters into her mocktail when I twist round to look behind me.

Typical! I'm out on a Friday night for the first time in ages and
Finn, in bright red chinos, chooses the very same evening to grab
a pint. He's standing at the bar of The Pheasant, trying to attract
the barman's attention while winking at every young woman who
catches his eye.

'Back in the sixth form, I honestly didn't think he was attractive,'
muses Sarah.

'Oh, please. He wasn't your type but you knew he was attractive.'

'I did not. I thought he was a right nerd. Everyone did, really.'

'Huh. Everyone got hot under the collar when he was around.
And I remember you throwing a right old strop with Alicia when she
refused to believe he'd asked you out. Even though you weren't in the
slightest bit interested in him.'

Sarah puts her glass down and peers at me down her long, straight
nose.

'I did not throw a right strop, even though I had every right to
because Alicia was a cow. And still is – I bumped into her in Oxford
a couple of weeks ago and she asked when the baby was due. I almost
clocked her one outside the Ashmolean.'

She smooths her jersey dress over her ample curves. 'Anyway, I'm not talking about Finn. I'm talking about *him*.'

When she gestures over my shoulder, I twist again in my seat and there, coming out of the Gents', is Noah. He's wearing tight indigo jeans and a pale blue polo shirt that matches his eyes.

'Eek!' My stomach starts fluttering with nerves.

'Did you really say "eek"? Honestly; one sighting of Noah Shawley and your vocabulary does a nose-dive. Maybe it is best that you're keeping away from him.' She takes another sip of her pink drink and her eyes narrow. 'You are keeping away from him, aren't you?'

'Why would you ask such a question?'

'Because you're scratching the back of your neck, like you always do when you're feeling guilty.'

Damn my scratchy hands. I place them firmly in my lap.

'Noah and I did meet recently for a short while.'

'Where? Why don't I know this? Did he come into the shop?'

'Not exactly.' Ooh, the back of my neck is itching like mad. 'He invited me round to the manor house to see an old shoe that was found while they were renovating the place.'

'A shoe?'

'Yes, a child's shoe that was hidden in the house centuries ago to ward off bad luck.'

'He invited you round to look at a shoe.' Sarah finishes her drink in one huge gulp and licks her lips. 'Well, I guess it makes a change from *come up and see my etchings.*'

'It wasn't like that.'

Every nerve-ending in the back of my neck is now on fire.

'How was it then?'

'Fine.'

'Here we go with the "fines" again. Just tell me what happened.'

'It was all very civilised. He took me up to the bedroom to show me where the shoe was found hidden in the fireplace.'

Sarah's left eyebrow is disappearing into her choppy fringe. 'He took you up to the bedroom? Then what happened? And remember that I can tell when you're lying.'

'Nothing really. We looked at the shoe and chatted about trees and he kissed me a bit and Finn came in and showed me around the house. And then I left,' I reel off at top speed.

'No, no, no,' splutters Sarah, jumping up and down in her chair. 'You can't just drop in "and he kissed me a bit" and then move on. That's not what friends do. You owe me full details as compensation for not ringing me immediately after it happened. Which is what you definitely should have done. Oh, my!' She claps a hand to her mouth. 'You didn't sleep with him, did you?'

'Keep your voice down! Of course I didn't sleep with him,' I hiss. 'It was just a kiss.'

'What kind of kiss? Good, bad, passionate, indifferent?'

'It was very nice.'

Even I'm not convinced Sarah is going to buy this lie – not when the kiss was out of this world and even thinking about it makes me shiver.

'It was more than nice. Your pupils are dilating.' Sarah thrusts her face forwards until our noses are almost touching. 'Yep, definitely dilating. That never happened when you talked about Liam. So how do you feel about Noah now?'

'He's going back to the States any day now so it doesn't matter how I feel about him.'

It doesn't matter one jot seeing as he'll be mixing with sophisticated, cosmopolitan New York women whom he presumably doesn't think of as 'rough'.

'But how does he feel about you?' asks Sarah, totally ignoring the impracticalities of the situation.

'I don't know.'

'Let me guess. You haven't talked to him about the kiss.'

'I couldn't because Finn came in.' I sigh. 'And I did a bit of a runner 'cos my head was all over the place.'

'Typical. Didn't he ring or text you?'

'He sent me one text but I sent a polite reply back and he didn't pursue it.'

'Polite? After he's just thrown you on the bed and French-kissed the life out of you?'

'He didn't throw—' I stop and wag my finger in Sarah's face because she's fishing for details. 'But since then I've been thinking about what happened, and I guess Noah and I do need to talk it through.'

'Uh, you think? You can't let him go back to New York without discussing it.'

'We haven't had a chance yet.'

'What good fortune that he's in the pub, then. Coo-ee!' yells Sarah, waving in ridiculous girly fashion across the packed pub.

'Stop it, or he'll come over.'

'That's the idea,' mutters Sarah like a ventriloquist through her wide, bright smile.

'Just remember that I don't need you to get involved.'

'You definitely do,' says Sarah, still waving wildly. 'Look lively 'cos he's coming over.'

'You. Cannot. Say. Anything. About. Anything. Nothing that happened eight years ago and nothing that happened this week,' I mutter through clenched teeth.

'Not anything about anything? That's going to severely impact on my conversational abilities.' Sarah grins, gesturing for Noah to take a seat opposite me.

'Noah! How lovely to see you,' she gushes. 'You remember me, don't you? We used to sit near each other in geography. It really is fantastic to have a chance to chat after all these years.'

Oh, dear. Sarah doesn't gush. She's not a gushy person at all so this doesn't bode well.

'Of course I do,' says Noah in his soft deep voice. 'It's Sarah, isn't it?'

'That's right. And you know Callie, of course. You two were thick as thieves at one point. Just before you both went to uni and everything mysteriously changed.'

She moves her leg, which I'm kicking under the table.

'That was a long time ago.'

'Years ago, but some things are never forgotten,' says Sarah, in an ominously low voice. 'Like, not ever.'

It's always a bit touch and go whether Sarah's about to start speaking her mind when she lowers her voice. She reckons it makes her sound more authoritative. But she winces and gives me an *OK, you win* shrug when my foot connects hard with her shin.

Noah catches my eye and smiles. 'How are you doing, Callie?'

'I'm good, thanks. And you?'

'Yeah, good.' Noah picks up his pint and takes a few gulps. He wipes froth from his upper lip. 'And what about you, Sarah? What are you up to these days?'

'This and that. Getting married.' She waggles her sparkly ring in his face. 'I'm living in Cheltenham now and working for a hairdressing business. It's slave labour but I get my hair dyed for free.'

'That sounds worth the slavery.' Noah grins.

'It helps. I hear you're living in New York now. I went there recently with my girlfriend.'

Sarah starts gabbling about Central Park and the Staten Island ferry and the 'awesome view' from the top of the Rockefeller where Gemma proposed, while I sip my drink and steal glances at Noah.

His long fingers are wrapped around his pint and I suddenly remember how he pushed them through my hair during that kiss. Oh, crikey. I knock back the rest of my lemonade and shudder at the fizz-pain in my nose. The sooner Noah and I discuss the elephant in the room and can move on, the better.

'Don't you think so, Callie?' Sarah is staring at me across the table. 'Sorry?'

'God, nothing changes. She's still got her head in the clouds.' Sarah leans towards me and speaks very clearly as though I'm deaf or daft. 'I was just saying to Noah that Finn's hotel will be good for the town.'

'I'm sure it will be.'

'Anyway.' Sarah pushes her chair back and gets to her feet. 'I need to get home to my fiancée so I'd better head off. You can keep Callie company, can't you Noah?'

'Um' – Noah hesitates – 'sure.'

He stretches out his long legs while Sarah kisses me on the cheek. 'Bye, babe. See you again soon. Be good. And if you can't be good…'

She winks at me and then at Noah and sashays out of the pub.

'I get the feeling that we're being set up.' Noah grins and settles back in his chair with his pint against his chest.

'Sarah's never been a subtle sort of person.' I pick up a beer mat and start tearing it into tiny pieces. 'I think we need to talk.'

'I think you're right.' He stares at the tiny shards of beer mat that are piling up on the table. 'Why don't I put some music on and we can have a drink together first.'

I nod, heartily approving of working our way up to the kiss conversation rather than launching straight in.

He fishes in his pocket for a pound coin and heads for the jukebox in the corner. Leaning his long frame over it, he makes his choice and wanders back. The strains of 'Life on Mars' waft across the old coaching inn.

'This brings back memories,' he says, with a lopsided smile.

It certainly does – we played David Bowie on a loop in our teens. I'm immediately transported back to his bedroom, with him lying across the bed with a textbook in his hands and me sitting on the floor with books spread out around me.

'It reminds me of being at your house. Any more news of your mum and dad?'

'They're all right, I think. Dad's still away on business most of the time, and I doubt he'll find time to visit the hotel which Finn is determined will be the most successful country hotel in the UK. He's always desperate to impress Dad and being *one* of the best isn't good enough. He's quite vulnerable really.'

Noah frowns and looks so much like the Noah I used to know, I don't scoff at the thought of Finn being vulnerable.

'Anyway.' Noah does a 'someone's walking over my grave' shiver. 'How's the café going?'

'OK. Well, mostly OK.'

I pause, thinking of the latest critical tweet that sent Becca into a tailspin this morning. It was from a man who said he'd called into The Cosy Kettle but hadn't bothered staying because the place smelled 'gross'.

His complaint's ridiculous because the café's always filled with the gorgeous aroma of coffee beans. But I spent an hour scrubbing every surface in the loos, just in case.

'Are you having business problems?'

'Not really. We've had a few uncomplimentary tweets and Facebook messages recently.'

'That's surprising. How many?'

'I don't know.' I think back – we've had at least three snarky comments on Facebook this week and at least the same number of negative tweets. 'About half a dozen.'

'All from different people?'

'Yeah, and all complaining about different things – the taste of the coffee, the prices, the décor, the smell.'

'Smell?'

'Apparently the place smells "gross".'

I laugh to cover my embarrassment but Noah's face clouds over.

'That's a mean and unnecessary thing to say so publicly. Try not to let it bother you, Callie. Some people seem to enjoy making other people miserable.'

'It doesn't bother me so much. Well, it does because it puts off new customers. But it's Becca who's really suffering. She set up the social media accounts for us and thinks the bad publicity is her fault. It's not, of course. It's mine but I'm doing the best I can. I'm just not sure what I'm doing wrong, and I don't want the café to fail.'

When I shrug, Noah reaches across the table. Is he going to touch my hand? I could move it – pick up my drink, perhaps, or pretend to blow my nose – but I leave it there. Because – lightbulb moment – I really want him to touch me.

Right now, I realise, I want him to put his arms around me and tell me that everything is going to be OK, because I'm suddenly overwhelmed by loss. The prospect of losing the café has sparked a cascade of thoughts about people I've loved who are no longer around – Dad and Gran are gone, Mum has a new life in Spain, Gramp won't be here for ever, and I lost Noah a long time ago.

Good grief, no wonder I've been keeping all this damped down. How do people who wear their hearts on their sleeves cope with all this crap?

I breathe deeply to quell the swirling tide of emotion that's come out of nowhere. And register a pang of disappointment when there's a burst of laughter from the bar and Noah pulls his hand back.

'Every business has teething troubles, Callie, but I'm sure the café will be a great success. You deserve it.'

Concern is etched across his handsome face, and Beyoncé starts belting out of the jukebox, as my emotions keep on swirling. OK, I'm going in…

'You were right,' I tell him. 'We need to talk about what happened at the manor house on Tuesday. So why did you kiss me, Noah?'

'Why do you think?' He pushes his glasses up his nose. 'I kissed you because…' Suddenly alarm flickers across Noah's features. 'Oh, no. I think we're about to be invaded.'

Julia's overpowering perfume hits my nose before I turn my head. She and Sorrell, wearing very short skirts, are bearing down on us with drinks in their hands.

'Look, I was thinking of visiting Blenheim Palace on Sunday, for old times' sake,' says Noah, quickly. 'Why don't you come with me? It'll be quieter there and we can talk without interruptions.'

Sorrell and Julia are almost upon us and I have only a couple of seconds to make up my mind.

'OK, it's a date.'

Aargh, I didn't mean to say that. But it's too late to take the D-word back because Julia is pulling up a chair so close to Noah's, she's almost sitting in his lap.

'Fancy seeing you here, Mr Shawley,' she says, fluttering her false eyelashes. 'We thought we'd come and rescue you from Callie, who's not half as much fun as we are.'

'Not even a quarter,' slurs Sorrell, who's totally wasted. 'We tried to have a word with your brother but he's in demand.'

She waves her arm at the bar where Finn's surrounded by a gaggle of locals who are hanging on his every word.

'I just want to tell you,' says Sorrell, slumping in her chair, 'you are a very handsome man. A very handsome man indeed. You weren't always like that. Oh, no.' She gives a tiny burp. 'I used to think Callie was welcome to you. But now...' She pauses for so long, I wonder if she's fallen asleep. 'Now, I wouldn't say no, Mr Shawley. Nuh-oh.'

Noah smiles and gently removes the arm she's flung around his neck.

'That's good to know and I'll bear it in mind but I'd better be getting back to my brother. He gets antsy if I'm away from him for too long.'

'Does he really? Aw, that's so sweet,' drools Sorrell, batting off Julia, who's trying to haul her to her feet. 'Leave me alone. I'm enjoying myself.'

'You're making a total tit of yourself,' hisses Julia, putting her arms beneath Sorrell's armpits and dragging her up. 'Come on, let's go and see if Finn's free.'

'What a good idea.' Sorrell has linked her arm through Noah's and pulled him up with her. 'Come and introduce us, though he won't recognise Julia 'cos she never slept with him. Unlike me. I slept with him loads.'

'Do put a sock in it!' hisses Julia, as the three of them stagger towards the bar.

Noah looks back over his shoulder and mouths: 'Pick you up at nine thirty.'

Should I go and rescue him? He's virtually holding Sorrell up and Julia's hand is perilously close to his backside. Nah, I reckon grown-up Noah can handle himself around women, if that kiss is anything to go by.

I gather up my belongings and slip out of the pub, half-dreading Sunday's 'date' but already missing Noah as soon as he's out of my sight.

Chapter Nineteen

Finn has poked his head inside the shop.

'Just look at how well you ladies are doing this fine Saturday afternoon! You should both be very proud of yourselves.'

It's amazing how he manages to sound patronising even when being complimentary.

'Come on in.' Flora pushes the door open wider and beckons him inside.

'I don't want to keep you from work when you're so busy,' he insists, but steps inside anyway and unzips his brown leather jacket. 'I didn't realise it would be so hectic in here.'

Several people are browsing the bookshelves and, with fabulous novels piled up everywhere these days, it doesn't take a lot for us to look rammed.

'That's OK. We're always happy to see you,' says Flora, which is a tad presumptuous.

I'm more wary than happy about seeing Finn because he's tricksy. Most people take him at handsome-face value but I sense more beneath the surface, especially since Noah 'fessed up about his daddy issues.

Finn picks up one of the book-jacket postcards Flora's started selling and flaps it beneath his artfully stubbled jaw to create a breeze.

'I was passing and thought I'd nip in to check out how my book's selling.'

'It's a bit sluggish at the mo,' says Flora, diplomatically. 'These things are a slow burn sometimes.'

'Slow?' repeats Finn, who's more used to life in the fast lane. 'I suppose this is a very small town. Well, just let me know when you need more copies and, seeing as I'm here, I might treat myself to a cheeky murder mystery.'

'We've got plenty to choose from over there.' Flora points at the shelves near the window that are jam-packed with crime thrillers. 'How's the hotel coming along?'

'Yeah, you know. Still a few bits and pieces to finish off before Noah heads back to New York.'

'Noah didn't fancy coming out for a walk with you, then?'

'Nah, he's busy supervising the tiling in the bathrooms or something equally tedious.'

Finn winks, not at me or at Flora but into mid-air – just in case there's a passing female he's not aware of. Then he glances at his watch. 'I might have a quick coffee before browsing the bookshelves, if there's one going.'

'Of course. Callie will show you through to the café, seeing as it's her baby.'

Flora gives me a none too gentle shove in the back and I reluctantly lead Finn through to The Cosy Kettle. He takes a seat near the door to the garden and scans the room while I'm making him a macchiato.

Two tourists are gossiping nearby and looking through leaflets for the falconry centre, a young newly married couple are holding hands in the corner, and Becca is carrying out two slices of marble cake to customers in the garden.

We're paying her to give us a hand in the café on Saturdays and she's doing a great job. Though she doesn't believe it and needs lots of reassurance.

'Well done indeed,' says Finn, taking a sip of his coffee and raising his eyebrows in approval. 'You've made a real go of this. I didn't think you would, to be honest, but you've proved me wrong. And that doesn't happen often, believe me.'

'You've been a great success yourself, from what I can see online.'

'Someone's been Googling me.' Finn grins, obviously no stranger to Googling his own name. 'You don't want to believe everything you read online but, in this case, it's all true. Did you see the article about my property ventures in Sheffield? They were ground-breaking. He who dares wins!'

I don't remember reading anything about Sheffield but I nod anyway.

'It's good to hear work's going well at the hotel. How long do you think Noah will be here?' I ask as casually as I can but Finn's eyes narrow across the top of his frothy coffee.

'Not too much longer. He'll be heading back to the States as soon as he's checked that the work at the hotel's been done to his satisfaction.' He carefully places his coffee cup into its china saucer. 'How's that old bloke, by the way? Did you say he was your granddad?'

'Yes. He's fine, thank you.'

'No more protests planned? I hope you're working hard to keep him out of trouble.'

I think of the demon flyers now banished to the shed.

'You have no idea. But he's still upset about the trees.'

'Why? They're just trees.'

'They've meant a lot to him and his wife over the years.'

'Whatever. Trees are good for the environment, and all that. But those trees are past it and a good-sized car park will mean more to my customers – customers, by the way, who will be injecting money into the local economy and, more specifically, buying coffees and cakes in your café.'

'Which I do realise.'

'Good. As a businesswoman yourself, you need to appreciate the benefit of every opportunity.'

'Talking of opportunities, have you had any more thoughts about setting up a coffee house at the hotel?'

'Lots of thoughts but nothing's definite. It might happen, it might not. Maybe I'll turn it into a sitting room instead. Anyway.' Finn pushes his half-finished coffee towards me. 'Must dash. There are business deals to make and workmen to berate. Shall I give your regards to Noah?'

'If you like,' I say, relieved that tomorrow's Blenheim Palace trip hasn't been mentioned. Presumably Finn knows nothing about it.

He's already on his feet and waving to Flora, who's come into the café.

'Bye, ladies. Take it easy.'

He sweeps out, leaving a fug of expensive aftershave and we hear the shop door ding behind him.

'I thought he was going to buy a book.' Flora sinks into the chair that Finn has just vacated. 'What was that all about, then?'

'I don't know. It was a bit odd, really. Maybe he was making sure Gramp wasn't going to be picketing his place again.'

'Your granddad's a real case. I hope I'm like him when I get to his age. How old is he again?'

'Eighty.'

'Unbelievable.' Flora twists the gold bangle on her arm. 'And if it's not being too nosy, what is it with you and Noah?'

'I don't know what you mean.'

'Maybe it's Finn you've got the hots for then?'

'Oh, please!'

'I didn't think so.' Flora's soft black bob swings around her face when she shakes her head. 'I can be a bit oblivious at times but the sexual tension between you and Noah positively crackles. I thought he'd be in and out of the shop all the time but he seems to have disappeared.'

When I don't say anything, Flora pushes herself up from the table. 'Sorry. It's none of my business.'

'That's OK. You know already that Noah and I had a bit of a thing a long time ago.' Flora drops back into her seat and leans across the table. 'But it didn't last long. His family were serial movers – his dad's something big in business – and they came to Honeyford when I was sixteen. Noah was in my class and Finn was the year above. Everyone was obsessed with Finn – you can imagine the excitement whipped up among a host of hormonal teenaged girls when he suddenly appeared – but I always got on better with Noah.'

'I'm not surprised.'

'He was softer and kinder and less showy.'

'So you started going out?'

'Not for ages. We were just friends but good friends, the kind of friend you tell things to. He made me laugh when Robert Callard dumped me and I took him to the pub when Janey Silverston said she'd go out with him but then went out with Finn instead.'

'Ouch!'

'Noah was used to it. He always felt eclipsed by his brother.'

'I can imagine. Finn is an eclipsing kind of person. So what happened between the two of you?'

'Exams. We ended up spending more and more time together in the run up to A levels and I started to realise how attractive he was, in lots of ways.'

'He's that, all right. Less brash than Finn and less showy. Definitely more a keeper than just fling material.'

'Flora! You're happily married.'

She frowns slightly before brushing her fingers across her plain gold wedding ring.

'I might be married but I'm not blind. Noah Shawley is a very attractive man. He's got that slightly nerdy vibe going on but you know underneath his shirt he's got muscles of steel.'

'Good grief!' I can't help laughing, or picturing Noah shirt-less. Flora giggles at my discomfort.

'So what happened?'

'We went out together for a few weeks but it fizzled out when we went to different universities.'

'Why? Oh, for goodness' sake.' Flora's shoulders drop with frustration when Joan from the local grocery store scurries into the café.

'Hi, Callie,' she calls. 'Any chance of a coffee and a quick chat to cheer me up? I've had the morning from hell.'

'Of course. Take a seat and I'll bring one over.'

Poor Joan's been up to her eyes recently with work and also caring for her husband, who's had a stroke. She often calls into the café for a breather.

'Can you finish the story later?' pleads Flora.

'There's nothing to tell. We were young and we grew apart. That's it. That's the story of me and Noah.'

'The unfinished story. I think there'll be another chapter with a happy ending,' says Flora, going all dreamy-eyed. Funny; I've never taken her for a romantic.

'I think the final chapter is Noah living the high life in New York and me in Honeyford, selling books and serving coffee to people who need a bit of cheering up.' I shrug. 'And that is a happy ending for both of us.'

Kind of.

Chapter Twenty

By the time Sunday dawns, I've resolved to forget the café for a while and concentrate on my date (that's not a date) at Blenheim Palace. Maybe Noah and I can manage a pleasant day out before he jets back to New York, even if we do need to discuss The Kiss. But my plan is severely tested before I've even got out of bed. I'm still in my PJs and half-asleep when my phone beeps with a message from Becca.

It's short and to the point: *Check Twitter and Facebook. So sorry. Feel awful.*

Propping myself up against the pillows, I click on the Twitter icon and spot two mentions for The Cosy Kettle.

The first tweet is from a London woman called Erika and has a photo of our lemon drizzle cake next to a steaming cup of coffee. It says: *A slice of heaven at The Cosy Kettle café in gorgeous Honeyford #CosyKettleHoneyford #yum #LoveTheCotswolds*

That Tweet is more than OK! I send up a quick prayer of thanks for Erika and her sweet tooth.

But the second tweet, from someone called Chester, takes my breath away: *Horrible coffee. Stale cake. Rude waitress. Don't bother #CosyKettleHoneyford #Honeyford*

Chester may as well have stepped into my bedroom and slapped me around the face. I scroll through his other tweets but he's only been on Twitter a short while and his tweets are mostly photos of places he's visited – Aberdeen, Manchester, Norwich and Milton Keynes.

Feeling sick, I log onto the café's Facebook page and read a new comment from a woman called Frances.

Visited the new Cosy Kettle Café in Honeyford today and was so disappointed. Below average coffee and poor service. Lots of potential but it doesn't make the grade. Shame.

As if that's not bad enough, she's tagged various other people into her comment, including the local tourist organisation. Frances is not only disappointed, she's also an absolute cow.

But what if she's got a point? Sunbeams pool under the curtains and track across the worn carpet while I read her post over and over, trying to work out where I'm going wrong. Maybe I'm just not up to running a business.

Time's ticking on so I head for the shower, pull on jeans and a floaty grey top from Zara, and slap on some make-up.

I'd planned to spend a good ten minutes on my face this morning – properly blended blusher, two coats of mascara, lip liner, the lot. But this social media mess needs to be sorted. I glance at my stressed, pale reflection in the bathroom mirror and sigh.

Gramp's already pottering about downstairs. His forgotten toast set the smoke alarm off while I was in the shower. So I perch on my bed and call Flora on my mobile. She answers on the third ring.

'Callie? You're up bright and early. Is everything all right?'

'Not really. I'm so sorry to bother you but Becca sent me an anxious message, first thing. Have you seen the café's Twitter and Facebook accounts this morning?'

'Surprisingly, I have better things to do on a Sunday.' Flora laughs. 'But I'm on the computer so let me have a quick gander.'

Computer keys clack and then Flora breathes out slowly.

'Good grief! That tweet from Chester is a right doozy, and Frances seems to have tagged loads of people into her nasty update. Why would anyone do that?'

'I'm so sorry, Flora. I'm absolutely gutted by what they've written and it's such bad publicity for the café. Something's obviously gone terribly wrong and I've done a rotten job.'

'Do you think so?'

'I don't know what to think. People keep telling me they love the café but the complaints keep coming on social media.'

'Does anyone actually complain to your face?'

'Only Millicent, who doesn't approve of the mismatched crockery. She insists coffee should always be drunk from John Lewis white bone china.'

'And yet she keeps turning up in the café! No, something's gone wrong, all right, but I don't think it's you. Take a look at Chester's Twitter photo. Do you recognise him?'

I click on the pic of Chester, who's the sort of bloke you'd pass in the street without a second glance. Middle-aged, brown hair, glasses – pleasant-looking, which is ironic.

'I don't think so. I couldn't swear to it because we get busy sometimes, but I don't recall seeing him in the café.'

'And what about Frances?'

Where the picture of Frances should be is a photo of a big black dog. And the account has a private setting so I can't check out her other posts. That's odd.

'There's nothing here to show me what she looks like. The whole thing seems a little off.'

'I'd say so. Hold on, Callie.'

There's the sound of a door being closed in the background, and Flora lowers her voice when she comes back to the phone.

'I'd rather Malcolm didn't hear any of this but I think we have a problem. Look at what these people have posted. Horrible coffee and stale cake? Unlikely, but maybe they caught us on an off day. But Frances mentions poor service and Chester talks about a rude waitress. He's got to be kidding. You're the opposite of rude and Becca wouldn't say boo to a goose. You're both ridiculously nice to everyone, which means' – she gives a deep sigh – 'we're being trolled. I read about it often enough in the papers.'

'But why would anyone bother trolling us? We're a tiny café in the middle of nowhere.'

'Who knows why? Fun, envy, boredom. Just because they can.'

'I was so busy feeling upset and guilty about doing a bad job, I didn't stop to think about trolls. There are some nasty people out there.'

'Indeed. But the more important question is, *who* would bother trolling us? Can you think of anyone? You know lots of people around here.'

I do, and some of them can be difficult sometimes. But I can't think of a single person who would do such a thing. Except maybe sour-faced Lesley, who used to run The Pheasant – but she didn't even have a mobile phone so trolling would be beyond her.

'All we can hope is that whoever it is has had their fun and will leave us alone,' says Flora, when I can't come up with any names. 'If not, we might have to close down our social media for a while.'

'Which could impact on the number of new customers. Three people yesterday said they'd called in after seeing Becca's posts.'

'But bad publicity could impact on the number of customers in a negative way so we'll have to balance out the pros and cons.' Flora pauses. 'Who on earth could it be?'

'I don't know and it's horrible to think that someone dislikes us enough to be so unkind.'

I glance out of the bedroom window, in case Noah decides to turn up early. Gramp's still disgruntled about the trees and putting him in close proximity with a Shawley could be unwise.

Plus, I haven't actually mentioned that I'm going to Blenheim Palace with Noah. Gramp automatically assumed I meant Sarah when I said I was going with a friend, and I've let him carry on assuming.

The sound of a car engine in the distance makes me jump. I need to be ready to run out of the front door the moment he arrives.

'Flora, I'm sorry but I have to ring off because I'm going out. Can we talk more about this later?'

'Of course. I'll post polite replies for now and we can discuss the situation at work tomorrow.'

'What about Becca? She was upset in her text and she takes all this so personally.'

'Don't worry about Becca. I'll give her a call to calm her down and suggest she gives our social media accounts a wide berth for a day or two. Are you off out somewhere nice?'

'Just to Blenheim Palace with a friend.'

'That wouldn't happen to be a Noah-shaped friend, would it?' asks Flora, who's far more astute than I'd like her to be.

When I don't reply, she laughs.

'The troll will wait but Noah won't. Get yourself off to Blenheim Palace, have a good time and try not to worry. Oh, and Callie, write yourself a good final chapter.'

Chapter Twenty-One

The sight of Blenheim Palace always takes my breath away. It's the sheer bonkers scale of the place that strikes wonder into my heart. And the what-the-hell grandeur that could have tipped into vulgar but came down just on the right side of good taste.

I turn to Noah, who's standing next to me in a huge, gravelled courtyard thronged with tourists.

'This place is utterly amazing. I reckon even your dad would be impressed if Finn turned this into a hotel.'

'I don't know. Dad's hard to please. But yeah, even he might send a few compliments Finn's way if he took on this place.'

He turns slowly on the spot, taking in the palace in all its glory.

Ahead of me, vast pillars support a carved portico above the entrance to the building, its stone glowing orange in the sunshine.

Behind me, past gold-tipped gates and an avenue of trees, is a statue of the first Duke of Marlborough. He looks lonely, standing on a dizzyingly high column that spears the cloudless sky.

'I haven't been here for years, not since our trip with Mr Baldwin,' I tell Noah as we're walking up a flight of stone steps towards the main door.

'Me neither, but I think about Blenheim quite often. Seeing what Vanbrugh did here centuries ago helped me make up my mind about becoming an architect.'

'Would you like to work on a project this big?'

'That would be great. In New York it's mainly apartment houses and loft buildings that keep me busy. But if they ever want a palace, I'm their man.'

He stops to grab a couple of audio guides and his hands brush my hair when he slips the strap of one of them over my head.

So far there's been nothing but small talk between us. The Kiss seems off-limits at the moment, and I'm glad. It'll come up soon enough but, right now, everything feels easy. Like it used to years ago when Dad and Gran were alive and life seemed simpler.

'After you.'

Noah stands back to let me step ahead of him through heavy oak doors into the palace, and I gulp at the sight that greets me.

I'd forgotten the elegant sweep of the Great Hall that welcomes visitors. My eyes travel up and up over rows of arches cut into pale stone walls and settle on the painted ceiling, high above our heads.

According to the audio guide, the ceiling was painted by Sir James Thornhill in the early eighteenth century. But my attention wanders as I wonder how on earth he managed to paint in such detail without falling and breaking his neck. I feel sick with vertigo simply thinking about it.

Noah's craning up at the ceiling too, but we have to move because tourists are coming in behind us. So we wander on, through high corridors and opulent rooms filled with centuries of splendour.

We both have earphones on so don't speak. But I sneak glances at Noah from time to time, while he's gazing at crystal chandeliers hanging from ornate ceilings and portraits on silk-covered walls. He seems engrossed in the history of this house – far more engrossed than the last time we visited and sneaked away to make out in shadowy corners. Whereas, I can't concentrate at all.

I'm aware of Noah all the time, even when he's out of sight behind me. And bright spots of colour flare in my cheeks when I pass a gilt-edged mirror and spot him staring at me. It's like being a teenager all over again, only this time excitement and desire are blunted by the reality of our very different lives.

He smiles at me when we walk into the library. This room is long and airy and lined with leather-bound books behind metal grilles. It's all peace and order, unlike the noise and chaos in Honeyford Bookshop. Plus, we don't have an awesome organ whose silver pipes are topped by gilded cherubs. It looks at home in this fabulous space but might be a tad over the top in our café.

Noah taps me on the arm. 'Do you remember that corner near the queen's statue?' he asks, pulling off his headphones and hanging them around his neck.

I switch off my audio guide and shake my head. 'I'm not sure.'

'I do believe that was where old Baldwin caught us locked in a torrid embrace.'

'Poor Mr Baldwin, he must have been well fed up,' I gabble, thrown by the steamy memory that suddenly pops into my head, and unsure why Noah has brought it up. 'There he was, trying to interest us in this place and all we wanted to do was make out. I'm not sure hormones and history are a good match.'

When Noah grins widely, a young woman nearby flicks her hair behind her ears and catches his eye. She likes him, and I'm not surprised.

He's wearing jeans, trainers and a Climax Blues Band T-shirt today. His horn-rimmed glasses have slipped down his nose and his thick fair hair needs a cut. Rather than a hot-shot New York architect, he looks like a geek. A hot, fanciable geek.

I swallow and wonder when we're going to talk about what happened this week, rather than clandestine kisses a decade ago.

Noah glances at me and grabs my hand. 'Shall we go and get some air?'

He leads me through the modest bedroom where Winston Churchill was born and out onto a terrace.

The April sun seems extra bright after an hour indoors and I fish my sunglasses from my bag so I can see properly.

Below us, fountains are splashing into stone-edged pools flanked by low hedges in intricate patterns. Visitors are drinking coffee at tables set out next to the water and enjoying the view that sweeps down to a large lake.

The mellow, weathered stone of the palace fits beautifully with the greenery all around us.

'Do you fancy a drink in the café, Callie? Or we could have an early picnic if you're hungry.'

'I think I've had enough of cafés this week, and I didn't have time for breakfast. So an early lunch sounds great. It was good of you to think ahead and bring a picnic.'

'That's me,' says Noah, patting the small rucksack on his back. 'Dead organised.'

'You never used to be,' I say, raising an eyebrow.

'Maybe not, but I'm a different person now.'

Is that sadness in his pale eyes, or am I reading too much into the situation? Possibly. Talk of the café has made me feel jittery about our troll again so my judgement's probably off.

Noah's wandered away and I follow him, around the side of the palace and onto a vast expanse of grass that stretches into the distance. It's the biggest lawn I've ever seen in my life and it's been mowed to perfection.

He spreads his arms out wide and grins. 'Will here do? It's quite peaceful.'

When I nod, he pulls a thin blanket from his rucksack and spreads it across the grass. Then he takes out two packets of chicken sandwiches, a small tub of cherry tomatoes, two bottles of orange juice, a pack of sausage rolls and a box of expensive chocolate biscuits.

'I nipped into Marks yesterday and stocked up. Does it look all right? You haven't gone vegetarian, have you?'

'Definitely not. I still enjoy a good steak, and chicken sandwiches.'

I sit cross-legged on the blanket and take a sandwich from Noah, who's ripped open one of the packets. We eat for a while and gossip about people we knew at school, as children chase each other across the grass and tall trees cast shadows around us.

We must look to passers-by like a happy couple on a date. And, as I lie back on the blanket and watch Noah sip orange juice, that's how it feels. Everything's so relaxed and easy – surely that matters more than our different backgrounds, and Noah can feel it too?

'I want to apologise for what happened at the manor house on Tuesday, now we've finally got a chance to talk in private,' he says, suddenly.

Well, that brought me back to reality with a bump. I sit up and brush grass from my legs.

'Apologise? Are you sorry you kissed me, then?'

'I shouldn't have lunged at you like that and I don't want you to think I lured you up to the bedroom with that in mind. It just happened out of nowhere, really – it was spontaneous.'

'Like our first kiss in your kitchen?'

'Ah, that wasn't quite so spontaneous, was it?' The corner of his mouth lifts upwards. 'What gave me away back then?'

'The Polo you scoffed beforehand.'

'A classic schoolboy error.' He shifts his backside on the blanket. 'The kiss on Tuesday was different. It honestly wasn't planned and I thought you were OK with it at the time. You seemed OK. But then you left in a hurry after Finn's tour as though you were angry with me.'

'I was confused, that was all. I mean, you're going back to New York soon so why kiss me? But I wasn't angry – I don't get angry with people.'

'You never want to *admit* when you're angry.'

Noah's eyes lock onto mine and I bite my lip. We've been apart for almost a decade but he still knows me as well as just about anyone.

'I will admit that the occasional thing riles me a bit.'

'Like what? You keep everything so buttoned up.'

'I don't know.' I dredge my memory for repressed feelings. 'Being pigeonholed is annoying. Becca, who helps in the shop, is known for being anxious. That's the first thing people think of when they mention her. She's also really funny and clever, but that gets lost.'

'I can see that would be annoying.'

'Also, people in front of you who stop dead in the street.' Hhmm, I've been guilty of that one. Moving on… 'Or people who see life in black and white and ignore shades of grey. I thought Millicent was majorly up herself but actually it turns out she's only slightly up herself and mostly she's lonely.'

'OK,' says Noah with a frown. 'I'm not sure I know Millicent. Anything else you're annoyed about, while we're on the subject?'

Oh, yeah. There's plenty, and it seems so easy to open up to Noah. I start reeling them off.

'People who pick fights over nothing and make their kids miserable. That's really not on. Relatives who change overnight and expect you to go along with all the weirdness. And me, I hate myself for feeling awkward when my mum and dad came to parent evenings at school and weren't like the other parents. I should have been glad they weren't boring. Also, snobs! I dislike people who look down on others because of where they're from. And you, I'm really angry with you.'

Aargh. I didn't mean to say that last bit.

'Oh, I've really opened the floodgates now.' Noah sits back on his heels. 'I don't get it. Why are you so angry about me kissing you? You kissed me back, Callie. And if anyone should be angry around here, it's me.'

'You? What have *you* got to be angry about?'

'What about the way you treated me eight years ago?' A mottled red stain is spreading across Noah's cheeks. 'When you dumped me out of the blue via text to go out with someone else. That really hurt, yet *you've* been off with *me* since I got back to Honeyford. And now you think you have the moral high ground on being angry, just because I dared to kiss you? That's ridiculous, Callie.'

As he shakes his head, I'm sorely tempted to get up and walk away. He's got it all wrong. I'm not angry that he kissed me. It was the best kiss of my life. What I'm angry about is that he never thought I was good enough for him. I sigh because it's all getting too heavy, like it always does when you let the anger genie out of the bottle.

'What is it, Callie?' Noah grabs hold of my arm. 'Talk to me properly, like you used to, and tell me why you're so angry with me.'

'Because of what you said to Finn.'

Noah drops my arm and sits back on the blanket. 'What on earth are you talking about?'

Here it comes. Although this has been burning inside me for almost a decade, my voice is oddly calm.

'I heard you in the garden, the night before I left for university, telling Finn that you weren't serious about me. You were laughing and making fun of my family and where I come from, and you said our relationship was nothing serious or special because I was pretty rough. It was obvious you were going to break up with me so I simply helped the process along.'

Noah looks at me blankly but realisation suddenly sparks in his eyes and he clamps his hand to his mouth.

'Oh my God. You heard me say that? But I didn't mean it.'

'Of course you meant it, or why would you say it?'

Noah shakes his head. 'Because I was terrified that Finn would make a play for you.'

'Don't be daft,' I scoff. 'He wasn't interested in me. I wasn't his type at all.'

'*I* wanted you, which made you Finn's type.'

Noah closes his eyes for a moment before carrying on. 'It's all a game to Finn. He has to be the most successful at everything and, back then, that meant getting every girl. He was asking about you and I knew if I seemed too keen he'd make a play for you. And you were going to his university.'

'So that's why you said what you did?'

Noah nods. 'It must have sounded awful to you. You were never meant to hear it.'

'But why did you laugh about where I come from? That was so mean.'

A sob catches in my throat as buried hurt rushes to the surface. His casual dismissal of the people and place I loved was devastating.

'Because Finn's a snob, like Dad,' says Noah, pushing himself onto his knees as though he's praying, 'and I was trying so hard to put him off you.'

'But I wouldn't have wanted Finn, even if he did make a play for me.'

'Wouldn't you? Most women seemed to fall for Finn's charms.'

'But I'm not most women, and I liked you. I really liked you. Why didn't you trust me, Noah?'

'I didn't—' He swallows hard. 'I didn't believe that an amazing woman like you could possibly feel as strongly about our relationship as I did. I was terrified that you'd realise you'd chosen the wrong brother.'

A breeze ripples through the grass as it sinks in that we both misunderstood what was happening eight years ago. And our lives veered off on totally different paths because of it.

'Why didn't you tell me what you'd heard?' whispers Noah, putting his head in his hands.

'I was too upset and hurt and I found it hard to talk about stuff. I still do.'

'It's like you've got a shell around you and you don't let anyone in. If only you'd said, or I'd been confident enough to trust your feelings for me.'

'If only you'd stood up to your brother.'

Noah briefly closes his eyes and gives a sad smile that tugs at my heart. 'We missed our chance, didn't we, Callie? Eight years ago, we well and truly messed up and missed our chance.'

'And now your life is 3,500 miles away and mine is here, in Honeyford.'

He nods and, leaning forwards, cups my cheeks in the palms of his warm hands. Little shudders of distress and desire shake my body as he stares into my eyes with such longing, time seems to reel backwards. The sounds of birds chirping and children playing nearby all fade away. Then Noah blinks and I'm back in the present.

'I'm so sorry for what I said and for hurting you. I'll always regret what happened between us, Callie,' he says gently, 'but I don't see how we can go back. Not now. It's too late.'

'You're right,' I whisper. 'We've become different people, living lives that are so far apart.'

When tears start dribbling down my cheeks, Noah first brushes them away with his thumbs. Then I feel his lips pressed against the wetness on my skin.

'Don't cry, Callie. I can't bear it,' he murmurs into my ear, before his mouth moves to mine and we kiss; a soft, gentle kiss that speaks of missed chances, regrets, and goodbye. A final farewell to what was, what is, and what might have been. Closing my eyes, I try to imprint every feeling on my brain so this moment will last in my memory after Noah is long gone.

'Oh my goodness, I'm so sorry!' calls a high-pitched voice as something barrels into my legs and wriggles between me and Noah. We pull apart as an excited young spaniel starts hoovering up the crumbs on our picnic rug.

'Jessie, come here! Stop slobbering everywhere!' A teenaged girl with braces on her teeth and a plait down her back grabs the puppy's collar and drags him towards her while I run my tongue over my lips. They taste of my tears. 'She's so badly behaved and so greedy. I'm really sorry that she interrupted you when you were… well, you know.' She stops and flushes lobster-pink.

'That's all right,' I say, with a forced smile. 'I think we were done anyway, weren't we, Noah?'

'I think we were,' he says, in a low, gruff voice.

The girl glances between us and giggles nervously before clipping Jessie onto her lead and pulling her away.

Noah wraps up the remnants of his sandwich that hasn't been gobbled up by Jessie and drops it into the rucksack. The sun has disappeared behind a thick bank of grey cloud and the smell of rain is hanging in the air.

'The weather's turning so maybe we'd better tidy up and head back to Honeyford,' he says, pulling a carrier bag from his rucksack. 'I think we've probably had enough of Blenheim and reliving the past.'

Together, we start dropping our rubbish into the bag, being careful that our fingers never touch – not now we both know where we stand and how our lives will carry on separately.

But one unanswered question is still niggling at me.

'What I don't understand is why you're still helping Finn,' I finally say, as Noah ties a knot in the top of the carrier. 'Not when he's like he is.'

Noah sighs. 'What you see is not the sum total of Finn. He's my brother and I love him in spite of his faults. I feel sorry for him, I suppose.'

'But why, after how he's behaved?'

Noah bends his head and starts picking at his fingernail. He breathes noisily in and out, in and out, then he looks up. 'OK, if I tell you something private, you mustn't tell anyone else.'

'I think we've just established that I'm pretty good at not telling people stuff.'

'Finn's my half-brother. Mum was a single mother with a small baby when she first met my dad. They had a whirlwind romance and got married, and Dad took Finn on. He loves him, I'm sure he does, but he treats him differently from me. It's very subtle, but it's there.'

Noah rubs a hand across his face. 'It's hard to explain. Dad expects more from Finn and is harder to please. So Finn's always trying to match Dad's business successes and prove he's good enough to be his son. That's why he's always trying to be the best at everything.'

'That's awful,' I whisper, feeling faint stirrings of sympathy. My dad wasn't perfect but I never doubted that he loved me.

'I know. And I feel guilty, as though I've stolen Finn's share of Dad's affection. That's why I've always let him get away with things.'

'Your dad's behaviour isn't your fault, Noah.'

'I guess not, and I don't want to paint Dad as some sort of monster. He does care about Finn but they clash because they're very different characters. Though you'd never guess it. Finn spends his whole life trying to be Dad. He's basically pretending to be someone he's not.'

'That sounds exhausting.'

'It must be. He's always hopping between business deals in search of the next big opportunity. He's been haring around the country sorting out deals while working on the hotel. He was up in Aberdeen a couple of weeks ago, Norwich last week and Manchester a few days ago.'

Somewhere deep in my brain, those places seem familiar. Oh!

'He hasn't been to Milton Keynes recently, has he?' I ask slowly.

Noah shrugs. 'I don't know. Maybe. He was in Buckinghamshire a while back. Why? Does it matter?'

'Photos of those places were posted on Twitter by the troll who's been attacking my business. And I just thought…'

'You thought that Finn's the person who's been trolling you?' Noah screws up his face in disbelief. 'That's ridiculous.'

'Is it?' I shoot back, my emotions still all over the place. 'You said yourself that Finn has to be the best, and he's talking about setting up a coffee house at the hotel. In his mind, he'd have to draw customers away from my café to come out on top.'

'So he sets up a hate campaign on social media? That's mad, Callie. I know Finn's behaved badly in the past but he wouldn't stoop to anything that low. You're just angry about his part in what happened between us.'

I shake my head. 'It's more than that. You could always ask him if he's the troll.'

When Noah jumps to his feet and starts massaging his temples, a missed tomato falls from his lap and rolls across the grass.

'There's no way I'm going to ask my brother if he's trolling your business. I understand that you're angry with him but this trolling stuff is just crazy talk.'

'Are you sure about that?'

'Quite sure.' Noah stands over me and folds his arms across his chest. 'Have you considered that the people complaining about your café might have a point? That maybe it's you and your café that's at fault, rather than anyone else?'

Ouch, that hurts so much it takes my breath away.

'I'm sorry,' mumbles Noah, a deep furrow appearing between his eyebrows. 'I didn't mean to be so blunt. The last thing I want is to upset you, Callie, but you've got to understand that Finn would never do anything like that.'

I want this conversation to end so much my hands are shaking. I don't want to argue about the café or Finn with Noah. Not when my lips are still warm from his goodbye kiss.

'That's OK. I'm not upset. Why don't we forget the café and Finn and talk about something else,' I say as positively as I can, knowing that *maybe it's you and your café that's at fault* will haunt me for days to come.

'That's probably best,' replies Noah, his voice laced with relief. 'The most important thing to me is that we've talked about our misunderstanding and we can be proper friends again. We are friends, aren't we?'

'Absolutely,' I assure him with a shaky smile.

Large drops of rain start splattering on the grass while I fold the rug and push it into the rucksack that Noah swings over his shoulder. Then we trudge back to the car with our heads down, lost in our own thoughts.

It's ironic, I realise, glancing at Noah as he drives us in his comfort-able hire car out of the palace grounds. Heavy rain is bouncing off the windscreen and he's biting his lip in concentration as the wipers whisper back and forth. We can't put the clock back because so much has changed over the last eight years – and yet in some ways nothing has changed at all. Noah's still in thrall to his older brother, and he's about to walk out of my life again.

Chapter Twenty-Two

Flora is staring at me, open-mouthed, as though I'm crazy.

'Finn!' she repeats. 'You're accusing charming Finn Shawley, businessman extraordinaire, of trolling us.'

'That's right. I don't have proof so it's kind of a…' I flounder around for the right word.

'A hunch,' says Flora, wrinkling her nose.

'Exactly.'

'But why would he do that?'

'Because he's thinking of opening a coffee house at the hotel. He told me.'

'I know. You mentioned it. But I really don't think a man with the high profile business acumen of Finn Shawley would be bothered by our little café, even though it's popular.' She frowns. 'Or at least it was until Chester, Frances et al stuck their poisonous oars in on social media. You must be mistaken.'

'Maybe, but I can't get the idea out of my head. He's recently been to the places posted by Chester on his Twitter feed.'

'So have thousands of other people.'

'But Finn needs to come out on top, with everything. If there's even a chance of being second-best, he'll be ruthless. Hasn't Malcolm ever done anything dodgy to give himself a business advantage?'

'Not really, though there was the time he…' Flora purses her lips and pushes up the sleeves of her cream angora cardigan. 'Look, even if it is Finn who's the troll, what do we do if we can't prove it? We can't go around accusing the town's golden boy on a hunch. Did you speak to Noah about it?'

'Yes, a bit.'

'And what's his view on the matter?'

'He thinks I've got a grudge against Finn and I'm not seeing the situation clearly.'

'Why would you have a grudge against Finn?'

'No particular reason.' I shrug.

Flora folds her arms and gives me one of her best cold stares.

'I get the feeling you're not giving me the full story, Callie. Did you enjoy your visit to Blenheim Palace with Noah?'

'Yeah, it was nice.' I shrug again, trying to appear nonchalant and failing miserably. It's hard to pretend when you've been lying awake most of the night and feel wrung out with exhaustion.

'Hhmm.' Flora narrows her violet eyes before glancing at the elegant silver watch on her slim wrist. 'I've got a publishing rep coming in any minute, so you have to let your conspiracy theory drop, Callie. Finn is a well-respected businessman and I'll need solid evidence before I can believe he'd behave in such an underhanded manner. OK?'

I nod but remain unconvinced. What Flora's saying makes sense, yet I still feel in my bones that Finn's the culprit, whatever Noah might think.

While Flora's busy with the rep, I work in the café and keep an eye on my gramp, who's enjoying a double-shot espresso – his new drink of choice, which is not ideal, as the caffeine hypes him up to even higher levels of unpredictability.

At the moment, he's sitting in the courtyard in a little huddle with Mary, Phyllis and Millicent. The four of them are a pretty tight unit these days, and Millicent in particular spends ages in the café nursing a coffee. She even got up and helped me a couple of days ago when a coach party was disgorged in the town. Twenty people came in at once, and everything went manic.

'That's terrible,' says Millicent as I get closer with a sticky dripping cake that Phyllis ordered. 'I can hardly believe it.'

'What's terrible?'

'The café having a pixie,' pipes up Phyllis, taking the cake and giving it a prod with her finger.

'A troll,' says Millicent, rolling her eyes, but she gives Phyllis's hand a gentle pat.

'Gramp, really? I asked you not to tell anyone.'

He harrumphs and fidgets in his chair. 'These ladies aren't just anyone and, anyway, no one should be dissing The Cosy Kettle when you've worked so hard on it.'

'Dissing?'

'Isn't that what young people say these days?' He sticks out his bottom lip. 'It's so sad that everything's changing in Honeyford. People were nice when I was a lad, but now they whinge and moan about each other, and destroy our countryside by cutting down trees.'

'On Friday,' says Millicent, frowning at Phyllis, who's just shovelled in a very large mouthful. 'That's when Finn Shawley's having those trees you told us about cut down.'

'This Friday? Are you sure?' says Gramp.

'I think so. That's what Scott, the tree surgeon, told me. He keeps my vast garden under control and insists on telling me what's going on in his life. The last time he came round, he said he's been hired by Finn to cut down the trees on Friday afternoon.'

'Which is sad but those trees have to come down and there's nothing you can do about it,' I say quickly, putting my hand on Gramp's bony shoulder.

He sips his coffee with a mutinous expression on his wrinkled face while I inwardly curse both Millicent's enormous garden and her over-sharing tree surgeon.

The afternoon passes in a blur of worrying about my grandfather's next move in the tree war, swallowing my sadness over the never-to-be romance with Noah, and pondering on the identity of our 'pixie'.

I can't shake the feeling that Finn's involved but Flora's right. Solid evidence is needed before I accuse Honeyford's boy wonder of dodgy business practices.

Which is why, ten minutes after finishing work, I'm skulking about behind the manor house wall.

In the movies, spies on a mission feel steady and resolute. In real life, I feel like a prat. A total prat who's not sure what she's doing here. I should have gone straight home, rather than lurking about trying to gauge if the Shawleys are home. What am I going to do – break in?

Ridiculous schemes to prove my trolling theory run through my head. I could drip-feed Finn false information about The Cosy Kettle to see if he takes the bait and tweets it. Or ply him with alcohol to loosen his tongue while recording his confession on a device hidden in my bra.

MI5 isn't going to come calling any time soon, I realise, sliding down the Cotswold-stone wall and sitting on the dusty pavement. I put my elbows on my knees and my head in my hands.

How am I going to find out, one way or the other, if Finn is behind the trolling? I can hardly march in and just ask him. Although…

A red butterfly flits in front of me as I realise that's not the worst idea I've ever had. Though it brings with it the possibility of conflict. Lots of conflict.

There's no way Finn will go down without a fight if he's guilty. And if he's not guilty and I march in and accuse him, he's likely to go ballistic.

My stomach clenches at the thought of all that potential shouting. And who knows how long it might go on? My parents could bicker for hours about who left the milk out of the fridge, and accusing someone of being a business cheat is far worse than curdled milk.

But you're a grown woman now who can handle even the fiercest of feelings, I tell myself. *And confronting bad people is a good thing.* That's what Gramp would say.

I pull myself to my feet, brush down my dusty backside, and push open the manor house gate as courage, or possibly nausea, stirs in my soul. Maybe it's time to be my true self and confront the man I suspect of trying to ruin my business.

Or maybe not. Being brave while sitting on the pavement is easy-peasy. Maintaining that courage while walking up the driveway towards the house is another thing entirely. My resolve evaporates like morning mist with every step that brings me closer to the front door.

What's the point of putting myself through this? I ask, as gravel crunches under my feet. *And what if Noah's at home and this wrecks our fledgling friendship?* Finn's vehement denial of my accusations will make me seem bitter and deluded – and I don't want that to be Noah's last memory of me.

With one final glance at the windows, to make sure no one's watching, I turn on my heel and run for the gate. Confrontation be damned.

Chapter Twenty-Three

Gramp has gone worryingly quiet. I watch him like a hawk over the next couple of days and he seems resigned to the trees' imminent demise. But I've learned to my cost that he's unpredictable so I deliberately schedule a meeting of The Cosy Kettle Afternoon Book Club for two o'clock on Friday – crunch day.

The idea is that we can provide him with distraction and moral support as the trees come down. But it's now five past two on Friday and no one's turned up. Not even Gramp.

'I have a very bad feeling about this,' I tell Flora, watching the minute hand on the wall clock click closer to ten past the hour.

'It'll be fine. He's probably just handing out flyers at Finn's hotel. I still want to see one of those, by the way. They sound fabulous.' She laughs at my appalled expression. 'Oh, just go and see what he's up to.'

I've grabbed my cardi and am about to hurtle out of the shop when Becca rushes in.

'I was told not to tell you but it's making me horribly anxious. You've been so good to me and I don't want to deceive you,' she gabbles, almost in tears.

'Calm down, Becca. Tell me what?'

'I can't tell you because I promised I wouldn't. I've never been a grass. Not even at school when it meant I got into trouble with the teachers.'

I grip her shoulders and turn her round to face me. I'm feeling so anxious now, I could shake her.

'Telling me what's going on isn't being a grass, Becca. It's being sensible, so tell me exactly what you know.'

She swallows. 'It's Stanley and the others.'

'What about them?'

'They're chaining themselves to the trees so they can't be cut down.'

Behind me, Flora snorts with laughter. 'That is priceless! It's classic Stanley, bless him.'

'Bless him? I'm going to freaking murder him!'

But that just makes Flora laugh even more. 'Go!' she splutters between hoots and snorts. 'You'd better go and rescue him before he gets felled along with the trees.'

Honeyford isn't usually a busy town. It's only at the height of summer that pavements are clogged with tourists taking photos. But today, though it's only early May, people keep getting in my way.

I weave along the pavement, apologising as I bang into people and muttering curses under my breath.

Gramp, the silly old fool, will get himself arrested – or worse, if Finn cuts the trees down regardless. Which I wouldn't put past him because what Finn wants, Finn gets.

When I finally reach the manor house, there's a white van outside with *Scott Geraldson: Tree Surgeon* embossed across it in large blue letters. He's here already!

Shoving open the gate, I hurtle up the drive, past the new sign that has *Shawley Manor House Boutique Hotel* picked out in gold lettering, and around the side of the house.

Maybe Becca was wrong and my grandfather's safely at home, or in the pub playing dominoes and debating climate change.

But, no. There he is, flat up against the trunk of the tallest tree with a chain around his waist.

It's hard to imagine how this situation could be made worse. But Gramp always seems to find a way because Millicent is chained up next to him. And secured to the other two trees are Mary, Phyllis and Dick. The women are still but Dick is struggling like he's trying to escape.

A tall, wiry man – presumably tree surgeon Scott – is remonstrating with Gramp as I get closer.

'Come on, sir, this is utterly ridiculous and merely putting off the inevitable.'

He scrunches up his weather-beaten face like he can't quite believe what's happening. I doubt he's often faced with protesting pensioners attached to trees.

'I've got nothing against you, mate, per se,' says Gramp, who's red in the face and puffing heavily. 'You're doing your job. I get that. I used to be a working man myself. But this is wrong. They're cutting down these trees and turning this area into a car park. It's criminal! Here's my granddaughter – she'll tell you.'

'Gramp, what the hell are you doing? This isn't going to help.'

'That's where you're wrong, Callie.' His mouth sets into a firm line. 'They can't cut down the trees while we're attached to them.'

'That's true,' says Phyllis, whose wheelchair is secured to her tree via a chain through a spoke in one of the wheels. 'Stanley explained why the trees mean so much to him and it's such a beautiful love story. We came along to support him.'

'Not me,' huffs Dick. 'I came along to stop him being such an idiot but they pushed me against a tree and fastened me to it and won't give me the key.'

He tugs vainly at what looks like a length of silver bicycle chain that's tightly secured around his waist and the tree trunk with a padlock.

'Really?' I address all of them. 'You're imprisoning poor Dick against his will? And Mary, where's Callum?'

'My friend's looking after him so I can do something different for a change. Something non-mumsy.'

'This is non-mumsy, all right. And what about you, Millicent?'

Millicent raises a clenched fist. 'My children are always saying how boring I am, so I thought I'd show them there's life in the old dog yet. I'm hoping to be arrested. Let's see how boring they think it is when they have to stump up my bail.'

Jeez, they've all gone completely mad.

'But what about your husband, Millicent? What will he think about all this?'

'Quite honestly, I couldn't give a rat's ass what he thinks. He's probably too busy having his sordid little affair with his PA to notice.'

She blinks rapidly and flushes as though she can't quite believe what she just said. But she looks more alive than I've ever seen her – as though the stick up her backside has been removed.

I take a deep breath and let my cheeks cool in the breeze blowing off the hill behind us. 'What you're trying to do is all very admirable, but did my gramp mention that the trees are diseased and unstable?'

'That's not true,' says Phyllis, looking at Gramp for support. But Scott steps forward.

'It is true. I've inspected these trees thoroughly and they need to come down before they fall down.'

'But not today,' says Gramp, pulling himself up as tall as you can when you're tethered by a chain to a tree trunk. 'Moira wouldn't like it.'

'But she's not here any more, Gramp.'

Anguish flickers in Stanley's rheumy eyes but he shakes his head. 'I'm still not moving and you can't make me.'

'Right,' says Scott, who's reached the end of his tether. 'I don't get paid to argue with bonkers old folk so I'm going back to the van to sit in comfort while you lot sort this out.'

He marches off and almost bumps into Finn, who's crunching over the gravel in his socks and wincing with every step.

'What the hell is going on? Oh, it's you.' His eyes track from my face to the trees. 'Great, you've brought your bolshie granddad too. And his friends! You're on private property, you know. This is outrageous.'

'What is?' Noah appears beside him, puffing slightly after running from the house. 'Callie' – he nods warily – 'and Stanley too.' He walks up to Gramp and runs his fingers along the chain around his waist. 'You appear to be attached to a tree.'

'You don't sound surprised,' says Finn, wincing again as sharp pieces of gravel stick into his feet.

'Nothing Callie and her family do or say surprises me these days. And I see you've brought reinforcements. Afternoon, ladies and gent.' He nods at Millicent, Mary, Phyllis and Dick, who have gone very quiet.

'How can you be so calm about this harassment?' Finn puffs. He grabs Gramp's chain and tries to wrench it from the tree. It doesn't work and makes him look ridiculous, like the Hulk without his super powers.

'Gerroff!' yells Gramp. 'I'll have you for assaulting a senior citizen as well as killing trees.'

'Leave him alone, you bully,' shouts Phyllis, bouncing up and down in her wheelchair.

'Can I just say, for the record, that none of this is anything to do with me. I was coerced,' calls Dick as I'm trying to get between Gramp and Finn.

'Noah, can you help?' I plead.

But Noah holds up his hands and moves back. 'I told you, Callie, I'm not getting between you and my brother. I'm sorry but you need to sort this one out.'

He walks off, back towards the house.

'Right, I'm going to get a very large pair of bolt cutters and the police,' yells Finn in Gramp's face.

How dare he? 'Don't shout at my grandfather! He's a very old man.'

'He's an ancient maniac!'

'Not so much of the ancient,' gasps Gramp, who's going a very odd colour. 'Oh my.' He clutches at his chest and grimaces.

'What's the matter?' I ask. 'Are you in pain?'

Oh, God, what's happening now? He's gasping for air.

'Come off it! He's putting it on,' says Finn, but he sounds scared.

I scrabble in my pocket – damn, in the rush out of the bookshop I forgot my phone. 'Noah!' I yell.

Noah looks back and waves his hand. 'No way, Callie. You'll have to sort this out with Finn…'

He stops, his hand in mid-air, as he spots the anguish on my face. And then he's running towards me.

'What's going on?' he calls.

'I think Gramp's having a heart attack.'

'That's very convenient,' blusters Finn, but Noah shoulder-barges him out of the way and helps me support my gramp, who's slumped against the rough bark of the tree.

'Where's the key to his padlock?' I yell at Dick.

'All the keys are in his pocket, I think.'

Noah and I ferret through Gramp's trouser pockets which are bulging with handkerchiefs.

'Got it!' shouts Noah. His hand is shaking and it takes several attempts to fit the right key into the tiny silver lock.

As the lock finally falls open, Noah wrenches it from the chain and throws it onto the grass. Then we support Gramp, who slumps into a sitting position with his back against the trunk.

'Where's the pain?' I stoop down beside him.

'It's my damn chest. It feels really tight,' he gasps.

'Breathe, Gramp. Take deep, slow breaths.'

I hold his cold hand while Noah speaks to the ambulance service on his mobile phone. Finn stands behind him, shifting from foot to foot like a guilty ten-year-old in trouble for bad behaviour.

'I don't need a damn ambulance. I'm fine,' protests Gramp weakly, but no one takes any notice.

'Give me the key,' calls Dick.

I throw the bunch of keys to him and he fiddles with the padlock at his waist until he's free and can unlock everyone else.

'What can we do to help?' Mary puts her hand on my shoulder and squeezes hard.

'You can all go and flag down the ambulance and show the paramedics where we are,' says Noah. 'They're no use here, panicking,' he murmurs to me as they bustle off, Dick and Mary pushing Phyllis's wheelchair, which scores deep lines in the pristine gravel.

'Why don't you get Stanley a glass of water, Finn?' suggests Noah, crouching down beside me, loosening the collar of my gramp's shirt.

Finn nods mutely before hurrying towards the house and then it's just the three of us huddled beneath the tree where, five decades earlier, my grandfather enjoyed al fresco canoodling with the love of his life. *Please don't let it be where his life comes to a close,* I pray. Tears fill my eyes as I hug him.

'You daft old bugger,' I whisper. 'Where's that ambulance?'

'They'll be here any minute,' says Noah, his blue eyes meeting mine over the top of Gramp's head. 'Don't worry. Everything's going to be fine.'

Which is what he told me eight years ago when I was panicking about my exams. He was right. I did pass my exams and go to university but everything wasn't fine, was it? Not between us.

The wail of a siren cuts through the fresh spring air and two female paramedics are soon crunching around the side of the house. I've never been more relieved to see anyone.

'What's been happening here, then?' says the older woman, kneeling down next to Gramp. She picks up the chain and gives me a puzzled look.

'He chained himself to a tree and now he's got pain and tightness in his chest. He's eighty.'

'OK,' says the woman, calmly, as though she treats chained octogenarians every day of the week.

Noah and I stand back while the paramedics examine their patient.

Beyond us, verdant green hills rise into a china-blue sky and birds are chirping as they flit above our heads. It's a perfect day in paradise.

But a feeling of dread is flooding through me. Gramp drives me demented sometimes but I don't know what I'll do if I lose him.

'Are you all right, Callie? You must let me and Finn know if we can help with anything.'

Noah is standing so close, I can sense his body heat. I nod, but a big fat tear dribbles its way down my cheek.

'We'll be fine,' I gulp.

'For goodness' sake, Callie. You don't have to be brave all the time.'

He snakes his arm around my shoulder and pulls me in tight against his chest. My cheek nestles against the soft cotton of his white shirt and I relax as his arms go around me. He feels wonderful.

Oh. My. God. I'm getting turned on by an old boyfriend while my grandfather is possibly dying.

'I'd better go with him in the ambulance,' I say, pushing Noah away from me.

'Shall I come with you?'

I hesitate. There's nothing I'd like more than Noah's comforting presence but I can't cope with the extra emotional turmoil at the moment. My head and my heart are all over the place.

'There's no need. We'll be fine, but thank you.'

'The trees!' croaks Gramp.

'Don't worry. There'll be no tree felling today,' says Noah.

'We could still do it.' Finn's come back with Scott and both men are hanging around behind us.

'Not today, Finn. Scott can come back tomorrow.'

It's the first time I've heard Noah speak so assertively to his big brother.

'Yeah, yeah, that's fine,' says Scott, backing away as though the last thing he wants to do today is fell trees that might have cost an old man his life.

But Gramp is starting to look better. His face is still pale, but the grey tinge has gone.

'I don't need to go to hospital,' he insists to the paramedics. 'I feel fine, now, and my chest is all right again. It was just the excitement of it all.'

But they strap him into the back of the ambulance and I sit next to him, gently rubbing his arm. Noah stands watching at the manor house gates and I put my hand on my right cheek, which still feels flushed and warm from resting against his chest, as the ambulance door closes and we pull away into Church Lane.

Chapter Twenty-Four

'What the hell do you think you're doing?'

When Gramp jumps, cornflakes scatter across the worktop and onto the kitchen floor.

'What does it look like I'm doing? I'm getting myself some breakfast. That's allowed, isn't it?'

Gramp steps back and there's a crunch as golden flakes of corn are crushed under his bare feet.

'You're supposed to stay in bed. I came down to get you some food.'

'I'm not lying in bed all day,' he grumbles, sploshing milk everywhere. 'I'm not dead yet.'

He takes his bowl and sits at the dented table while I root through the cutlery drawer where decades worth of mismatched knives, forks and spoons are jostling for space.

'How are you feeling today?' I ask, handing him a spoon.

'Old!' Gramp starts stirring the flakes round and round. 'Though you all overreacted, taking me to hospital when there was nothing wrong with me.'

'That's not strictly true, is it? The doctors think it's angina brought on by stress.'

'So they say. I've never been poked and prodded so much in my life. And that doctor with the Magnum 'tache had very cold hands,' he complains. 'Shouldn't you be at work?'

'Flora's given me the day off to look after you and make sure you take things easy. Which means no more chaining yourself to trees and getting stressed out about things you can't change. OK?'

When Gramp continues staring into his bowl of fast-congealing breakfast, I scoot round the table and put my hand on his.

'I mean it, so listen to me. Anyway, you must be tired after all the excitement of yesterday.'

'No more tired than you are,' says Gramp, peering into my face. 'You're pale as a ghost.'

'No make-up,' I tell him, but he's right. I'm knackered. We were at the hospital for hours and then I had bad dreams all night. Well, not so much bad as disturbing. Dreams in which Noah pulled me tight into his chest but kept on squeezing his arms around me until I was suffocating. And I wanted to yell at him to stop but couldn't bring myself to shout. I woke up in a cold sweat.

'We'll be all right, girl.'

'We will, if you look after yourself and stop these one-man crusades.'

'Don't worry, Callie. My crusading days are over.'

When Gramp lifts his head, his tired old eyes are bright with tears, which breaks my heart. The last time I saw my gramp really cry was on a summer morning three years ago, at his beloved Moira's funeral.

'You can still stand up for what you believe in. But just do it in a less stressy and' – I search for the right word – '*chainy* kind of way.'

'It won't happen again. I thought I could be someone different, someone who achieved something, but I'm just a daft old fool reading a self-help article that hasn't helped me much at all.'

'You've achieved loads, Gramp.'

He brushes away a tear furrowing its way down his cheek.

'Hardly. I've lived in the same house for decades, my son's dead, I worked hard but never earned enough to take Moira on a decent holiday, and now she's gone and I can't even save the trees that meant such a lot to her.'

'I'm so sorry. They have to come down.'

Gramp shrugs. 'It doesn't matter. Moira's gone and will soon be forgotten, and I'll be forgotten too because my life hasn't amounted to much. That's my true self.'

'Your true self is amazing and I'll tell you what you've achieved. You raised a son and a granddaughter who love you. And you and Gran were always here when I needed you, when life at home got a bit stressful.'

I spent my childhood avoiding taking sides when my parents were bickering, and always smiling in the hope my apparent good mood would be infectious. When it all got too much, I'd scuttle round to my grandparents for a hug, a slice of Battenberg in front of the telly, and perfect peace.

'You and Gran saved me from a life of constant squabbling. That's an achievement, isn't it?'

Gramp gives a sad smile. 'Helping to raise you is the best thing I ever did, apart from marrying your grandmother, obviously.'

'Obviously.'

He sniffs while I thank my lucky stars that he's still here and a part of my life.

'Noah's good for you, you know,' he says, suddenly.

Whoah; that came out of nowhere.

'I thought you didn't approve of the Shawleys.'

'Noah's all right. He looked after me well enough until the ambulance arrived, and I saw the way he looked at you. It's such a shame he lives in New York. Why would anyone want to live there rather than Honeyford?'

'I can't possibly imagine.'

'Do you think you might move to New York? I want you to go if you'd be happy.'

Gramp's bottom lip is trembling and I feel an overwhelming rush of love for this exasperating, exhausting, irreplaceable man.

'I'm not going anywhere and leaving you. I promise. Things are complicated between me and Noah, but we're friends now and that's good enough.'

'Really? Friends won't keep you warm at night.'

'Maybe not, but I've got the café to keep me busy, and I've got you. I'm happy enough with my life in Honeyford.'

Gramp places the palm of his hand against my cheek and smiles.

'You're a good girl, Callie. The only bright spot in my life.'

'What about the wild swimming and the parachute jump?' I smile. 'They're bright spots too.'

'They're madness. I'm an old man and old men don't do that kind of thing.'

'Dick bought a sports car.'

'Yeah, there is that, the daft old fool.' He winks and pushes his uneaten breakfast to one side. 'But you don't have to worry about me doing daft things any more. Do you know, I am quite tired so I think I'll go back upstairs and lie down for a while.'

He walks slowly out of the kitchen and clumps up the stairs while I pour myself a bowl of cornflakes. Gramp's wrong. I'm even more worried about him now.

*

A little later, while he's still in bed, I slip out of the front door and go for a walk. My phone's been beeping non-stop with messages from people enquiring about Gramp's health, and I need to clear my head.

It's one of those bright blustery spring mornings that often burn themselves out. But right now the air is warm and sweet with the smell of blossom as I climb the hill that rises behind our house. Other walkers are out enjoying the sunshine too and wave as they go by.

At the highest point of the hill, I sit on a wooden bench and retie my shoe laces. All around me, rolling countryside stretches into the purple distance, scattered with huddled villages. Roads wend like arteries across the landscape and church spires soar high above banks of trees.

You never go far in the Cotswolds without stumbling across some gorgeous gem of a village, and I love it here. I'd find it hard to leave Honeyford, even if Gramp was gone and Noah and I had the sort of uncomplicated relationship that promises happy ever after.

The peace and breathtaking beauty of the rolling countryside fill a hole in my soul. Though I'd never admit that to Sarah, obviously, or she'd label me a pretentious weirdo.

Spread out at the foot of the hill is Honeyford, with the church at its centre, the long winding High Street, and our little estate of houses grouped at the village edge, almost like an afterthought.

And there, beyond the old Baptist chapel, are the tall, butter-yellow chimneys of the manor house. Where Noah is right now.

I push my sunglasses up into my hair and sit for a while, feeling glum. It's not surprising I'm subdued after yesterday's events and the realisation that my gramp isn't going to be around for ever. But I also can't help feeling that my life's a bit of a cock-up.

There's no one around so I list the evidence, speaking out loud.

'You launched The Cosy Kettle with no proper experience, you're using Flora's money and you don't really know what you're doing.'

Hhmm, that's a biggie.

'You've let one spiteful troll come close to knackering your confidence and your plans. If the trolling ramps up and customer numbers drop, the café might fold, shop profits will suffer, and the whole place could close. Then what happens to Gramp, Flora, Becca and the book club?'

I'd rather not think about that.

'Also, you got things horribly wrong with Noah by not speaking up all those years ago. Though he sparked things off by not standing up to his stupid brother. Whatever. Now you're going to have a frigid life and die alone. Way to go, Callie.'

Behind me, trees rustling in the wind sound like whispered voices confirming that my life is indeed one humungous cock-up.

I squint and lean forward when I spot someone walking up the hill towards me. It's… oh, no! It's Noah.

My stomach starts fluttering as he strides up the hill, dressed in dark jeans and a grey sweatshirt with his fabulous fair hair blowing all over the place.

'Who are you talking to?' he calls out as he gets closer.

Great! He just saw me talking to myself like the Mad Woman of Honeyford.

'No one. I was just thinking out loud.'

Noah raises his eyebrows and stops in front of me.

'Very wise. I do it all the time 'cos it beats talking to other people.'

He gestures at the bench that's so hard it's making my bum go numb. 'Room on there for another one?'

I shuffle along and he sits next to me. His thigh is against mine so I shift along a bit because all this touching and lusting and longing for what's behind us is pointless.

'What are you doing up here?'

'I called round to see how Stanley is. No one answered and his bedroom curtains were closed so I guessed where you'd be. You always did your best thinking up here. So how's he doing?'

'OK. They think it's angina, like I said in my text. So he's resting today but he'll be fine if he looks after himself.'

'No more chaining himself to trees, then.'

'That's definitely off the cards so you can report back that Finn can cut down the trees, protest-free.'

Noah bristles beside me. 'I don't go reporting stuff back to Finn.'

'Sorry, wrong choice of words.'

'But I'm afraid the trees are gone now anyway. Scott came back this morning and felled them. Can you tell Stanley I'm sorry, and say goodbye because I'm heading back to New York in a few days' time.'

Of course he is. I always knew he'd be going back to his real life – so why do I feel like crying?

'I wish you all the best, Callie,' says Noah, staring straight ahead at the magnificent view.

'Thank you. I wish you every happiness too.'

And it's true. We've had our differences – some real, some entirely in our own heads – but I feel a connection to him that I can't ignore. I want him to be happy and have a good life, even though my heart is hurting.

He turns his head and looks at me. 'I'm sure your café will be a great success, and I hope your troll will leave you alone.'

'Thank you. Hopefully he's had his fun and will move on. Or she has,' I add, so it doesn't sound as though I'm still focusing on Finn.

To be honest, my conviction that it's Finn has started to waver and I don't want another argument with Noah, not just before he leaves.

'Has the trolling stopped?'

'I hope so but with everything that's been going on I haven't checked our social media accounts for a while.'

I find my phone in my pocket and click on Facebook. Everything looks fine – a new pic's been posted of Phyllis's potted pansies which are a riot of yellow and purple. And there's an update about the evening book club which starts next week.

As for Twitter… Noah hears my sharp intake of breath and peers over my shoulder at a tweet posted yesterday.

A bookshop should stick to doing what it does best and sell books, not mediocre coffee in a shabby storeroom #CosyKettle-Honeyford #rubbishservice

That's so mean it takes my breath away.

'Good grief, that's awful,' says Noah. 'A really rotten, low comment.'

'Yeah,' I say, shakily. 'I have no idea how we've managed to annoy Chester quite so much.'

'What's his name?' Noah snatches the phone from my hand, clicks on the tweet and starts peering at Chester's photo, before scrolling through his Twitter feed. Then he clicks on the café's Facebook account and scrolls some more.

Suddenly, he shoves the phone back at me and jumps to his feet. 'I owe you an apology. Come on!'

'Where are we going?'

'To see Finn.'

He grabs hold of my hand and starts pulling me down the slope, taking such huge strides I can hardly keep up. After a while he slows down a little and I fall into step beside him. But he still keeps his fingers wrapped around mine which feels wonderful, even though I haven't got a clue what's going on.

Noah lets go of my hand when we reach the road that skirts the bottom of the hill but he keeps up a cracking pace. He marches through the town, along the manor house drive, and barges through the front door which bangs behind us. Then he stops so abruptly I almost barrel into his broad shoulders.

'Finn!' he yells at the top of his voice. I begin to wonder if me being here is a good idea. I get the feeling there's about to be an almighty row.

'What the hell is going on?' yawns Finn, appearing at the top of the stairs in tight black boxer shorts that leave little to the imagination. 'I was having a lie-in until you started making so much noise.'

'I need to speak to you. Now.'

'All right, bruv. Keep your hair on. Let me get some clothes on first.'

He wanders off towards his bedroom, scratching his backside. Many women would be all a quiver at seeing Finn Shawley in his underkecks but, nope, he just doesn't do it for me. On the other hand, lovely nerdy Noah…

I steal a glance at Noah, who's pacing up and down on the Persian rug, circling the table and its vase of tall, cream lilies. His cheeks are flushed, he looks annoyed as hell, and so gorgeous I can't bear the thought of him leaving for New York. The strength of my feelings for him is suddenly undeniable.

'Can I say something?' I blurt out.

Noah stops pacing and looks at me expectantly. Ooh, I haven't thought this through. I can hardly say: *Please give up your high-flying career in New York and stay in sleepy Honeyford because I've just properly realised that I'm still hopelessly in love with you.* Not when we missed our chance a long time ago. What good would that do?

I'm saved from saying anything at all by Finn padding down the stairs, thankfully fully clothed in grey tracksuit bottoms and a white T-shirt.

'Hi, Callie. Sorry for giving you an eyeful.' He glances down at his crotch and gives me a huge wink.

Urgh. He never lets the flirting drop. It must be exhausting to spend your whole life trying to get off with people, and lonely, if every relationship is based on superficial lust. I feel a stab of sympathy for Finn and his successful, shallow life.

'So what's this all about?' he asks, rubbing his eyes.

'Callie has a very important question to ask you, about your dodgy business practices.'

'You're going to have to be more specific. Which particular dodgy business practices are you referring to?'

'This isn't a joke, Finn.' Noah's voice is ice-cold. 'Go on, Callie, ask your question. It should come from you.' He looks at me and his face softens. 'Sometimes confronting people is the right thing to do.'

When Finn turns to me and folds his arms I realise that Noah is wrong – hideously, horribly wrong. Avoiding conflict and people-pleasing until your teeth are so gritted you can't speak is the right thing to do. But there's no backing out now.

'Someone's been trolling The Cosy Kettle on social media and'– I swallow, loudly – 'I think it might be you.'

No one moves as my wobbly words hang in the air between us.

Then Finn splutters: 'What? That's an outrageous suggestion. As if I'd waste my valuable time on your little café when I've got this place.' He swings round to Noah and laughs. 'Honestly, mate, this girl's delusional.'

'So you're saying that the people who complained about horrible coffee, stale cake and poor service weren't you?' I say in a low voice.

'Of course not. They're customers who thought your coffee and cake were crap. Criticism happens in business and you have to suck it up. You're being totally over-sensitive and hysterical.'

'One man who's been complaining had photos on his Twitter feed of places you've recently been to on business.'

'Is that your proof?' Finn snorts. 'Your disgruntled customer posted photos of places that I happen to have visited, along with millions of other people? I can't believe you're here accusing me of this.'

I can't believe it either. I've stepped outside my usual boundaries and am desperate to get back to my non-confrontational comfort zone. Gramp can stick all his true self nonsense.

'I'm sorry,' I squeak.

'I think you'd better leave,' says Finn, striding to the front door and flinging it open. But Noah puts his hand on my arm.

'Who posted the latest tweet this morning, Callie?' His voice is still cold and level.

'Chester.'

'That's an unusual name, wouldn't you say, Finn?'

Finn gives a nervous laugh and starts shuffling from foot to foot. 'Not really. We know loads of people called Chester.'

'I don't know anyone with that name. The only Chester I've ever known is our black Labrador when we were growing up. The dog Dad bought us that you doted on.'

'What's that got to do with anything?' blusters Finn, letting the front door swing shut.

'It would be a name that might spring to mind if you were creating a fake Twitter account and making it look authentic by posting photos of places you'd visited. That wouldn't have been enough on its own to convince me but then I looked at Frances' profile pic on Facebook and, rather than posting a picture of herself, she's used a photo of a black Labrador that looks strangely familiar.'

'That's ridiculous! I know nothing about Frances or Chester and I'm hurt that you'd even—'

'Stop it! Just stop it!' Noah's shouts echo through the house. 'I know you're lying.'

Finn takes a deep breath, ready to deny everything, and hesitates before expelling the air in one loud *oof*.

'OK, I've been rumbled.' He shrugs and opens his arms wide. 'It's a fair cop – it was me who posted a couple of tweets and Facebook posts. Remember that all's fair in love, war and business, and it's only a piddling little café, at the end of the day.'

'But it's *my* piddling little café,' I say in a loud voice.

Finn's mouth falls open at little mouse Callie speaking up. He's shocked, though not as shocked as I am. I have the strangest sensation that I'm on the ceiling watching myself lose control as overwhelming anger finally boils to the surface. I was right – this man has been sabotaging my business.

'Tell me, Finn, why you think setting out to ruin a business that has nothing to do with you is acceptable.' My voice has got even louder.

'God, you're overreacting. So my tweets and comments might have put a few customers off. But if you think about it, it's a compliment that I thought your café was worth the trouble. Honestly, what I did isn't a big deal.'

When I move towards Finn, he takes one look at my face and steps back behind Noah.

'It is a big deal if the bookshop might have to close because the café isn't making enough money. It is a big deal if a young girl with a difficult life is breaking her heart because she set up our social media accounts and feels responsible. And,' I shout, 'it is a ginormous deal if my dream is going down the pan because you're a selfish, arrogant dick with no ethics who's desperately trying to impress his father all the time.'

I'm shocked that this feels good – weird and a bit scary, but good. I never knew that saying what you truly think so loudly could be this… liberating. I'm quite tempted to go the whole hog and smash Finn's fancy-ass vase of lilies all over the flagstones.

'Why did you do it, Finn?' Noah has moved to stand beside me. 'Surely it's no skin off your nose if The Cosy Kettle is doing well? It wouldn't have much of an effect on a coffee house set up here.'

'But it would have *some* effect,' says Finn, his mouth turned down like a sulky child. 'I could see the café was doing well and would pull in more and more customers, especially with Callie here and her touchy-feely hands-on style which people seem to like these days. That could affect my coffee house's profits and, as Dad says, it all comes down to the bottom line. It's nothing personal.'

Noah lifts his chin and looks so disappointed, I want to hug him.

'It's all personal with you. What about when you've made a play for my girlfriends in the past? That was personal. You always have to win, whatever the cost to those around you.'

'It's just a game, mate. You know I'm a serial flirt and don't mean anything by it,' blusters Finn, his face shiny with a thin sheen of sweat.

'But it isn't a game to me. You enjoy making a beeline for women I'm interested in to prove you're still the best. You'd have done the same with Callie at university which is why I...' He presses the heel of his hand to his forehead. 'Callie's right. I should have called you out on this a long time ago but I've always made excuses because of Dad.'

'What's Dad got to do with this?'

'Everything,' says Noah, suddenly icy calm again. 'You always have to come out on top to impress him. You always have to win to shore up your own self-esteem. I've put up with your behaviour and ignored any misgivings about the way you do business because you're my big brother. But you're hurting me and the people I care about and I can't ignore it any more. So I'll be heading back to New York tonight.'

'It was just a few stupid tweets,' protests Finn. 'It didn't mean anything.'

'It means everything. You have no idea of the damage you do with your games and what people lose because of them.' Noah glances at me and there's such pain in his eyes, I can't hold his gaze. 'We need to have a talk, Finn, a long overdue talk.'

'I'd better leave you to it if you're talking about family stuff,' I say, briefly running my fingers down Noah's arm.

He smiles faintly. 'That's probably a good idea. My brother's sorry for trolling your business, Callie, and it won't happen again.'

'Are you speaking for me now?' mutters Finn who looks punch-drunk. But he adds, so quietly I can hardly hear it: 'No, it won't happen again. Sorry.'

'And you'll delete the comments you've already made,' I tell him.

Finn just hangs his head and nods.

I'm halfway along the drive, walking so fast my breath is coming in little gasps, when I hear crunching on the gravel behind me and swing round.

Noah's running towards me. He stops several metres away and pushes his hands into his jeans pockets.

'I'm sorry I didn't believe you about Finn. I didn't want to believe he could behave like that. It's all a mess, isn't it?'

'It is, thanks to your awful brother.' I sigh as my anger cools and retreats. 'Say what you have to say but don't be too hard on him. Your dad's messed with his head and I know what it's like having parents who do that.'

Noah grins. '*You* gave him a pretty hard time. I've never heard you shout like that. In fact, I've never heard you shout at all. You scared the life out of me.'

'I scared the life out of myself but it felt good to say what I really think. My people-pleasing days are well and truly over.'

'Completely over?'

'Hhmm, maybe not. There's a lot to be said for getting on with people and having a quiet life, but maybe I'll pick the occasional fight just to prove I can.'

'That's my girl.'

Noah scuffs at the gravel with his foot, and small stones ping off the paintwork of Finn's purple Porsche.

'Are you really going back to New York tonight?'

'If I can bring my flight forward. I need to get back and Finn can make finishing touches to the hotel without me.'

'Well, while I'm speaking my mind – I'll miss you horribly.'

I bite my lip hard to stop myself blurting out any more, and a tremor of emotion flits across Noah's face.

'If only we hadn't gone such separate ways, Callie. I think we could make a go of it and be so good together, but New York's far away and my life is there now.'

'I think we would be great together too,' I say, weighed down with sadness. 'But you're right; my life is here, with Gramp and the café.'

'I know.' Noah's mouth twists into a shaky grin. 'But at least when I leave Honeyford this time, you and I are parting as friends.'

'We are,' I reply, longing to be more than friends – to hare across the gravel and throw myself into his arms. But that would make this even messier. So I stand still as a statue, next to the hotel sign that's glinting in the sunshine. 'When will you be back?'

He shrugs. 'Not for a while. I'm heading up a big new project that'll keep me in the States for months. Maybe you could come over to the Big Apple and visit some time?'

'That would be great if I can find someone to keep Gramp out of trouble while I'm three thousand miles away.'

Noah nods, knowing as well as I do that finding someone able to do that will be nigh-on impossible. And even if a Good Samaritan came forward and I saved up and made it to New York for a few days, being 'just friends' would be torture.

'I'd better get back to the house. I've got a brother to shout at and a case to pack. So I guess this really is goodbye.' He holds my gaze across the space dividing us. 'Take care of yourself, Callie, and be happy in Honeyford.'

'You too. Have a fabulous life in the big city.'

'And keep telling people what you really think. It suits you.'

'I will,' I gulp. 'Bye, Noah.'

Then I turn on my heel and march off towards the gate at top speed so he won't see the tears pouring down my face.

Chapter Twenty-Five

'I don't believe it.' Flora bangs her hands on the counter so hard, the till drawer rattles. 'You have got to be kidding me. It really was Finn who was posting those horrible tweets and Facebook comments? Charming, successful Finn Shawley?'

'The very same. But it's been dealt with and it won't happen again.'

'Are you sure? The café and shop can't cope with more bad publicity.'

I remember the astonished look on Finn's face when Noah confronted him and nod. 'I'm absolutely sure.'

'Wow.' Flora drops onto the stool behind the counter. 'Just, wow.'

'I know, it's crazy. But you can't tell anyone.'

'Why not? He deserves to be outed. What he did was appalling and the whole town should know.'

'You can't tell anyone because it'll reflect badly on Noah.'

'But you say he had nothing to do with it.'

'You and I know that but people think the Shawley brothers are joined at the hip and people will gossip that it was Noah too. Please.'

Flora runs her bead necklace through her fingers and tilts her head to one side.

'He still means a lot to you, doesn't he, this Noah? In spite of all your protests to the contrary.'

'He did. He does. But he's back in New York now so there's no point dwelling on it.'

Even though I'm doing nothing but dwelling on it. My eyes are prickling and I bite my lip so hard it draws blood. When I start crying these days, I find it hard to stop and spending all morning sobbing at work would be totally unprofessional.

Flora thinks for a moment, her forehead wrinkled in concentration. 'All right. I'm not happy about it but I'll keep quiet for you and for Noah. But Finn had better not show his weasley little face in here or I'll tell him what's what in words of one syllable.'

Eek, I must never get on the wrong side of Flora, who appears to be in healthy touch with her inner anger. But the anger drains away as she hops off the stool and walks towards me.

'How are you doing, Callie? First it was Stanley in hospital, then Finn behaving like a complete ass and now Noah's gone. Are you all right?'

'Mmmm.' I nod, furiously, willing her to walk away.

But she carries on towards me, puts her arms around me and pulls me close.

I know she's my boss and not that much older than me but she feels like my mum as she hugs me tight. And I really need my mum right now. The floodgates open and I sob on her shoulder.

Thank goodness no one comes into the shop while I'm having a mini-meltdown. The gossip would be all around town by lunchtime. But no one comes in until after my sobs have subsided into little hiccups and I've fled to the loo to sort out my wrecked face.

For the rest of the week, I throw myself into my work. The bookshop has never been so proficiently stocked and the coffee machine has never been so gleaming. I chat with customers and laugh at their jokes and no one knows that two little words are whirling constantly around my head. *If only.*

If only I'd tackled Noah eight years ago about what I'd overheard. If only he'd been less in thrall to his older brother. If only Finn wasn't a total tit. And if only Noah hadn't kissed me in the manor house bedroom and left a hole in my heart.

But, as Gran used to say when I sat on her kitchen table, drumming my heels: *If onlys are a waste of time. You might as well howl at the moon.*

So I pull myself together and get on with life which, now the trolling has stopped and the café's getting busier, would be pretty good, if only I didn't feel so sad.

Aargh, there I go again with the *if onlys.*

I'm making caffè lattes for Joan and her recuperating husband a few days after Noah has left when raised voices drift in from the shop.

'Can you take over?' I ask Becca, who's working in the café two days a week now that the tourist season is hotting up. 'I won't be a minute.'

Heading into the shop, I spot Flora near the door standing legs astride with her hands on her hips. In front of her is Finn, dressed in black from head to toe.

'You've got a damn nerve,' hisses Flora. 'I know what you did and you're not welcome in here. Go and get your books elsewhere.'

Finn rolls his eyes but doesn't move. 'Look, I'd rather not be here either but I need to make sure you won't mention our little, um, misunderstanding when the journalist gets here.'

'What journalist?' I ask, edging forwards.

Finn shoots me a nervous look before pointing at the door which has just tinged open. 'That one.' He lowers his voice. 'I'm sorry for what happened. I'm trying to make things better.'

Two women have walked in – one in a flowing summer dress with sunglasses perched on her head and the other in tight jeans with a large camera slung around her neck.

'And who are you?' asks Flora, her face furrowed with annoyance.

'I'm Philippa and this is June. We're from *Breathe* magazine,' says the woman in the dress, flicking back her long, brown hair. 'Have you heard of it?'

Flora nods. *Breathe* is the magazine that comes through the door with Gramp's favourite regional newspaper, *The Tribune.* It's the magazine that carried the article about being your true self which he found so enthralling.

'We're doing a piece on Finn and his new hotel. Eligible bachelor comes to rural backwater and shakes the place up, kind of thing.'

'He's shaken us up all right.' Flora glares at Finn, who gives an almost imperceptible shake of the head. 'So why exactly are you all in my shop?'

'Finn's giving us a tour of the town and is insisting that we include a mention of your shop and café. It's all very quaint, apparently.' Philippa glances around the shop and gives a wide, bright smile. 'Yes, this is lovely. We'd like to take a few photos if that's OK. Can we have a quick look around?'

'I don't think so,' says Flora, folding her arms.

'Really?' Philippa turns to Finn and frowns. 'OK. Maybe we can find somewhere else to take a few pics.'

I think quickly. 'How many people read your magazine?' I ask.

'I can't remember what the paper's circulation is these days. What is it, June? Thirty thousand, something like that? Lots, anyway. We're online too and a significant proportion of our readership lives in or visits the Cotswolds and might like to stop by your shop and café.'

'So it would be good publicity.' I raise my eyebrows at Flora.

'Absolutely, and it's free.'

'Flora?' I step in front of Finn, who's trying on a pair of the reading glasses we've started selling. 'What do you think? We could do with some positive publicity.'

'I don't know.' Flora eyeballs Finn but unfolds her arms. 'I suppose there's no harm in it but it's your café, Callie, so it's your call.'

Everyone turns to me as I quickly weigh up my dislike of Finn against my ambitions for the café. The café wins.

'A mention in your magazine would be lovely, thank you.'

'Great!' Phillipa heads for the café door, peers inside and calls to June, who's staring out of the window, looking bored. 'This will be perfect for photos and there are some locals here which is fabulous. Come and have a look, June. You too, Finn.'

'Keep an eye on him,' hisses Flora. 'Seeing as he's such a snake in the grass.'

'I can hear you,' says Finn, 'and I'm not a total bastard.'

'The jury's still out on that one,' calls Flora after him.

Finn's shoulders drop as he walks towards the back of the shop and I can't help it, I feel a twinge of sadness for him. He doesn't think his dad loves him, he's lost his brother, and now he's persona non grata around here.

'Callie, is it?' calls Philippa from the café doorway. 'Can you come and have your photo taken by the coffee machine? It's absolutely gorgeous in here and perfect for highlighting Finn as a much loved member of the local community.'

Flora gives an ironic snort as I head for the café.

If only you knew, Philippa. If only you knew.

Chapter Twenty-Six

Life gradually goes back to normal in Honeyford, because life always does. But, for me, it's a new normal.

Business in the shop really picks up after *Breathe* is next published. Its double-page article includes several photos of Finn, who's described as a 'thrusting young business entrepreneur with the face of a young Johnny Depp' – a comment that has me reaching for the sick bag. And there's a particularly fetching pic of him draped across our coffee machine, with the café looking cosy and pretty behind him.

Visitors who've read the article come in to buy books, linger in the café over espressos and sit in the courtyard, delighting in the pots of bright blooms that are lovingly cared for by Phyllis.

In fact we're getting so busy, Becca is taken on almost full-time and it's lovely to watch her confidence grow as she hands out macchiatos and chats shyly to customers.

We also have a few guests from Finn's newly opened hotel coming into the café. Though that will tail off as soon as his coffee house is open too.

According to local gossip, a business partner is coming in to set up the coffee house and run it because Finn's so often away in London. Now the hotel's actually open, he seems bored with Honeyford and is rarely spotted in the town.

So I get Gramp up in the mornings, go to work, do Pilates in the Town Hall on Tuesday evenings, and walk by the river as the sun gets hotter and May slides into June. But some things are different. I'm different.

'You've turned into a right bolshie mare,' is Gramp's verdict. But he grins as he says it to show he's not being critical. He approves of me uncovering my authentic self.

Am I being authentic? Who knows, but I certainly feel more confident and assertive these days. I've started complaining if people cut ahead of me in a queue or provide rubbish customer service in shops.

I haven't turned into one of those rude, difficult people who say 'that's just the way I am' as they have a go at all and sundry. But I give my opinion and stand up for myself much more than I ever have before.

Which is all great and *why didn't I do this years ago* lovely. But I'm lonely. It's the same loneliness I felt at university just after Noah and I fell out.

We've been in touch intermittently via email and social media since he left. But that makes it worse somehow. Do I really want to see photos of the man I care about – my missed chance – laughing in a rooftop bar in New York without me?

'How are you doing, Callie?'

Flora has padded up behind me while I'm ordering a batch of cakes, flapjacks and Cotswold-cream biscuits for the café.

Calculating how many calorie-laden treats we'll need isn't an exact science and takes a lot of concentration. We got caught out earlier in the week when a minibus stopped outside the shop and disgorged a dozen hungry pensioners from Wolverhampton. They'd read about us on *The Tribune's* website and wanted to experience our 'quaint Cotswolds charm'.

'I'm all right, thanks,' I mumble, sucking the end of my pen as I try to get the order right. There are only so many leftover cakes that Gramp can eat. He's put on a few pounds recently.

'No, really.' Flora plonks herself directly in front of me and closes the lid of my laptop. 'Only you're not yourself these days.'

'That's ironic because my gramp reckons I'm my true self at last.'

'Stanley cracks me up with his New Age speak. How's he doing these days?'

'He's getting his spark back now his health's improved and he's resigned to the trees being gone. Turbo-charged Stanley is re-emerging, which is great actually. I kind of missed him.'

'Me too. But how are you really? You keep saying you're fine and you've seemed more confident and assertive recently. But you've been a bit sad since Noah left.'

'No, I'm feeling great.'

That didn't sound convincing at all.

Flora tilts her head and gives me the same sympathetic look that Gramp got for ages after Gran died. The one that drove him mad after a while.

'How's Noah doing in New York?'

'I'm not sure.'

'Why? Aren't you friends on Facebook?'

'Yes, but I've changed my settings so I don't see the posts he's tagged in.'

'Why? And tell me the truth.'

No need to stress that, Flora, because it's all I seem to do these days.

I take a deep breath. 'Because I was turning into an awful person who didn't want him to be happy.'

'OK, that's extremely truthful. In what way, awful?'

'I felt mutinous every time I saw him in some bar surrounded by high-powered New York goddesses with perfect teeth. I preferred the photos where he looked a bit lost and lonely, which makes me a horrible person because I do want him to be happy. He deserves it after putting up with Finn all these years.'

I glance at Flora to make sure she's not horrified by this confession.

'Anyway, that's my deep, dark secret. Underneath this pleasant, small-town girl exterior is an embittered old bag.'

'Oh, sweetheart.' Flora puts her arm around my shoulders and gives me a hug. She smells of country-garden roses. 'What does Noah say in his emails?'

'We're hardly emailing. He's busy with his new project and I don't want to bombard him with tales of Honeyford. What could I say? *Hi Noah. I sold a lot of coffee and took Gramp to the cinema to see the latest Bond film which he reckoned was pants. The big news in town is that Mrs Jones is giving up running the newsagents and moving to be near her daughter in Cirencester because her arthritis is giving her jip.* He's living in one of the most vibrant and exciting cities in the world, for goodness' sake.'

'That's true but it doesn't mean he's not interested in what you have to say. You could always tell him exactly how you feel about him and how miserable you are without him.'

I open my mouth to protest that I'm pretty much over Noah Shawley and he was just a passing fancy. But in the spirit of being my true self, I press my lips tightly together.

'I mean it,' says Flora, her pretty violet eyes open wide with concern. 'Tell him.'

'What good would that do? His life is in New York and mine is here, and there's nothing more to say about it.'

When I lift the lid of the laptop, Flora stares at me, biting the inside of her cheek. But any urge to sort out my impossible love life is scuppered by a customer coming into the shop. She talks to him for a minute and leads him to the local maps displayed on the back wall.

Talking about Noah has made me feel wobbly inside, like one of Gran's milk jellies, and thinking about my beloved Gran finishes me off. I tap at my keyboard with tears dripping off my nose and order enough flapjack to feed a small army.

'Ahem.'

A tall person is standing in front of me and casting a shadow across my computer. I brush a hand across my face before glancing up.

'You're not crying, are you?' Finn loosens the collar of his snow-white shirt. 'Why do women turn on the waterworks?'

'Menstrual hormones.'

That does the trick. Finn decides not to probe my low mood any further. Instead, he starts inspecting his nails and picking at stray bits of cuticle but he doesn't move away.

After a while, I close the laptop lid with a sigh. Flora is watching us from the back of the shop in between chatting with her customer.

'What do you want, Finn?'

'That's not much of a welcome for your favourite customer?'

I give him a shrug and my best WTAF look.

He takes a breath and holds it, as though he's about to do something unpleasant. Then he blurts out, 'I need to speak to you right now.'

My heart starts hammering in my ears as my mind floods with images of car crashes and terrorist attacks.

'Is Noah all right?'

'Yeah, I presume so. He's still peed off with me so we don't talk much. I just need a quick word with you.' He notices Flora and her thunderous expression. 'A quick word in private.'

When I don't move, he leans closer and mouths: 'It's urgent.'

I hesitate, weighing up whether I want to give him the time of day or not. On the one hand, there was the outrageous trolling, but on the other, the magazine publicity he organised has really boosted profits.

'All right,' I say at last. 'You'd better come with me into the café.'

Finn follows me without another word into The Cosy Kettle and, in spite of my low mood, pride fizzes through me. The place is buzzing. Millicent is in the corner with her daughter, Celeste, who's home for a few days. In the centre of the room, a group of women with babies in buggies are sipping coffees and laughing. And both tables are full in the garden.

A couple of the young mums wave at me and one calls out 'Hi, Callie', while Becca works the hissing coffee machine. Thick viscous liquid is dribbling from its chrome spout.

'Is this too noisy?' I ask Finn, who's scanning the room.

'It's fine,' he says, flashing a megawatt smile at the mums' table as we walk past. He really can't help himself.

'Would you like a coffee?'

Finn pulls out a chair at the café's only empty table and nods. 'That would be nice. White, no sugar. Please,' he calls after me as I head for the counter where Becca's watching us and scowling. Neither Flora nor I have told her he was the social media troll but she seems to have the measure of Finn Shawley.

'What does he want?' she asks, wiping drips from the coffee machine spout. 'I hear he's opening his own café? Is he spying on us now?'

'I don't think so. Does he look like James Bond?'

'Well…'

Finn chooses that moment to shoot the cuffs of his shirt and wink at Celeste. He does look a little like Pierce Brosnan in his younger years.

Becca and I both laugh. She laughs a lot more these days and she's growing out her severe hairstyle – currently a vibrant shade of orange.

'Give me your best caffè latte for our esteemed visitor, Becca, and then I'll send him packing.'

Becca makes the coffee and places it on the counter in front of me. It's a beaut – the snow-white milk is frothy and perfectly edges the rim of the bright red cup. She picks up the silver chocolate shaker.

'Would Mr Shawley like a heart on top of his coffee?'

I grin. 'Yeah, go for it.'

Finn watches me walk back and inspects the drink I put in front of him. He raises an eyebrow.

'A heart, Callie. Are you trying to tell me something?' He takes a sip and wipes froth from his upper lip. 'Nice coffee. Nice café, in fact. You've done a great job here.'

'Thank you,' I say, slowly, waiting for the sucker-punch follow-up which inevitably follows a compliment from Finn. But he just sips his coffee with a thoughtful expression on his handsome face.

'I don't mean to be rude but why are you here?'

'Very direct. I like that in a woman.' He winks and does that clicking sound that men sometimes make at the same time.

'Please just stop flirting for a few minutes, I implore you. It's incredibly trying after a while.'

'Really?' Finn looks surprised, as though the thought a woman might not find him irresistibly attractive has never crossed his mind. 'Do you know what I like about you, Callie?'

'My fabulous charm?'

'The fact that you don't bullshit me. You say it like it is and that's not something I encounter very often.'

'That's because you either flirt or bludgeon people into submission with your arrogant personality or dodgy business ethics,' I point out.

Whoops. Although I'm enjoying this new truthful, more confrontational me, I think I may have gone too far. But Finn nods as though I've passed a test.

'That's more or less word for word what Noah said to me when he went off on one before flouncing off to New York. Maybe I am a bit much at times and a little blinkered and selfish when it comes to business.'

He waits for me to deny it and stirs his coffee with a small sigh when I stay silent. The young mums gather up their bags and their babies and leave the café, but Finn keeps on stirring.

'I do love my brother and I want him to be happy,' he suddenly says. 'Noah implied that I was involved in splitting the two of you up years ago. He was shouting all kinds of stuff and I didn't take it all in, to be honest. But I hope it wasn't my fault, although meeting up with you again has had a disastrous effect on him. I can't believe he left me and went back to New York early.'

He takes another sip of coffee but almost spits it across the table when another thought hits him. 'Hell's bells, I didn't sleep with you, did I?'

'No, Finn, that definitely did not happen.'

'Phew, just as well.'

'How's your hotel doing now you're open for guests?'

I'm keen to veer away from Finn's extensive but obviously hazy love life.

'So-so. It takes a while for these things to get going.'

'Has your dad been to see the place yet?'

Finn's face clouds over. 'Not yet. He's so busy with his successful businesses, he finds it hard to… oh, what's the point? I presume from what you yelled at me that Noah told you about the' – he puts the next two words in air quotes – '*daddy issues* that I apparently have.'

I wince. 'He did mention them.'

'I just want to make him proud of me and there's nothing wrong with that, is there?'

'Nothing at all and I'm sure he is proud.'

'Not as proud as he is of Noah, who's always been the golden boy. Fruit of his loins and all that.'

When Finn gives a bitter laugh, I get an urge to reach across the table and hold his hand.

'Parents can mess you up.'

'Even when they're not biologically your parents.'

'Even then.'

Finn blows out his cheeks and fixes his sad eyes on mine. He's not flirting or screwing a business rival or pretending to be what he's not. It's like seeing Finn Shawley for the very first time.

'What did your parents do to you?' he asks, breaking eye contact.

'Nothing awful. They were good parents but they bickered constantly which was miserable when I was growing up. I didn't want to be like them so from an early age I've kept my mouth shut in arguments and never spoken my mind.'

'You didn't do a very good job of that round at my place.'

'I've decided not to live like that any more. I don't want negative stuff from my past getting in the way of my future – though it's a bit of a learning curve. You should try it.'

'What, speaking my mind?'

'Hell, no. You do enough of that already.'

Tiny lines fan down Finn's face when he smiles. 'How's your granddad doing?'

'He's OK, thanks. Still a bit of a handful, but his health is all right.'

'That's good. Noah told me that the trees meant a lot to him because of his wife who passed away. Moira, was it?'

'That's right. She was ace. Gramp misses her like mad and worries that she'll be forgotten when he's gone.'

'My grandmother, Constance, was ace, too. She was my dad's mum and knew all about my background but she never treated me any differently from Noah. She never loved me any less.'

This time I do reach across the table and put my hand on Finn's. His fingers wrap around mine for a few seconds before he pulls his hand away and sits up straight.

'Anyway, enough of reminiscing and family talk.'

'That's a shame. I rather like you when you're being vulnerable.'

'Vulnerability is the kiss of death in business and I'm here with a business proposition for you.'

'For me?'

I can't help laughing but Finn seems deadly serious.

'I've been let down by the man who was going to set up the hotel's coffee house and run it for me. I thought he was a friend but it turns out I don't have too many of those. Anyway, I don't have the time to faff about with it and my hotel staff don't have the expertise. So I thought you could do it.'

'Me? Let me get this straight. You want me to set up your coffee house and run it.'

'That's right.'

He leans back in his chair while myriad emotions flit through my mind.

Entrepreneur extraordinaire Finn Shawley is asking me to run a business for him. It's flattering and exciting and most people would leap at the chance. But I look around the café which is bustling with people I care about and shake my head.

'Thank you for your offer but I can't abandon The Cosy Kettle or Flora. She had faith in me and I owe her my loyalty. Anyway, you need someone with far more business credentials than me.'

Finn shudders. 'Blind loyalty even when it's detrimental to you? I just don't get it. But consider my offer properly before you make a decision. I can see the touchy-feely approach you have is a great advantage when it comes to a customer-focused business such as this. Quite frankly, it's not my thing but it seems to be yours. So don't do yourself down and out of a great opportunity. You said that running The Cosy Kettle was your dream. I'm offering a chance for that dream to expand.'

'I can't just leave here.'

Finn sighs. 'You could set up and run my coffee house as a sort of upmarket offshoot, maybe. Get that miserable-looking goth girl to manage this place day to day and you can oversee and build up both businesses.'

I hesitate because it just might work but then a thought strikes me.

'Did Noah put you up to this?'

'Would it matter if he did?'

'Possibly. I want to be offered this on my own merits, rather than it being a pity proposal.'

Finn laughs. 'Callie, I don't ever do business out of pity. Noah didn't suggest anything. We've hardly spoken recently – he's still angry with me and busy with his new project, and I wouldn't be surprised if he's busy with a new woman as well. I promise this is all my own idea because my project would benefit from your expertise and local contacts. Plus, I get the feeling you wouldn't ever screw me over.'

Finn's presumption that Noah has a new girlfriend has made my throat constrict and it's hard to get the words out.

'I'd have to speak to Flora about it because it was her money that allowed me to set up this place.'

'She could be a sort of sleeping partner in my coffee house venture if she wants, I suppose. We could work something out. Though she looks like she'd rather kill me. How old is she, by the way? She's pretty hot.'

When I shake my head, he shrugs. 'Sorry. Reflex action. Talk of the devil.'

Flora is walking towards us and she doesn't look happy.

'I'd better go before I outstay my welcome but will you at least think about my proposal?'

He smiles when I nod at him, and he and Flora pass each other without a word.

'What was that all about?' Flora takes the seat Finn has just vacated and pushes his half-drunk coffee to one side. 'Watch out, he's coming back.'

'I've got something to tell you,' says Finn, marching over and standing in front of us. He wrings his hands together and swallows. 'I'd like to apologise, Flora, for my appalling behaviour which I know Callie has told you all about. I behaved extremely badly and I regret it.'

Flora stares at Finn with her mouth open until I give her a gentle kick under the table.

'Your behaviour was absolutely dreadful and completely out of order. But there's no lasting harm done, I suppose, and the magazine article has helped to drum up business.'

'I hoped it would, and I've been advising my hotel guests to call in and buy a book and a coffee.'

'We've had a few of your guests here.'

'Good. OK, that's all I wanted to say. Thank you.'

With that, he turns on his heel and walks swiftly out of the café.

'What the hell just happened?' asks Flora.

'I think he's trying to turn over a new leaf.'

'That's great but I'll believe it when I see it. What was he saying to you?'

'He had a business proposition for me – for us, really.'

As I explain Finn's proposal, Flora's jaw drops again.

'Let me get this straight. He is suggesting that you set up and run his coffee house as an offshoot of The Cosy Kettle. It's mad.'

'That's what I thought initially, but now I reckon that it just might work.'

'With Finn as a business partner? I don't think so.' Flora shakes her head and sits back in her chair.

'I agree he's slippery but I've got the measure of him now, and he knows it. Finn is an experienced businessman with plenty of successes under his belt and this could be a great opportunity for both of us – an expansion of our café business, rather than his coffee house always being in direct competition with us.'

'That all sounds good, but I don't have lots of capital to put into the venture.'

'I get the feeling that wouldn't be a problem. He seems very keen for us to accept his proposal.'

'Because he reckons it will ultimately make money for him.'

'Definitely,' I say, slowly. 'But also because I really think he's trying to do the right thing for once.'

'Hhmm.' Flora drums her fingers on the table top. 'With sufficient legal safeguards in place to protect our interests, I suppose it might just work. If you're really up for it.'

'I am. I feel quite excited about the whole thing already. So what do you reckon? Will you tell Finn that you agree?'

'Personally, I'd rather tell Finn this.' I laugh in disbelief when Flora holds up one perfectly manicured middle finger. 'But from a business perspective it could make sense, and you deserve this chance, Callie.'

Do you know what? I do deserve this chance after all my hard work in the café. It's good to spend time doing what's best for other people but sometimes you have to step up and do what's best for you – and for your true self. Gramp will be proud of me.

I take a deep breath and look around at what we've already built up in the back of a bookshop in a small Cotswold town.

'OK,' I say, with a huge grin. 'Let's go for it.'

Chapter Twenty-Seven

Let's go for it is all very well as a mantra. It trips off the tongue and sounds enthusiastic and confident. But it doesn't take into account the hard work and fear involved when building up a coffee house from scratch that's so different from The Cosy Kettle.

The atmosphere in both businesses will be similar, I hope – warm and welcoming with efficient service, lovely coffee and fabulous Cotswold cake.

But a café in a posh country hotel is very different from one that was cobbled together at the back of a small-town bookshop, and I have plenty of sleepless nights.

The next few weeks pass in a flurry of sorting out regulations, choosing white tablecloths – who knew there were so many different shades of white? – setting up the hotel kitchen with the right coffee-making equipment, appointing staff, and hyperventilating.

Finn dips in and out but mostly keeps out of the way and lets me get on with it. Which is brilliant and terrifying in equal measure.

'We need a name,' he says during one flying visit from London to see how things are going. 'I was thinking The Manor Coffee House.'

'Maybe.'

'Why, what did you have in mind?'

Finn taps on the polished hardwood table nearest to him and nods in approval. Thank goodness he likes them because I've ordered two dozen.

'Seeing as the bookshop café is named in memory of my gran, I thought maybe this one should be named in honour of yours. What about The Constance Coffee House?'

'I think…'

He hates the idea! Finn turns his back on me and takes a few deep breaths. 'I think that would be perfect,' he says in a shaky voice. When he turns back, he's smiling and his eyes are bright. 'Absolutely perfect, and I'm going to be much more involved in setting it up.'

But of course he isn't. He's already moved on to his next big enthusiasm – transforming a run-down warehouse in north London into top-end offices and making a shedload of cash in the process.

Fortunately Simon, the hotel manager he's appointed from Cirencester, is a decent bloke and we work well together.

Right at the start of the project, I dropped Noah a line to let him know I was setting up the coffee house and double-checking it wasn't his idea.

He sent a lovely reply confirming it was all down to Finn and saying he was proud of me, which made me cry. There was no talk of him coming back to England any time soon, or of new girlfriends – and I didn't ask. Missing your chance with the man you can't stop thinking about is hard enough without finding out some other woman is grabbing her chance with him.

People say that hard work helps to mend a broken heart. That's rubbish. You just end up broken-hearted and knackered.

But at least working day and night to keep The Cosy Kettle doing well and The Constance Coffee House on schedule leaves me less time to think. And seeing as my work-free thoughts are still full of Noah and *if onlys*, that has got to be a good thing.

It's two o'clock on a beautiful June afternoon. The coffee house doors are flung open, the pale blue sky is scattered with wispy clouds, birds are chirping outside – and I'm bricking it. I look around me and gulp because my mouth feels like the Sahara during a particularly dry spell.

Any minute now guests will begin arriving for the official opening of The Constance Coffee House and I'm about to throw up. Why wasn't I content with running The Cosy Kettle?

Callie Fulbright, born and brought up on the Berry Estate and still living there with her gramp, was never meant to run a café empire. Damn stupid Finn and his ridiculous business proposals!

I have a sudden childish urge to run home and mash huge chunks of Battenberg cake into my mouth. But it's too late because someone has just tinged the bell on the reception desk.

At least the coffee house is looking great. A soft breeze is ruffling pristine white tablecloths, the huge windows are glinting in the sun, and two large fans above my head are gently wafting air around the room.

A long table along the back wall is covered in silver platters piled high with iced cupcakes, and rows of sparkling champagne glasses ready to be filled. Behind them are dozens of china cups for our best steaming-hot coffee.

I did this. In spite of my nerves, a warm glow of accomplishment rushes through me and I smile. Eek, my smile freezes into a rictus grin as Simon shows in our first guest. Here we go.

*

'It's a bit posh.'

Gramp, dressed in his only suit, wipes a smudge of buttercream from his chin and grabs another cake from the long table. 'You'll be turning into one of them, next. Now you've got a taste for how the other half lives.'

'One of them?'

'Yeah.' He gestures at Mr and Mrs Hartington-Smythe, who are staying in the hotel. 'People who are posh and a bit up themselves, with more money than sense. Talking of which…' He whips two sheets of folded A4 paper from his pocket.

'Definitely not. You can't use the coffee house opening as a chance to tout your sponsorship form round the guests.'

'Shame.'

Gramp shoves it back into his pocket. He's walking several miles next week, dressed as Ginger Spice, for The British Heart Foundation in memory of my dad. And he's already raised over a hundred pounds from people coming into The Cosy Kettle.

I'm also helping him find out if he's allowed to do a parachute jump now he's been diagnosed with angina. Watching him leap into space will give me kittens, but I can hardly stop him following his dreams when I'm following mine.

He stops scoffing cake, runs his finger under the collar of his shirt and pulls it away from his neck.

'I'm still not sure about you being in business with Finn. And if it wasn't for this place being your project, I wouldn't have come today. There's nothing for me here now the trees are gone and I'm definitely not apologising to him for my perfectly reasonable protest. I might chain him to one of his stupid car park bollards instead.'

He grumbles on while I grab Sarah's arm and whisper in her ear.

'Can you try to keep Gramp and Finn as far apart as possible? I don't want a punch-up.'

'Why not? It would liven up this do immensely, and Finn could do with a slap.'

'He's all right.'

When I catch Finn's eye, he gives me a thumbs-up from across the room.

He's loitering near the door in case his revered father deigns to grace us with his presence but so far he's a no-show. Mr Shawley senior was invited as guest of honour but replied saying he 'couldn't commit to an event in advance due to business pressures'.

Finn was outwardly understanding and I agreed with him that business pressures can be terribly demanding on one's time. But personally, I think Mr Shawley is a heartless idiot.

'You've changed your tune about Finn,' says Sarah, smoothing down her scarlet bodycon dress which keeps riding up her thighs. She flicks her glossy hair over her shoulder. 'Mind you, you're all about change at the moment. I don't recognise the new, improved, speak-your-mind Callie. But I like it, so keep it up.'

'Yes, ma'am!'

I give her a mock salute and take a glass of the champagne being handed out by hotel staff. Then I wave at Phyllis, who's sitting in the corner with Millicent, Mary and Amy who runs the sweetshop. Becca's holding the fort at The Cosy Kettle because she doesn't like large gatherings, and Dick's precious car has broken down so he's at the garage.

Phyllis waves her glass of champagne at me and blows a kiss towards my grandfather.

'How are things with you and Phyllis these days?' I ask Gramp, who has stuck his finger into the middle of his chocolate butterfly cake and is licking off the cream.

'Fine, thank you. Why, what are you implying?'

He grabs a glass of champagne as the waiter walks by and takes a gulp.

'Nothing. Just that you and Phyllis seem close and that would be fine, you know. Moira wouldn't mind if the two of you had a relationship.'

'She probably wouldn't. She always was a very understanding woman. But I'm far too old for another woman to see me naked. I couldn't hold my stomach in for long enough. Anyway, Moira was the only woman for me. Sometimes there's only one person you're supposed to be with – your one and only – and that woman was your gran. You'll feel the same about someone someday.'

I already do, but he's 3,500 flaming miles away.

Gramp narrows his eyes when he spots my face fall but, before he can quiz me, Finn taps a teaspoon on the side of a cup.

'Here we go!' sighs Gramp, shoving his finger back into his cake.

The tinkling sound carries across the conservatory and a sudden hush descends. Finn is about to make a speech and then, heaven help us, it's my turn.

I've been practising for days so I won't cock it up in front of everyone. Gramp's heard me run through it a few times and yesterday fell asleep halfway through, which didn't do a lot for my rising anxiety levels. But my nerves have suddenly vanished because all I can think is: *What if Noah is my one and only? What a complete pain in the backside that would be!*

Finn's voice pierces my self-pity.

'It's wonderful to be here this afternoon to celebrate the opening of The Constance Coffee House, which is named in honour of my wonderful grandmother. I had rather hoped that her son, my dad, would be with us today, but' – he pauses – 'anyway, he can't make it but we can all celebrate this marvellous space.

'Shawley Manor House Boutique Hotel is putting Honeyford on the map and this elegant coffee house will help to cement the hotel's reputation as the best place to stay in town. Thanks to Simon for running the hotel so efficiently while I'm busy doing business deals in London, to Flora from Honeyford Bookshop, who's backed this venture, and, of course, to Callie, whose vision has brought our ideas to fruition.'

There's a cheer from the people around me and my face starts to burn. Fabulous! I take long, slow breaths, hoping my face will feel less like someone's set fire to it.

'That's enough from me,' concludes Finn. 'I'm sure we'd love to hear from Callie, who, may I say, is looking particularly gorgeous today.'

He stares at my bare, tanned legs and gives me a huge wink.

Really? He's making inappropriate comments at our grand opening? I resist yanking down the hem of my short blue dress.

'Go on, girl!' whispers Gramp, rather loudly in my ear. 'Stuff it to the posh folk!'

Flora's standing on the other side of him and snorts but covers it up with a cough.

Pulling my shoulders back, I launch into my speech. 'Thank you so much for coming to the grand opening of The Constance Coffee House.'

'Hooray!' shout Phyllis and Millicent. I think they've been working their way through the champagne.

'I'm very grateful to Finn and to Flora for giving me the chance to set up and run this coffee house which, along with The Cosy Kettle, will be a fantastic meeting place for hotel guests, local people and visitors to Honeyford.'

Finn shrugs, not too keen on local people besmirching his lovely new coffee house but knowing it makes good business sense.

'Thanks to everyone who's been involved in getting this amazing place off the ground. Lots of the people involved are here today and I couldn't have done it without you. Special thanks to entrepreneur Finn, who asked me to take on this project, and to Flora, who's the best boss ever and an inspiration to me.'

I grin as Flora delves into her handbag for a tissue and starts dabbing at her eyes. Her usual composure has deserted her.

'Thanks also to six special people who helped give me the confidence to set up and run The Cosy Kettle, which led directly to me being here today. Becca, who can't be here this afternoon, Phyllis, Mary, Millicent, my lovely loyal friend Sarah, and, of course, my young at heart and very handsome grandfather, Stanley. He made me put that bit in.'

He nods to confirm the fact and everyone laughs.

'Finally, my gran used to tell me to fulfil my potential and follow my dreams. It's taken me a while to fully follow that good advice but I'm getting there with The Cosy Kettle and now this wonderful coffee house. So, let's all raise our glasses to…'

'You came!' yells Finn, rushing out of the conservatory into the hotel hallway.

'It's his dad,' I tell our puzzled guests, inwardly delighted that the old curmudgeon has decided to put in an appearance. It's the least Finn deserves after all his hard work on this place. 'As I was saying, let's all raise our glasses to The Constance Coffee House.'

There's a cheer and everyone swigs back their drinks.

'His dad came then,' says Sarah, sidling up with a champagne glass in each hand. 'I thought you said he wouldn't show? Nice speech, by the way.'

'Thank you. I didn't think he would turn up but I'm glad to be proved wrong. Are you holding a glass for someone else?'

'Nope, they're both mine. I love a spot of free booze. Are you a good enough friend to take me home if I get horribly rat-arsed?'

'No.'

'Good to know. See you later,' says Sarah, necking one glass and making a beeline for the waiter with the drinks tray.

Gramp's chatting in the corner with Phyllis, and Flora's busy discussing thriller writers with a hotel guest so I head for Reception. I haven't seen Mr Shawley for years and it's about time I renewed my acquaintance with the man who's had such a disastrous effect on Finn.

The two men are leaning on the Reception desk with their backs to me. And blood starts pounding in my ears when the taller man turns round, because the Shawley standing next to Finn isn't the Shawley I was expecting.

'Hi, Callie,' says Noah, running his hands through his hair. 'I hear I missed your speech. Sorry about that but my plane was delayed.'

'I didn't know you were coming. Finn didn't say,' I stutter, trying desperately to stay cool, calm and collected. It wouldn't do to lose it in front of dozens of invited guests.

'I wasn't sure until the last minute that I could get away. How are you? You look great.' His eyes crinkle in the corners when he smiles at me, and my calm starts to slip.

'You too,' I gulp.

Noah looks tanned but tired in jeans and a cotton jacket. A pair of sunglasses are hooked into the V-neck of his thin black jumper.

'Isn't it great that Noah came to support me!' Finn throws his arms around his brother and hugs him tight and when he mumbles, 'I really appreciate it, bro,' I swear his bottom lip is trembling.

'I'm sorry that I'm not Dad.'

'That's all right. You'll do just as well,' sniffs Finn. 'Now come on in and see what we've done with the place.'

He leads Noah towards the conservatory while I take a few moments to calm down and gather my racing thoughts.

Chapter Twenty-Eight

I've tried to gather my thoughts. I really have. But they refuse to be reined in. Noah's been chatting to people and eating cake for the last ten minutes which is plenty of time for me to have got a grip. But it's just not happening.

'So what are you going to do about nerdy Noah turned hunky Noah?' demands Sarah, swaying slightly beside me. 'Now you've sorted out your pre-uni misunderstanding, you should be snogging the life out of him.'

'Keep your voice down. I'm not going to do anything. It's a lovely surprise to see him again, but he's here on a flying visit so I doubt we'll even have a proper chance to chat.'

'Shame,' says Sarah, really loudly, pushing out her bottom lip. 'Hey-up, he's coming over. So it's head high, tits forward and ass tucked under.'

She really is as bad as Finn in her own way.

'Hi again, Callie, and hello, Sarah,' says Noah in his soft, low voice. Sarah just giggles.

'Finn's in the garden and has asked if you and Stanley will join him,' Noah says to me.

'Why?'

Noah shrugs. 'I have absolutely no idea. He's being very secretive but he said it's important and I have to get you out there.'

'I'm not sure Stanley will want to go into the garden with Finn.'

'Probably not.' When Noah grins at me, my stomach does a flip. 'But see if you can persuade him. Finn was very insistent. I'll see you out there.'

Gramp is not ambivalent about whether or not he should go into the garden with Finn.

'If you think I'm spending any time on my own with that tree-murdering hooligan, you've got another think coming,' he snorts, when I find him emerging from the toilet. 'I'd rather watch *Mamma Mia* again.'

It wasn't one of his favourite films.

'Come on, Stanley. Let's find out what he wants,' booms Sarah, who's standing right behind me, swigging yet more champagne. Everyone else has moved on to coffee but she's been sweet-talking Simon.

'I don't care what he wants,' mutters Gramp, but I can tell his curiosity's piqued.

'It's a bit awkward leaving him waiting outside,' I insist.

'OK, stop nagging. But he'd better not have another go at me or I won't be responsible for my actions.'

He troops with me and Sarah out of the French doors and into bright sunshine. It's gorgeous out here – there's an expanse of raked gravel without a weed in sight and huge ceramic pots of purple geraniums dotted everywhere. But there's no Finn.

'I'm not playing hide and seek,' says Gramp, turning to go back inside, but I grab hold of his arm.

'Let's have a look around the corner and if we still can't see him we'll go back inside. I promise.'

Gramp huffs and puffs but walks with us around the back of the house towards the car park. I rarely venture round here because I walk to work and I'd forgotten, until we round the corner, that we're close to where Gramp's beloved trees once stood.

'Maybe we should go back inside,' I mutter to Sarah out of the side of my mouth, but she's already striding towards Noah, who's waiting for us near the stone fountain. He's wiping his glasses, which are spattered with water spray that's caught in the breeze.

'What's the point of all this?' I ask him. 'Isn't it a bit cruel showing my gramp the space where the trees once were?'

'Just come with me and you'll see.'

His hand brushes mine as though he's about to grasp it, but he turns and sets off with me, Gramp and Sarah following.

Beyond the fountain is a little huddle of people I recognise – Finn, Mary, Millicent, Phyllis and Flora. They smile and move aside in a single wave when we get closer.

'What on earth is going on?' I ask, but no one answers. Instead, Phyllis points to what's behind them.

It looks amazing! Where the trees once stood, the meadow has been transformed. A long raised flower bed with a wooden border now stands where branches once arced into the sky, and it's a rainbow of colours. Vivid yellow, pale blue, deep red and purple flowers are bursting from their bed. And behind them are three saplings with protective mesh around their slender stems.

'They're crab apple trees,' says Finn. 'It'll take them a while to grow, but one day they'll be tall and beautiful.'

'I don't understand. I thought this was going to be an overspill car park.'

'So did I, initially. But we can cope without it and I thought a garden here would be pleasant for our guests.'

Millicent shoves her handbag over her shoulder and does a little clap. 'It's absolutely lovely. Bravo!'

'Stanley,' says Finn, turning to my gramp, who hasn't uttered a word. 'Would you do us the honour of unveiling this?'

He guides him to what looks like a tablecloth draped over a large object. It's all very mysterious – apart from the large object, which is very obviously a wooden garden bench. Its legs poking out from under the cloth rather give the game away.

'What do I have to do?'

'Just pull the cloth,' says Noah, standing next to me.

Gramp shuffles forward, takes hold of the fabric and gives it a tug. He steps back as it flutters to the ground and puts his hand to his mouth which has formed into a perfect 'oh'.

Screwed into the back of the wooden seat is a brass plaque, and etched in deep, chunky letters are the words: *Moira's Garden. In memory of Moira Fulbright, who loved it here. Never forgotten.*

I glance at Noah, who shrugs as a ripple of applause breaks out. Did he know about this?

'That's really wonderful,' says Mary, sniffing into a tissue. 'Quite the gesture.'

Everyone's talking and smiling and crying but Gramp's still as a statue, staring at the permanent memorial to his beloved wife.

'Gramp, are you OK?'

When I touch his arm, he gives a weird little gulp before taking hold of Finn's hand and pumping it up and down.

'Thank you, sir. My Moira would love having a garden named in her honour, especially in this spot where she—'

'Spent so much time,' I butt in, blinking back tears.

'You're welcome,' says Finn, gruffly, extricating his hand from Gramp's. He looks acutely embarrassed, especially when Phyllis grabs his tie, yanks his head down towards her and plants a kiss on his cheek.

Noah laughs and traces the letters in the plaque with his fingers. 'I'm sure you can visit the garden whenever you like, Stanley.'

'Yeah,' sighs Finn. 'Just so long as you don't chain yourself to anything, have a heart attack or frighten the guests.'

'I promise, though I might tell your guests about my Moira if that's all right. She was a wonderful woman.'

'She was,' wails Sarah, bursting into tears and throwing herself into Noah's arms. Heaven knows how much she's drunk. He pats her awkwardly on the back and gives me a 'what the hell' grin.

Chapter Twenty-Nine

It's two hours later and Flora is driving my gramp, Phyllis, Mary and Millicent home while I'm tidying up the conservatory, ready for our first paying customers tomorrow.

Prising Gramp away from Moira's Garden was hard work and only achieved when Finn promised he could come back the next day to weed the flower bed. There aren't any weeds in the flower bed but he can sit on Gran's bench, eat a picnic lunch and remember the woman he loves.

Sarah's also gone, after spending ages huddled over a washbasin in the toilets and informing anyone who came near that she would never *ever* drink again. Gemma came to the rescue in her car when I rang and told her how wasted her fiancée was. Boy, is she going to have a bad head tomorrow.

I sweep cake crumbs off the long table into my palm and tip them into the black rubbish sack at my feet. Dozens of dirty cups and glasses are already in the hotel's huge dishwasher and Simon has cleared up discarded cupcake cases.

'What do you reckon?' Finn steps into the conservatory. He's changed into his jeans though I doubt he's here to help with the clear-up.

'I reckon it went very well and, with any luck, the coffee house will be a great success. What do you think?'

'I think you're right and you've done a great job, Callie.'

He grabs a leftover choc-chip cookie and an avalanche of crumbs cascade onto the floor when he takes a bite.

'I haven't had a proper chance to thank you yet.'

'For what?' he mumbles, with his mouth full.

'For Moira's Garden.'

'That's all right. We both know how important ace grandmothers are.'

He catches my eye for a moment before taking another bite of biscuit.

'Gramp's really thrilled with the garden and so am I. It was a really kind and selfless thing to do, Finn.'

'Shhh!' He leans close. 'Don't let my business rivals hear that or my reputation as a ruthless operator will be wrecked and any advantage I hold will be scuppered.'

'I won't scupper your bad-boy reputation, but I know the truth – that underneath that arrogant exterior you do have a heart.'

'Maybe. Though I'm still going to quash my rivals, flirt far too much and sleep with as many women as possible.'

'I would expect nothing less.'

Finn gives me a salacious wink before shoving the last of the biscuit into his mouth. He wanders to the window and stares at the garden while I fasten the top of the rubbish bag and dump it in the corner of the room.

'I'm sorry your dad didn't make it to the coffee house opening.'

He looks round and shrugs his shoulders. 'To be honest, I never really expected him to turn up. But hey, the one person I can always count on did put in an appearance. It looks like Noah's forgiven me so I'm happy – and here he is.'

Noah's walked in through the open French window and is standing with his back to the sun.

'How are you doing?' he asks. 'I was kind of hoping we could go for a quick walk, Callie, but I can help if there's still lots to do.'

'There is still a fair bit,' I say, pushing a strand of hair behind my ear and feeling wobbly at the thought of being alone with Noah. 'I need to vacuum and put the tables back in the right places so we can open at nine on the dot tomorrow.'

'Ah, go!' says Finn, with a wave of his hand. 'I'll do it.'

'Really?'

'Nah, I'll get Simon or one of his minions to do it. But you should both go out for a walk. You've had a long flight, Noah, and Callie, you've worked like crazy. So go and get some fresh air – or something.'

He waggles his dark eyebrows and gives a filthy laugh.

'If you're up for a walk, Callie, shall I meet you by the front gate in a few minutes?' asks Noah.

'Sounds good,' I squeak.

When Noah's walked off, his feet crunching on the gravel, I rush to the Ladies' for a quick tidy up.

Sarah spent ages twisting my hair into an intricate French braid but strands have started escaping so I brush it out. Then I reapply my lip gloss and take a look in the mirror. Pink spots are burning in my cheeks even though I forgot to bring my blusher.

It's just a walk, I tell myself, resting my hot forehead against the cool mirror. *It can't be anything else because we live on different continents. It's just a walk and a catch-up between old friends and absolutely nothing to get uptight about.*

That's all true but, boy, do I feel uptight when I see Noah leaning against the garden wall, waiting for me. And when he spots me and smiles, it feels as though my heart skips a beat. Literally skips a beat, like I'm the heroine in a romantic movie, or something.

Hell's bells, Callie. You have got to get a grip!

I breathe in to the bottom of my lungs and plaster on an *I'm looking forward to our no-strings platonic walk* expression.

'Where shall we go?' asks Noah, straightening up and wiping away tiny chips of stone that have stuck to his arm. 'I was thinking maybe by the river as it's still quite hot. It'll be cooler down there.'

'Sounds good to me,' I reply in a jaunty voice that I don't recognise.

At the old toll bridge, we clamber down to the water's edge and follow the path as it mirrors a bend in the river. Noah's right, it is much cooler down here. Tall trees lining the path cast shadows into the clear water, and the air is thick with the smell of damp earth.

We wander on, past clumps of comfrey and butterbur, making small talk. We talk about the screaming baby on Noah's flight, the weather in New York, Gramp's sponsored walk, and Sarah's inability to hold her drink. And despite my reservations, I begin to relax and enjoy being in his company.

After a while, during a discussion on the merits of Netflix, Noah stifles a yawn.

'I think my jetlag's catching up with me. Is it all right if we sit down for a bit?'

He flops onto the grass in a patch of sunlight and lies back, hands behind his head, while I slip off my sandals. It's been a long, hot, frazzling day and the cool river is calling me.

Sitting on the bank's edge, I trail my toes in the shallow water and gasp. Cool? It's freaking freezing! But my toes go numb after a while so it's all good.

Noah is breathing deeply behind me – I think he might be asleep – and sunlight is dappling through the branches of a willow on the opposite bank. All I can hear is the whoosh of the breeze in the trees and the call of a chaffinch nearby, and I'm happy.

Noah will be back in New York within days but he's here with me now and I can pretend for a while that our lives turned out differently. I tilt my face to the sun, close my eyes and dream.

The distant revving of a car engine brings me back to earth and I open my eyes. A cherry-red car is zooming along Chalford Lane which leads into the back of Honeyford. I can just see its roof from here.

Noah stirs, sits up and rubs his eyes.

'How long was I asleep? Sorry.'

'I have no idea. I kind of drifted off myself.'

He shuffles his backside across the bank until he's sitting next to me.

'It's beautiful here, isn't it? And so peaceful after the coffee house launch and the grand unveiling of Moira's bench.'

'Did you know anything about that?'

'Nope. It was all Finn's idea and I was as surprised as you were.'

'And you definitely had nothing to do with him proposing that I take on the coffee house?'

'I swear on Finn's ultra-successful life that the first I knew of it was when you emailed. You've done such a fantastic job. It looks amazing and I'm sure it'll do a roaring trade. Great name, too. My grandma would have loved it.'

'Thanks. It's been a real challenge but it's been great, actually. Becca's doing brilliantly in The Cosy Kettle, Flora's selling lots of books, and The Constance Coffee House opens for business tomorrow. I still can't believe Finn asked me to take it on.'

'I think you impressed him.'

'What, by yelling in his face?'

Noah throws back his head and laughs. 'That's the kind of thing that does impress my brother, sadly.'

He lobs a handful of twigs into the water and watches the current carry them away.

'It was good of you to come back for the launch. It meant a lot to Finn, especially as your dad couldn't make it.'

I steal a glance at Noah, who's shielding his eyes from the sun and staring across the water. You can see the chimneys of the manor house from here, above the tops of the trees.

'I don't regret falling out with Finn. It was about time I told him a few home truths, but he's still my brother and I love him. Was he all right after I left?'

'He was sad about falling out with you and about the situation with his dad. He opened up to me a bit when he came into the café and asked me to go into business with him.'

'Did he?' Noah twists round and stares at me with his perfect pale eyes. 'Finn never opens up to anyone. You really do have a special way with people, Callie.'

'Thanks,' I gulp. 'Um, how's life in New York?'

'OK, I guess. Busy.'

'How's your new girlfriend?'

Why did I ask that? Only a total moron would ask that.

'What girlfriend?' says Noah, sounding puzzled.

'Finn said he reckoned you had a new girlfriend.'

'Finn knows nothing about my love life in New York.'

'There must be loads of women throwing themselves at you over there – a successful, good-looking man who sounds like Prince Harry? I expect you're fighting them off with a stick.'

Shut up, Callie. Shut up!

Noah raises his eyebrows at me while I briefly contemplate throwing myself into the river. But then he grins.

'My accent is a bit of a babe magnet, to be fair. But none of the women I meet measure up to you.' He hesitates and then says, softly: 'I miss you so much, Callie.'

His hand slides along the bank until his fingers cover mine but I pull my hand away and jump up, my wet toes squelching in the spikey grass. My heart can't take this much pretending that everything's all right.

Noah clambers to his feet, anguish etched across his face.

'I'm so sorry. I didn't mean to upset you. I know we said we couldn't turn back time but I thought – I hoped – you might still have strong feelings for me.'

'I did. I do. But this is so unfair, Noah,' I wail. 'We both know now what really happened eight years ago and you're not a total wuss when it comes to your brother any more, no offence. All that's great, but, as you said yourself, we missed our chance and now you're settled in New York and I'm settled in Honeyford. So why are you here being all smouldery and hand-holdy and "let's go for a walky"?'

Did I really say 'walky'? Am I losing the power of coherent speech?

I hear a loud sigh and realise it came from me. 'You have no idea how hard the last few weeks have been for me, Noah, and how often I've thought about you. You're breaking my heart all over again.'

It's funny, really. I've spent years suppressing how I truly feel about everything – Noah, Mum and Dad's parenting skills, rude shop assistants, cold callers who insist I've recently had an accident. But now I just open my mouth and every damn feeling I've ever had comes tumbling out.

And there's more.

Noah takes a step towards me but I hold up my hand to stop him.

'You should also know that I'm different these days. I'm more like my'– the words stick in my throat – 'true self. It's not always pretty because I speak my mind more and disagree with people and get angry sometimes. You might not like the real me.'

'Jesus, Callie. I've only ever seen the real you.'

His body's suddenly hard against mine, his fingers are weaving through my hair and he's kissing me as though his life depends on it. My bones feel like they're melting.

'What are you doing?' I gasp, when we finally break apart. It took a while for us to break apart because my arms were around his neck and I was kissing him back. 'Didn't you hear what I just said?'

'I heard the bit about me breaking your heart.' His breath is warming my neck and his arms are around my waist. 'I wasn't sure how you really felt about me.'

'I'm in love with you, you stupid ass,' I blurt out, taking speaking my mind and sharing my innermost feelings to a whole new level.

Noah laughs out loud and cups my flustered face in his hands.

'That's good because I'm in love with you, too.'

My emotions are now officially fried. Joy, fear, excitement and sadness – all at a full, fierce one hundred per cent – are fighting for space. Noah Shawley, who lives 3,500 miles away, loves me.

'You say "good" but it's totally impractical. It'll never work if we're on different sides of the world.'

'What about if I was just up the road?'

'What the hell are you talking about?' I splutter, now veering between elation that Noah definitely loves me and anger that he's told me he loves me just before he jets back to America. Basically, I've become completely emotionally incontinent.

'I've been headhunted by a respected architects' practice in Oxford,' says Noah, still holding me close. 'I used to work with one of the partners and he's offered me a job.'

'You can't accept it.'

His watch catches on my skin when I pull away from him.

'Why not? Don't you want me to?'

'Of course I do, but it's too much. You can't give up your dreams for me, Noah. Here I am, finally following mine, and you'd be giving up everything.'

'What sort of everything? I've lived in New York for three years and it's been great but I've been feeling homesick for a while. I miss England and I miss Honeyford because I was happy here. Coming back to the town reminded me of that.'

'What about the big new project you've taken on at work?'

Noah shrugs. 'It's quite tedious, to be honest, and I'm dealing with the client from hell. Walking away will be a relief and plenty of the people I work with will be happy to take my place. I want to come home, Callie.'

'Honestly?'

A beam of sunlight falls across Noah's fair hair and broad smile.

'Honestly. But if you're feeling overwhelmed by everything, we can take things slowly. What do you reckon?'

I gaze at the man who stole my heart so many years ago and has held it captive ever since. Take things slowly? I don't think so.

When I fling myself back into his arms, we almost topple into the river and two moorhens drifting lazily by paddle off in fright.

'Whoah!' laughs Noah, squeezing me so tightly against him I can hardly breathe. Then his lips are hard against mine and we don't say another word for a long time.

A Letter from Liz

Thank you for choosing to read *New Starts and Cherry Tarts at the Cosy Kettle*. I hope Callie, Noah and the inhabitants of Honeyford have entertained you and made you smile. This book has an extra-special place in my heart because I grew up in the beautiful Cotswolds – and hopefully I've imagined Honeyford as the sort of gorgeous place you'd move to in a heartbeat. I've also loved creating a host of new characters, especially Stanley who's just the sort of eighty-year-old I one day hope to be.

I'm still writing about Honeyford and, in particular, what happens to Flora (think, marriage upsets, baking contests, and handsome strangers) as summer sets in. You can find out when that book will be published by signing up at the following link. Your email address will never be shared and you can unsubscribe at any time.

www.bookouture.com/liz-eeles

Before I go, can I ask a favour? If you enjoyed *New Starts and Cherry Tarts at the Cosy Kettle*, I'd be really grateful if you could write a review. I know life can get busy, but even a quick line or two can make a huge difference and encourage more people to give my books a try. Thank you in advance.

And please do get in touch if you'd like to say hello. There are lots of ways to contact me – on my Facebook author page, via Twitter or Instagram, and through my website.

Right, I'd better get back to Flora's story. Take care – and I hope to see you again in Honeyford, very soon.

Liz x

lizeelesauthor/

@lizeelesauthor

lizeelesauthor

www.lizeeles.com

Acknowledgements

This book would never have seen the light of day without the faith shown in me by Bookouture. I couldn't ask for a more professional and supportive publisher, and I absolutely love being a part of the Bookouture 'family'.

Before I signed my first publishing contract, I thought that editors just… well, edited. Boy, was I wrong! Abigail Fenton and Ellen Gleeson, as well as being brilliant editors, have also been cheerleaders when I doubted myself, kindly taskmasters when I started flagging, and founts of knowledge when I asked (sometimes very daft) questions. I'm so grateful to both of them.

Thank you to Paul Sweetman, who runs City Books in Hove with his wife, Inge, and to Steve Leslie who runs Beach Bakery in Shoreham-by-Sea. They generously gave their time to chat with me about running a book shop and a café in real life, and provided a flavour of the satisfaction and sheer hard work involved. If you're on the south coast and love good books and great coffee, do call in and see them. Of course, Honeyford Book Shop and The Cosy Kettle are figments of my imagination, and any inaccuracies in how these kinds of businesses operate are mine alone.

My family and friends are fab and I really appreciate their support and interest in my writing. And I'm very grateful to everyone who takes the time to read my books, to review them, and to blog about them – you're all awesome. Finally, a special mention and thank you to my children, Sam and Ellie. And also to my rock of a husband, Tim, who reads first drafts of my books in bed and helpfully points out all my spelling mistakes and plot holes as I'm falling asleep.

Printed in Great Britain
by Amazon